CIRCLE of TERROR

CIRCLE OF
TERROR

A Novel

Larry Powalisz

New York

CIRCLE OF TERROR

A Novel

© 2017 Larry Powalisz.

Published in New York, New York, by Morgan James Publishing. Morgan James and The Entrepreneurial Publisher are trademarks of Morgan James, LLC. www.MorganJamesPublishing.com

The Morgan James Speakers Group can bring authors to your live event. For more information or to book an event visit The Morgan James Speakers Group at www.TheMorganJamesSpeakersGroup.com.

Shelfie

A **free** eBook edition is available with the purchase of this print book.

CLEARLY PRINT YOUR NAME ABOVE IN UPPER CASE

Instructions to claim your free eBook edition:
1. Download the Shelfie app for Android or iOS
2. Write your name in **UPPER CASE** above
3. Use the Shelfie app to submit a photo
4. Download your eBook to any device

ISBN 978-1-63047-976-3 paperback
ISBN 978-1-63047-977-0 eBook
Library of Congress Control Number:
2016902262

Cover Design by:
Chris Treccani
www.3dogdesign.net

Interior Design by:
Bonnie Bushman
The Whole Caboodle Graphic Design

In an effort to support local communities and raise awareness and funds, Morgan James Publishing donates a percentage of all book sales for the life of each book to Habitat for Humanity Peninsula and Greater Williamsburg.

Get involved today, visit
www.MorganJamesBuilds.com

Habitat
for Humanity®
Peninsula and
Greater Williamsburg
Building Partner

Lynn, you've been my best friend for over thirty-eight years, through thick and thin. Thanks for pushing me to finish the manuscript.

Krista and Ryan, thanks for the joy you've provided us, for marrying wonderful people, and for bringing God's most precious gifts into our lives.

Chapter I

HOLY CROSS CEMETERY: MILWAUKEE, WISCONSIN

A morning breeze sent a mixture of orange and brown leaves tumbling across the neatly trimmed grass. The sun beamed in November splendor as the cool night air slowly dissipated. The first hints of an early winter shrouded him. On one knee, Detective Declan Tomczyk measured the length of a shoe print left behind by an unwanted visitor.

"Size elevens," the detective told a uniformed police officer standing near him. "At least one of the suspects had on a pair of size eleven boots with four grooves across the middle. And look at this notch on the outside corner of the sole. Must have caught it on something during one of his nightly escapades. If we find this boot, we have one of our suspects."

Tomczyk slowly stood, patted some dirt off the knees of his blue jeans, and surveyed the cemetery. "How many did you say were damaged, Jerry?"

Holding a small, brown notebook in his left hand, the young officer moved a black pen downward and flipped the page. "I count thirteen."

"Thirteen?" asked the detective rhetorically. "Not that I'm superstitious, but coincidentally, kind of an unlucky number of gravestones damaged in a cemetery on Halloween night, isn't it?"

"Sure is. My money's on the group of neighborhood teenagers too old to trick or treat for the first time," responded the officer, providing a theory for the crime.

"Who knows? You could be right," Tomczyk admitted. "If you want to take off, I'll handle it from here. We'll use the cemetery as the complainant. Do me a favor and file a short supplementary—you know the drill: why you were sent, who called it in, and that you secured the scene until I arrived. Just check with a couple neighbors living by the entrances to see if they saw or heard anything. If you get something good, call me."

The dark circles under the uniformed officer's eyes and the beard stubble told a story of someone who had worked all night.

"Thanks, Ski. Mind if I file the report tonight when I come in? I'm beat and still have to make ten o'clock court on a crummy subpoena for a preliminary hearing; it's my third day of court in a row. My wife's ready to hang me out to dry."

"No problem, man. Promise me you'll go home and get some sleep after that. You look like hell. Consider this a grim reminder that they don't call it the 'graveyard shift' for nothing."

The officer smiled. Nodding his head in agreement, he walked toward his marked squad car parked on a nearby cemetery roadway, looking carefully for anything that might reveal the identity of the perpetrators.

Tomczyk visually examined each headstone. A total of eight had been kicked over and defaced by pentagrams made with bright red spray paint. Four others were still standing, but had the same red, spray painted pentagrams. The final headstone, a three-foot-high brown marble, was lying at an awkward angle against one of the other stones. A twelve-inch inverted cross had been spray painted on it, and the word *PIG* was manually inscribed, using some sort of chiseling tool. Someone took particular fascination in that one. The detective diligently noted the last names of the departed souls: MALICKI, GRACZYK, KILOGORE, STANISLOWSKI, STAWICKI, WENDT, CZAJKOWSKI, SLAMMS, LIGHT, BALANSKI, SCHNEIDER, REINER. That final headstone was of a Harold SCHLUNDT: "1900-1982, Loving Husband and Father." In his mind, Tomczyk divided the small area into sectors and performed a methodical search of each grid. Inside a well-groomed bush about thirty feet away from the area lay a partially hidden can of red spray paint. *Good, at least I found something helpful,* he thought to himself.

Just then, he felt the presence of somebody behind him. He turned and saw a woman—attired in a black pant suit and white blouse, covered by an unbuttoned beige trench coat.

"Can I help you?" asked the temporarily startled detective.

"I'm sorry. Didn't mean to sneak up on you like that," said the woman as she walked closer. "Don't think we've ever met before. My name is Anne Dvorak. I'm a special agent with the FBI." She opened a black leather wallet displaying her shield and credentials.

Slightly confused, Tomczyk extended his right hand. "FBI? What a pleasure, I think. A-ah, hi, I'm Detective Declan Tomczyk. I'm guessing you already know I'm with Milwaukee PD. So, do you usually get all dressed up and hang out in cemeteries on beautiful fall mornings in good ole' Milwaukee, Wisconsin?"

"Not too often," Dvorak replied, her shoulder-length, brown hair gently moving about in the breeze. "I'm new here in Brewtown, just a little over two months. I was on the way to get my morning shot of caffeine when I received a call from my office about this assignment.

Thought I'd stop by and see what you had here before facing the stack of paperwork on my desk. Not to be rude on our first visit, but Declan Tomczyk? That's quite an interesting handle."

"I'd be a liar if I said you were the first one to ever ask. Suffice it to say my proud Irish mother wanted to make sure her children had some identity. She gave us very Irish names to go with our Polish last name. Please, call me Ski."

"I get that."

"So, a federal agent gets sent to check out a vandalism complaint in a cemetery? Okay then." Tomczyk wanted to scratch his head and ask why the FBI would have the slightest interest in this case, but decided to just go with it. "Just started poking around. I'm guessing kids. But something is bothering me here," he said, pointing to the headstone of Harold Schlundt. "Why would someone take the time to etch the word *PIG* on a headstone and to spray paint an inverted cross instead of a pentagram like the others? I'm sure there's a story behind it. It's the first case of this type I've investigated. I've only worked this gig for ten months. Left the robbery squad to seek my fame and fortune in the intelligence unit."

"Ah, makes sense. You know what they say," Dvorak added. "Your first hunch is usually the right one. These types of cases are usually juveniles, but there are always exceptions."

He watched as she looked intently at the downed headstones. "I'm sure there are," Tomczyk grinned. "Halloween night is the night to visit your local cemetery and do crazy things."

"Don't let Halloween jaundice your investigation," the agent warned.

"I'm not from internal affairs, Anne," he jokingly added, "so I won't try to make square pegs fit into round holes."

"That's good," Dvorak commented. "I sure would appreciate it if you would forward a copy of your report to our office. Did you find anything suspicious around here, besides the obvious?"

It was the way she said it that struck him as strange. "Should I be looking for anything in particular? I'll make sure you get copies of the report." Tomczyk reached into his badge holder, retrieved a business card, and handed it to the agent. "If you haven't heard from me in a week, shoot me an email or give me a call and remind me. They keep me busy, so I forget things. Hard to be both handsome and smart."

"A rare breed if you were," Dvorak smiled as she gave him a business card of her own. The infamous gold-foil shield and FBI logo protruded brightly from it. "Thanks, Detective. It was a pleasure meeting you."

"Likewise." Tomczyk watched as the agent made her way back to a black Dodge Intrepid, partially concealed behind the cemetery's mausoleum. In her mid-thirties, the female agent cut a stunning figure. *What a knockout. I'll have to work on getting to see her again.*

Reality struck when a white evidence van with MILWAUKEE POLICE and a blue, horizontal stripe stenciled on the side pulled up. An identification technician in a navy blue windbreaker and black cargo pants walked toward him. "What's up, Ski?"

"Oh, just your normal vandalism of headstones in a cemetery on Halloween night," he smirked. "I'll need the usual once over, Kim. If you can dust some of the smooth headstones for prints, that'd be fantastic. I have a can of red spray paint over in that bush and a boot print I'll definitely need your expertise in making a cast for. That's way past my rudimentary evidence-collection skills. Guess we're lucky to have this small patch of dirt here instead of all grass. Sure makes for a great print. And, if you have a couple of those colorful, yellow evidence numbers of yours to place around here to take a couple pictures, we'll be good to go. Even CSI would be proud of us then. You on your regular squad?" As he spoke, Tomczyk wrote on his steno pad: Squad 2385, ID Tech Kim Robertson.

"You got it. That's a great boot print; let me get the kit out of my van."

Tomczyk grabbed the half-full bottle of orange juice from his coat pocket and took a gulp. At the same time, his handheld radio squawked, "Squad 7376 to 3531 on channel seven."

"Removing the radio from his belt, he answered. "Squad 3531 here; go on, channel twelve."

"Roger."

Tomczyk turned the channel on his handy talkie from the Criminal Investigation Bureau radio frequency to a side channel. "Go ahead, Jerry."

"Yo, Ski. I knocked on about eight houses. All but two were home. None heard or saw anything, so I drove back into the cemetery and saw a small, brown paper bag floating around in the wind by the south entrance. Looked inside and found a receipt for two cans of spray paint. They were bought yesterday at a small hobby shop a couple blocks from here."

"Beautiful."

"There's more. It appears our rocket scientists also spray painted both brick pillars on either side of the entrance with the same red paint. On one side is the word *REMHAD* and on the other is *REDRUM*, printed out in all capital letters."

"Well, that makes this case a little more interesting. Do me a favor and hang out 'til I'm done with the evidence tech here. We'll be over as quick as we can. I'll take the paper bag and receipt off your hands. You may have uncovered another piece of the puzzle. Per usual, you're the man."

"Copy that, standing by."

As Tomczyk secured the radio back onto his belt, his gaze returned to the strange way two of the gravestones had been placed on the ground. That's when he saw it. The dark green wire blended in perfectly with the manicured Kentucky bluegrass—except where the two brightly colored orange and red maple leaves crossed its path. He got down on his knees to get a closer view. Shock enveloped him as he followed the wire under the brown marble. He couldn't believe no one had tripped the wire while they were searching for clues or evidence. *Why would someone put an improvised device in a cemetery while defacing and knocking over some headstones? This case just took a really crazy twist.*

"Big favor, Kim?" Tomczyk called over to the ID tech to shut off his handheld to avoid possible detonation from two-way radio transmission. "Get over to the south cemetery entrance and meet the uniformed squad. They have evidence for you to photograph. Throw it in a bag for me to inventory later. But first, give the Detective Bureau a call on your cell when you get over there. Tell them to get the bomb squad over here ASAP. Possible IED. I have some experience with explosives from my deployments over in the Middle East, but never went through the formal training. I specialized in butt-kickin', not bomb defusing. We need the EOD experts."

"You're kiddin' me—an IED?!"

"Wish I were. This thing's set to go off if someone moves the headstone or trips on the wire. We're lucky none of us set this dang thing off. Gotta wonder if the intended victim was a cemetery worker or a cop."

"Think I'll wonder about that when I move my butt out of the way. How about if I throw a pylon over the boot print and take the cast after the place is secure?"

"That'll work."

"Okay, I'll get back to you."

"Fair enough. Appears I won't be going anywhere."

Tomczyk sat in his squad for what seemed like half his shift. He looked at his watch and logged that it was now ten thirty. His notion of this being a quick assignment was fading fast. As he was pondering a hike to a safe area to call the dispatcher and see where the bomb tech was, he saw the dark blue MPD bomb squad truck. It was followed by an unmarked, light green Ford Crown Victoria driving over to his location. His good friend John 'Lurch' Lemke exited the driver's side of the 2010 Chevy 3500 Heavy Duty truck.

"Sorry, Ski. All the bomb techs are in training this week at the quarry in Muskego, blowin' stuff up. I even brought along one of the feds to show him what real police work looks like."

FBI SABT (Special Agent Bomb Technician) Kevin Cleary stepped out of the passenger side of the truck. He wore a navy blue, insulated nylon jacket with large FBI letters stenciled on the left breast and standard, federal-agent-tan 5.11 pants. Feds love to don 5.11 pants when they're not in their business attire—any size, any color.

"Easy Lurch, or I'll refuse to play with you again. I'm one of the only feds who actually thinks you're human." They chuckled at the comment.

"This makes two FBI agents I saw in one day." Tomczyk rubbed his chin. "Does that make for a bad omen?"

"Depends."

"What do ya have?" Lemke had been a detective for over twenty-two years, and a bomb tech for twenty. He didn't appear to be the brightest bulb, and everyone, including Tomczyk, was amazed he still had all his digits—even more so that he was still alive. Lemke had picked up the dubious nickname of "Lurch" from the scary "you ra-a-ng" character on *The Addams Family*. He stood six-foot-five, solidly built, with a slow, deliberate manner of speaking. There was no arguing he knew everything about explosives, WMDs, and anything remotely associated with them.

"This one kind of freaks me out, Lurch. The district squad was dispatched in response to a vandalism call, and I was sent to meet them because of possible cult connections. As I was checking out some of their spray painting art, I saw a green wire protruding from beneath that brown headstone leading over to the overturned black granite one. Underneath it," as he pointed to the target headstone, "is a micro switch and wire connected to some kind of hidden container. Thank God no one went in too close or moved anything. At that point, it was time to call for the experts."

"You got it, buddy. Good thing we brought our secret weapon today." Lemke raised his right arm and gave a slight wave. With that, a man in green army camouflage came out of the driver's side door of the Crown Victoria. He opened the back door and out leapt a sixty-five-pound yellow Labrador Retriever. "Ski, meet Austin, Department of Defense's bomb dog extraordinaire. That's her handler, Sergeant Rick Vasquez. These EOD guys either have some of the biggest balls on the planet, or they're missing a number of brain cells. Remember the crazy guy in *The Hurt Locker* and all the stuff he did? There you go, proof positive."

"I heard that, Lurch. Don't hurt Austin's feelings; she's sensitive." Sergeant Vasquez attached the leash to Austin's collar and came over to the group. Lemke briefed him on what they had.

"I can't get too close with Austin in case she missteps and hits the wire, but I can go in from the other side. Wind's from out of the north. If there's any explosive material here, Austin'll smell it."

He led the dog over to the area of the pushed over headstones and spoke to her. Her tail wagged excitedly, and she sat down next to a section of grass near the headstones, signifying a "passive alert" to the presence of explosive materials. The sergeant flashed a look over at the three investigators. "Okay, Austin smells something. Looks like we have a live one. Do you guys mind if I have my try with this? I'm going back to the 'Sandbox' in February, and those terrorist turds make deadly, but crappy, bombs. It's always good to get the training with someone who hopefully knows what the heck he's doing. You put enough explosives anywhere with a detonating device and something's bound to get blown up. Just hold on to Austin for me."

"Have at it, Rick," Lemke smiled.

Sergeant Vasquez knelt down and surveyed the situation up close. He didn't like what he saw. The green wire was wound around a metal stake that had been pushed into the ground and hidden under the angled black granite headstone. It went through an open area and under the knocked-over and defaced brown headstone of Harold Schlundt. He turned on his small penlight and saw a black, plastic micro switch attached to wires leading to a midnight black-colored plastic container directly underneath the headstone. A separate black wire, making a secondary detonation connection, also led to the container. He stood back up.

"This is not very promising, boys. The green trip wire is hooked up to the micro switch as the primary connection. There's also a black wire connection to the container, which I'm guessing is the secondary detonation. That doesn't even take into account a plunger, motion, or sensor device inside the box. Guess I'll go put on the bomb suit, since I worry about trying to maneuver the robot around these headstones and uneven ground. It's a job for the PAN. What do you guys think?"

"Totally agree," both Lemke and Cleary responded.

Lemke went to the back of the truck and grabbed the olive-green, colored bomb suit for Vasquez. Special Agent Cleary reached for the Percussion Actuated Nonelectric disruptor (PAN) from its prominent space on one of the shelves. It was used extensively by military and civilian personnel to remotely disable and render safe improvised explosive devices without detonating them. The disruptor employed a standard, commercial twelve-gauge shotgun shell with modified loads designed to provide general and specific disruption capabilities—the bomb technician's best friend. Equipped with a collapsible, adjustable stand, the PAN was activated remotely from various radio frequency devices using a shock tube initiator. Highly pressured projectiles, such as water, clay, sand, or other substances, were used to open the potential explosive at high speed. This disrupted the explosive and firing train, rendering the IED safe. It could also be attached to a robot and armed with video capabilities.

It took several minutes for Sergeant Vasquez to put on the cumbersome outfit. Fixed with a number of layers of Kevlar, the suit also contained ceramic inserts to protect the wearer from shrapnel.

"Okay, boys, wish me luck." Vasquez walked up to the knocked-over headstones and set up the PAN low enough to target the black container. After several minutes, he turned around, flashed the thumbs-up sign, and walked back to the group.

"I'd say we're good here at about 150 feet back to protect us from a blast, if there is one."

When everyone was safely positioned behind one of the larger headstones, Vasquez pushed the button, and the distinctive disruptor sound pierced the air, which was thankfully the only sound they heard. He slowly stepped over to the area, peered under the headstone, and saw a damaged but "safe" black plastic container. He moved the heavy SCHLUNDT headstone to expose the formerly intact container with wires still attached. He signaled "all clear" to his coworkers.

They walked over to Vasquez's location. Tomczyk was the first to speak. "Okay, bomb techies, talk away—I'm all ears."

Lemke bent over and scanned the container, noting some of the items and picking up one of the black plastic pieces.

"Looks to me like the maker devised several different ways for this thing to detonate. He was nice enough to omit one rather important component—the explosive load. See the cut-out opening here on top? Here's the pin he had that would've acted as a plunger to go off if the headstone was moved. He also had the trip wire and timing device here just to show that he could."

Lemke raised up an eight-inch cast iron pipe with a metal cap on one end and a blue piece of paper rolled up inside. Black and green wires protruded out from the ends, which were connected to a nine-volt battery attached to the inside of the container.

"This is where the explosive should be. Instead, our Mister Bomb Maker is sending pipe-bomb love letters. You have any secret admirers, Ski? Looks like someone is sending us a message or trying to make a statement." Lemke carefully removed the rolled up piece of paper with his rubber-gloved hands and unrolled it using only the ends of the paper. He read the note out loud:

This is a test, pigs. As you see, I can make bombs, and if I wanted your ass, I'd have it. The past is going to come back and haunt this shit city. Bombs away! The days of terror have returned to Brewtown.
TMB

"What the heck does all that mean?" Lemke said, scratching his large forehead.

"This message is as crazy as the rest of this case. Not sure you saw the artwork on your way into the cemetery. REDRUM and REMHAD were spray painted in red on the stone pillars at the main entrance. The days of terror are returning to Brewtown? What days of terror? Okay, I get REDRUM and REMHAD as 'MURDER' and 'DAHMER' spelled backward—whatever their connection is to this case. But what or who is TMB?" Tomczyk was completely baffled. *Wonder if that FBI agent had any knowledge of this. Why'd she show up at something like this anyway?*

"Better you than me, Ski. Had my share of 'whodunits.' I retire in a month, so I'm just cruisin' until then. Always a pleasure to do business with you, though. Since there isn't anything I need to take with me as evidence, can you handle the rest? We need to get back to training for our re-certs."

"You got it, Lurch. Thanks for the help, guys. I'd bet money that I'll be seeing you again soon."

"I won't take any odds on that one," Agent Cleary mused as they all shook hands. The three bomb techs started toward the bomb truck to put the equipment away.

"I'll catch up with you guys in a sec. I want to check something out." Lemke started walking off toward a large oak tree as if he were following something.

Tomczyk was watching Lurch when his attention was drawn to the sound of a car engine behind him. He turned his head and observed a newer-model green Ford Explorer about fifty yards away, edging slowly along one of the cemetery roads. The driver, a bald white male, was wearing sunglasses. Something seemed strange about him. There was a passenger in the front seat and two males in the back. Tomczyk turned around and spied the orange wire along the ground that Lemke must have been following.

For that split second, a feeling of déjà vu swept over him. "Lurch" was all he got out before the bomb went off. The explosion blew Tomczyk off his feet. He saw stars, but quickly regained his balance and stood up. He looked at the SUV. The driver pulled his glasses down, revealing an evil set of eyes as he gave a slow, deliberate middle finger while flashing a wicked smile. Tomczyk would never forget those piercing eyes or sinister smile, even from that distance. The vehicle sped off through the cemetery while the detective momentarily glared over at his friend, lying lifeless on the ground.

Chapter 2

MILWAUKEE

Special Agent Dvorak kept wondering why she was sent to the cemetery. The only similarity between what she was sent to check for and what was there was that it occurred in a cemetery. She ran over the details of her observations in her mind to see if she missed anything but came up with nothing. Hopefully the detective, Declan something, could come up with more. She drove into the secured garage of the Milwaukee FBI office on North Broadway Street.

Holy Cross Cemetery, Milwaukee

Tomczyk dashed over to where Lurch was lying, quickly joined by the two bomb techs. He touched his finger to Lurch's carotid artery. The pulse was faint.

"Squad 3521, officer down. Request an ambulance 10-17 to Holy Cross Cemetery! An explosion just went off. Have them enter at the east entrance. We're about two hundred yards southwest of there. Dispatch, request the air for a vehicle description."

"All squads, standby for a description. Go ahead, 3521."

"Squad 3521 to all squads. Wanted for attempted homicide of a police officer by means of an explosive device. Occurred in Holy Cross Cemetery, 7301 West Nash Street, several minutes ago. Wanted is a newer-model, dark green Ford Explorer with unknown Wisconsin license plates. Driver is a white male, bald and wearing dark sun glasses. Appeared to be in his twenties or thirties. Last seen wearing a dark-colored jacket or shirt. Three additional white males in the vehicle, with no further descriptions. Vehicle last observed fleeing at a high rate of speed toward the north entrance of the cemetery. KSA-536."

"10-4, ambulance is on the way. Just confirmed they'll be there in less than three minutes."

Sergeant Vasquez had a large first aid kit from the bomb truck opened up and was surveying Lurch's injuries. "Damn. Austin smelled the stuff, but didn't trail it away from the headstones over to that tree."

Tomczyk spun into "Marine Mode" as he feverishly tried to save Lemke. He said quietly, "I know, Sarge. Austin did her job by alerting us to explosives. Nobody expected this."

Over the course of his two tours served in Iraq, Declan had seen a number of fellow soldiers with life-threatening IED injuries. There was no way he was going to lose Lurch, who like many of the others was his friend. He elevated the concept of saving lives in the first seconds after an injury to a new level—the long and informative lifesaving classes he attended on his own time while in the Marine Corps flashed in his mind as he took the necessary steps of saving another life.

The sirens of the Milwaukee Fire Department paramedic ambulance were getting closer. Kevin Cleary was the first to see the vehicle pull into the cemetery entrance. He went to the bomb truck and flicked on the oscillating red and blue lights to gain the driver's attention.

"You're going to make it, Lurch," Tomczyk gently whispered in his friend's left ear. "Don't you dare stop fighting! I'll be with you every step of the way."

He was able to stop the bleeding on Lemke's head and arms before starting an IV of saline solution. The heavy ballistic level-four vest that Lemke was wearing deflected its share of shrapnel and destruction. It would have to be removed so he could be checked for any additional injuries after the MFD personnel placed him on the stretcher.

"We have it from here. Can you give us his vitals?"

Tomczyk turned around and observed the familiar MFD paramedics logo on the blue cloth jacket.

"IED detonated about five minutes ago, somewhere over there," pointing to an area fifty feet away. "Detective Lemke sustained percussion and shrapnel injuries to his head and extremities. He has a pulse, which was initially weak, but it started getting stronger after we administered the IV drip. We've stopped the obvious bleeding areas, but he's still unconscious. Please do your magic. I'll be riding with you to the hospital."

"Good enough, thanks."

The three paramedics, along with the help of the law enforcement professionals, were able to lift the athletically built detective onto the stretcher. No additional wounds were discovered when the ballistic vest was removed. As they placed Lemke in the ambulance to stabilize him before the trip to the level I trauma center, Tomczyk removed the radio from his belt and requested the ID tech go to the side channel.

"Go ahead, Ski; what's the game plan?"

"I know you heard that explosion. It was a secondary IED from the one I found initially. Lurch was hit when it exploded."

Kim noted the slight quivering in Tomczyk's voice and asked, "Damn, how bad?"

"He's in rough shape. I'm headin' out to Froedtert Hospital. Can you take care of the pictures and evidence recovery over there, then come back and finish the scene here? One detective from intel is on his way, along with a couple homicide guys. They'll help you out. I know it's asking a lot, but this is bad."

"Come on, man. You know I'd walk across hot coals for either of you. I'll see you downtown later. Looks like this is going to be a long day."

"In more ways than one! I owe you one, buddy."

"You know I'll collect," he said, trying to brighten up the serious mood. "Give Lurch a hug from me."

"Count on it!"

ID Tech Robertson went back to the job at hand and told Police Officer Jerry Boyek the bad news about Lemke.

Tomczyk opened the back door to the ambulance and climbed in. Several minutes later, after victim stabilization, the driver began the ten-minute ride to the hospital, red lights and siren blaring. A paramedic was on the phone to the hospital, providing vitals and taking important information from a medical doctor. One of Milwaukee's finest had his life in their hands. There was no room for mistakes.

Milwaukee FBI Office

Anne took the elevator to the sixth floor and key-carded her way into the FBI offices. As she was on the way to her cubicle, fellow Special Agent Matt Hacker walked over. "Anne, weren't you over at Holy Cross Cemetery to meet a detective for a possible case?"

"Yeah, Matt. I took care of that and left a while ago. What's up?"

"There was an explosion. They found a bogus bomb under one of the damaged headstones. An MPD bomb tech traced a wire over to a tree when some guys in a green SUV driving through the cemetery must have detonated a real one. He was hurt really bad. Some MPD detective, Tomczyk or something like that, saved the guy's life."

Agent Dvorak's jaw dropped. "I don't believe it. Detective Tomczyk had it well in hand. They must have found everything after I left. I feel terrible."

"Not our case, Anne. You did what you were supposed to. We're still in the dark about this investigation until we get more info."

"I still should have stuck around to help them." A sickening feeling came over her. "You're right. Probably nothing I could have done."

"I'll say. Cleary was there. He has the bomb training; you don't. Kevin gave Lee a call to tell him what happened. That's how we knew about it so fast."

Milwaukee, Wisconsin

It was three fifteen when seventeen-year-old Demetrius Simms turned the key in the lock on the front door of his house on Milwaukee's North Side. Football season at Rufus King International High School was ending soon, and he had just finished another tough practice getting ready for the conference championships that weekend. Coach Horner was a tough coach, but the proof was in the pudding. King had made the championships the last five years running. Even though there was only half a day of school today, Coach Horner held an early afternoon practice. "Can't waste a beautiful day by not practicing," he told his team as they pushed hard on the football field. As a junior, Demetrius still had one year left before hopefully landing a scholarship offer to a Division I college. He was taking advanced placement classes in the International Baccalaureate program, and his goal was to graduate from college in three years. Demetrius had already received about thirty letters from various colleges expressing interest in him.

"Ma, how ya doin'?" he asked as he walked up and gave her a big hug and a kiss on the lips.

"Blessed, D. Just cleaning up a bit. How was practice?"

"Tough, as usual. Coach wants us to kick it up a notch for Thursday's game. He gives a whole new meaning to wind sprints. They suck. Are you gonna go to the game?"

"D, I wouldn't miss my baby's football game. I'm expecting another three-touchdown game from you." She caressed his head lovingly for effect. "You know Johnny's got some homing device on that football for you, right?"

"Rig-h-t! He's sure a solid QB. Just so ya know, I have to work at the nursing home tonight from six to ten. Might as well get a couple hours of work in and earn some 'bank.' Can I have the car?"

"The 'bank' is down on the corner, honey. We could use some extra money, though. Of course you can use the car. Just get back home so you can finish the homework I know you have."

"C'mon, ma, you know what I mean. I started talkin' to this one old resident. He's a trip. Has to be in his nineties, but he's still smart as heck. Dude has some great stories."

"Dude? You mean *man*?"

"Yes, ma'am."

Demetrius ran upstairs, changed into his uniform, and was back down in less than five minutes. "Thanks, Ma. You're the best," he said as he grabbed the car keys from the counter and started for the door.

"Love you, honey. I'll probably be sleepin' when you get home. I have a six o'clock start at the hospital tomorrow. That four-thirty wakeup call comes early."

"Love ya more. See ya later." Demetrius walked out of the front door to the dark blue Chevrolet Tahoe parked at the curb in front of their house. Within three minutes, he was northbound on Interstate 43, on his way to River Hills Nursing Home.

Chapter 3

MILWAUKEE POLICE DEPARTMENT
HEADQUARTERS

The job's not done till the paperwork's complete. *How come all these TV cops never do reports? All they do is play* Action Jackson *their whole shift, then go home.* Tomczyk was thinking to himself as he perused over the bags of evidence piled on desks in the Detective Bureau. He was tired just thinking of all the reports he had to file. The time on his Timex Ironman digital watch showed 4:10 p.m. Lurch was in stable but critical condition in the ICU when Tomczyk left the hospital at three-thirty. He dialed FBI agent Anne Dvorak's cell number from her business card and her voicemail kicked on.

"Anne, this is Declan Tomczyk from Milwaukee PD. Please give me a call when you get this. We need to talk." He disconnected the call and went back to his work.

"Okay, Ski," the ID tech chimed in. "I have all the inventories signed out that we should need. I didn't get back to HQ until a half hour ago and had to pull teeth from my boss to let me stay to help you out. You'd think the overtime pay was coming from his wallet. One of our own is on life support at Froedtert, and he's worried what the chief's going to say because an ID technician got a couple hours overtime helping the detectives. The homicide guys did a hell of a job at the scene. Even you'd be proud of 'em."

"Well, that's a first. A homicide detective figuring a crime out." Tomczyk had the utmost respect for the tenacity of any detective who followed cold lead after cold lead to solve crimes, in between the various fresh homicide investigations that came his way. Homicide detectives had that knack.

"I'll have to tell them that. Anyway, after we finished the scene at the cemetery, a District Three squad found the Ford Explorer in the parking lot at Gille's on Bluemound Avenue. I drove there and processed it. Turned out to be a 'steal' taken two days ago when some 'brain child' left the keys in the ignition with the engine running to run into a gas station to buy some M&Ms. Go figure. Hopefully, the cop who took the complaint gave the idiot a car-key ordinance ticket. I know I would've. Anyway, I lifted a couple of prints from the interior, found some red spray paint marks on the seat, the floor mats, and on both of the passenger side door handles. I took some samples, so we'll see where it goes."

As they were talking and sorting out the evidence to be inventoried, the three detectives who had been at the cemetery walked into the Detective Bureau assembly. Each carried a number of brown shopping bags filled with additional evidence.

"Ski, my main man. How ya doing, and how's Lurch doing?"

"Hangin' in there, Robo. Lurch is still in critical condition, but they have him stabilized. I'm going back to the hospital when I'm done here. So, what have you high-priced and esteemed homicide detectives found out today that is going to solve this caper?"

Detective Scott Roblewski hung his suit jacket up on a hanger and straightened out his gun belt. "Well, according to Special Agent Cleary from the FBI, who swabbed some of the bomb residue, the explosive was methyl nitrate. You ever hear of it?"

"Methyl nitrate? Now that doesn't make any sense!"

"That's exactly what Agent Cleary said. He also said it's mega dangerous. Said it's like walking around with nitroglycerin because of its volatility."

Tomczyk, shaking his head in bewilderment, grabbed his notebook in case he needed to take some notes. "Did he also tell you that methyl nitrate has slightly less velocity than C4 explosive upon detonation, which is about twenty-five thousand feet per second? That's even faster than you can run, Robo. It's one of the most brisant explosives there is." Tomczyk went on to explain that brisance referred to the shattering effect of a high explosive. "When the explosion went off in the cemetery, I thought for sure it was C4 because of that distinctive cracking sound a high explosive makes. I heard it enough when our explosive ordnance boys would blow stuff up in training during my professional-soldier-playing days. Definitely a pucker-factor moment. Did you ever hear of triacetone triperoxide? TATP for short. It's the IED explosive of choice for terrorists."

"I've heard of it, but what's the connection?"

Tomczyk decided to share some of his knowledge: "Remember Richard Reid, who had it in his shoes on the plane a couple months after 9-11? Or the Al-Qaeda-trained turd who drove from Colorado to New York in 2009 with the intent of blowing up parts of the subway—until the feds caught up and arrested him? They both had TATP. Well, that has about a sixteen-thousand foot per second velocity, which packs about one-third less punch. I did some reading about methyl nitrate a while ago. It was invented by the Germans during World War II and used as a jet fuel. Someone got the wise idea to try to make an explosive out of it. The process of making it is almost exactly like nitro—and with the same volatility issues. Now that's scary stuff. Whoever is making and using this has to know about that fact, yet he's still crazy enough to use it. When it comes to explosives, methyl nitrate is definitely near the top of the ethyl-methyl-bad-stuff family.'"

"Cleary wasn't quite as graphic since he definitely didn't have as much info as you do about it. He used the term 'radio-controlled IED,' or 'RCIED,' to describe the device since the dirt bags placed it in a brown plastic container, secured it to a tree, and then used a two-way radio or cell phone to detonate it. You must have had your 'keen moment of observation' at about the time you saw 'em in the Explorer. The bomb techs found parts of a blasting cap, a receiver, and tiny bits of the container all around that tree during their post-blast investigation. By the way, the tree looked like it went through a 150-mile-an hour wind storm. We even found some wood splinters impaled in a plastic vase that must've been on top of one of the headstones. You guys are lucky you didn't get impaled by wood splinters."

"I didn't even think of it at the time. You're right. Explains why I saw a couple wood splinters stuck in Lemke's vest."

"The cops canvassed the heck out of the area where they found the Explorer. Can you imagine dropping off a hot vehicle like that in an ice cream custard stand parking lot —in Milwaukee? Every cop in the city is looking for the car, and that's where you abandon it? That's ballsy—and sacrilegious at the same time. Anyway, we found several witnesses who observed four white males wearing black leather jackets getting out of the SUV and walking southbound nonchalantly down 76th Street at about 11:35 a.m. I'm guessing they had another car sitting somewhere in the area or someone picked them up so they could make a clean getaway. Two of the witnesses provided great descriptions and were with a police artist from Wauwatosa PD, who volunteered to help us out on this one."

"That's a good start. Anything else?"

Roblewski perked up. "Agent Cleary said Lurch survived because of the way the device was placed. Since it was secured on the east side of the tree and Lurch approached it from the southwest, most of the blast force and shrapnel blew out in a different direction, so thankfully he didn't absorb the full brunt of the explosion."

"It was enough to knock me over, too, and I was a ways away from that damn thing."

River Hills Nursing Home: Suburb of Milwaukee

Demetrius arrived at 5:50 p.m. and punched in. He made his way over to the maintenance room and grabbed the brooms and other equipment he would need for his shift.

"What's up, D? How's my favorite homeboy doing?"

"You're trippin', Mrs. Howe. Is that any way for an RN to talk?" he said to her, smiling from ear to ear.

"Only because I love ya, kid." Mrs. Howe was the shift supervisor for the nursing home. Demetrius had been working there for six months and had become a favorite among the nursing staff on the p.m. shift because of his punctuality, readiness to work, and upbeat personality. He certainly had shattered stereotypes that employees and residents had of young black men. His friendly and helpful demeanor was also enjoyed and respected by the majority of residents with whom he came into contact, nearly all of whom were white. The very upscale suburb of River Hills, Wisconsin, located between the Milwaukee River and Lake Michigan, was heavily populated with white people. The same demographic was also prevalent in the nursing home.

"Thank you, ma'am. Tim left directions for me to start cleaning the rooms on the second floor. Is there anything I can get for you guys before I start?"

"Nothing at all. Things are going smoothly so far tonight. George was asking about you. Don't know what you did to gain his confidence over the last two weeks, but he sure has taken a liking to you."

"We found a common bond in football. He's a big Packer fan, so we relate well. Can't believe what a memory he's got for his age. Totally amazes me."

Demetrius walked down the hall with the broom and started cleaning the first five rooms. He then went and grabbed the mop bucket to wipe down the rooms and the hallway. "How you doin,' Mrs. Springer?"

Delores Springer looked up from the book she was reading and smiled at him. At seventy-nine-years-old, she enjoyed her time at the nursing home. "I'm doing well. You're looking perfectly happy tonight, I must say, Demetrius."

"Had a great day at school today, ma'am. How's the book?"

"An excellent mystery," she said, adjusting her glasses. "Love those mysteries."

"Love 'em myself. Good to see you, Mrs. Springer. Have a great night. If you get out of bed in the next fifteen minutes or so, be very careful of the wet floor." Demetrius finished mopping up her room and placed the WET FLOOR sign in the hallway just outside her door. Walking down the hall to the activity room, he saw George in his usual place, sitting in the brown leather chair by the corner. George's eyes lit up when he saw his newfound friend.

"Demetrius! How's it going? Did you see the Packers wipe out the Lions last Sunday?"

"Sure did, George. What about this weekend, though? They're playing the Giants."

"No problem. Their QB ain't that good. Our defensive coordinator has a couple tricks up his sleeve, and I can feel Rodgers throwing for four hundred yards and getting a couple TDs under his belt."

"Can I get you anything?"

"How 'bout a can of Dr. Pepper? It's in the fridge down the hall. Grab two so you can sit for a while and we can talk."

"Done." Demetrius came back in a few minutes with two cans of soda in his hands. He popped the top of both, handing one to George.

"Can't tell you how much I love Dr. Pepper. Been drinking this concoction for seventy years or so."

"You have any good stories for me?"

George sat silent for a minute or two. "Demetrius, I have a doozie for you. Happened in 1935 and affected my life in a big way. Heck, I even ended up going to prison because of my foolishness. I spent less than a year screwin' up my life, but it cost me pret' near six years. Coulda' been a lot more. Please, pull up a chair."

Demetrius didn't know what to think. He was on his break but had also been encouraged by the staff to make the residents happy by engaging them in conversation, even if it meant putting some of his job duties on hold. "Okay, George. But I can't spend my whole shift talking to you. You can call me 'D' like everybody else. It's a lot easier to say."

"Great. This is something I need to get off my chest. You're a good kid, and I don't want something like this to ever happen to you. Peer pressure's strong, ya know. I told that Richie kid who used to work here the same story six months ago. He doesn't work here anymore, so I don't know if he ever took my advice."

"Yeah, I remember the dude, from when I first started here. Guess he quit shortly after that." Demetrius pulled a wooden chair over from the table in the room and set it down next to George.

"I was born a week before President John F. Kennedy, in 1917, so you get a feel of how old I am—damn old!" He laughed a little at what he said. "When I was just a little older than you, I got involved with a couple guys in my neighborhood doing some things. The main guy was Idzi Rutkowski—not even sure what his first name was. Don't know where his nickname came from. He was a year or so older than me. We both went to Boys Tech High School and lived on the Sout' Side. The other kid's name was 'Shrimp' Chovanec. He was just a little shit, excuse my swearing, and was only about sixteen-years-old."

"That's okay. I've heard words like that before. By the way, they let girls go there now, and it's called Milwaukee Technical High School."

"Progress. Good thing 'bout Boys Tech back then, it gave you skills for an occupation: electrician, plumber, auto mechanic, stuff like that. Anyway, Idzi used to get arrested by the cops all the time, and he hated 'em. Always told us he was going to get revenge. We just figured he was blowin' smoke. One day he came to the garage we used to hang out at and told us his plan. He had gone to the CCC camp up in Estabrook Park and applied for a job, but they turned him down cold. Said his teeth were too screwed up."

"That's crazy! What's a CCC camp?"

"Sorry. CCC stands for Civilian Conservation Corps. It was a program started by President Roosevelt during Depression to get men back to work. They had 'em working on projects all over the country to give 'em a sense of self-worth, instead of just standing on the street corner drinking all day or getting in trouble."

"They sure could use some of that today. I see dudes standing on the corner in my 'hood all the time. All they're doing is selling drugs and drinking beer." He shook his head. "So what was the plan?"

"There you go, D. You're a smart kid. Idzi said he had some information they stored dynamite in a special building in the park, and he wanted to break into it and steal some. Said he had been casing the guards for a while and knew what they did. So he talked me into stealing a car. I had stolen one a couple months before and got away with it. That was some sweet ride. An eight-cylinder engine and it moved like a sonofabitch. Anyway, I picked Idzi and Shrimp up one night, and we drove up there, broke into the building, and stole three boxes of dynamite and a box 'a blasting caps. I was scared as hell, but Idzi—Idzi was like a demon on a mission. We drove back to the garage with the dynamite stuffed in the trunk. My fingers were glued to the steering wheel the whole time. They only had manual transmissions back then, and I didn't want to screw up the shifting or break any laws." George simulated driving with his hands on an invisible steering wheel and his eyes wide open.

"Didn't want the cops to stop us. We put the wooden boxes in the garage. Coupla' nights later, we took some sticks of dynamite and drove the same car out to some railroad tracks in 'Tosa to see if the stuff worked. Idzi set the charge and blew 'em up. Damn, it was loud. We got the hell out of there in a hurry."

"That's wild!" Demetrius was sitting on the edge of the chair, taking the whole story in.

"That's not the half of it. On the way back, Idzi says he has info about some guy who lived by us who had a bunch of guns in his house. So we parked the car down the street, and the three of us walked up to the house. It's like one o'clock in the morning, and all the lights were off. Idzi forced open a window in the basement, and we all climbed in. We went up to the first floor and found some of the guns hidden in the kitchen pantry—found a couple more upstairs underneath the guy's mattress. Turns out no one was home. They had an article about the house getting burglarized in *The Milwaukee Journal* the next day. Thought for sure the cops were gonna come out and arrest us. We got like five or six handguns, a shotgun, and a rifle. We hid 'em in the clubhouse garage that night. The next night, Shrimp and I stole another car and hid it in this garage Shrimp had rented a coupla' blocks away. I still don't believe someone rented a two-car garage to a teenage kid. We put one or two of the guns in the car and sold a couple on the street to some friends."

"You were busy dudes, George. My ma woulda' strangled me if she found out I ever did something like that!"

"I hit a wild streak for a while. It took prison for me to straighten out. I'll tell you something else and let you go back to work. We had one busy month."

"Okay."

"It was a Sunday afternoon sometime that October. I went over to the garage and Idzi showed me the shotgun we took in the burglary. He had sawed the barrel down about a foot, so now it looked like something you'd see in a gangster movie. He told Shrimp and me that he had this great idea. We got into the car and drove over to the East Side, you know, 'round Oakland Avenue, there in Shorewood."

"Yeah, I kinda' know it."

"Idzi told me to park the car outside this drugstore on Oakland and for Shrimp and me to stay in the car. So Idzi grabbed the sawed-off shotgun and got out. Just before he walked into the store, he put on a pair of sunglasses and a handkerchief over his mouth and nose. That's when it hit me. I was in way over my head and didn't know how to get out. He was in that store less than five minutes when Shrimp and I heard a loud pop. A coupla' seconds later, Idzi comes runnin' out, jumps in the car, and tells us to get the hell outa' there. All I remember is flyin' away from that curb with my foot stompin' on the gas pedal."

"Did Idzi tell you what happened?"

"Oh yeah. He was laughin' about it and breathin' hard, all at the same time. Said he went to the back of the store and demanded money from the clerk. When he told the guy a second time, he fired a round from the shotgun and missed, but hit a clock right behind the guy's head. Idzi said he got pissed off, so he ran out of the store and didn't even take any money. The next day, we saw an article in the newspaper and a picture of a cop standing next to the clock on the wall that Idzi hit. Laughed our asses off!"

"Unbelievable." Demetrius looked at his watch. It was a quarter till nine. "Dang, George. I've got to get going before Tim goes crazy on me. I have to mop the rest of the rooms and hallway before leaving for the night."

Laughing, George put his hand out to Demetrius and embraced it warmly. "You're a great listener, kid. When you working next?"

"I'll be here all day Wednesday 'cause we're off school. Our next game is Thursday night."

"Great, D. Can't wait to talk to you again. Remind me where I left off. You're a little younger than me—with a better memory."

"Come on! Who's got the memory? I don't remember what I had for dinner last night."

"You're funny. Thanks for making my time here more enjoyable."

Demetrius grabbed the mop and bucket in the corner of George's room and walked back to where he had left off. *I can't wait until he tells me more of his story on Wednesday.*

Chapter 4

MILWAUKEE PD HEADQUARTERS

dentification Technician Scott Kamble sat at his desk on the third floor of the Police Administration Building located on the southwest corner of West State Street and North James Lovell Drive in downtown Milwaukee. The four-block-long street was named after Milwaukee native and former astronaut, James Lovell. Kamble used scissors to cut open the large, brown paper bag where the white evidence tape had been securely wrapped during the sealing process. He looked at the photo copy of the Milwaukee Police inventory form attached to the bag and matched the inventory number with the one inked on the bag to be sure he had the right items. Inventory# 4618349 was listed in both locations. He noticed Detective Declan Tomczyk's name listed on the inventory and his initials and date inked on the white tape next to the dried red seal wax. Kamble peered into the top of the now-opened bag to see what goodies had been placed inside that needed to be checked for latent fingerprints.

"Mike, here's another big caper from Declan Tomczyk, that bombing at Holy Cross Cemetery from the other day. Man, he's a great

31

guy, but what a crap magnet. Collects more evidence on cases than all the detectives on *CSI Miami* combined."

"I know. Had two cases last week with him. We pos-ID'd both through prints. He called and thanked me, then mentioned that he got felony warrants on both suspects. If we had more guys like him, they'd have to bring a couple more ID techs up here per shift."

"Copy that." *Let's see what we got. A can of spray paint, white paper receipt, and a brown paper bag,* Kamble thought as he gently pulled out each item from the bag with his blue rubber-gloved hand. He first dusted the can with a fine-haired brush, using silver oxide powder. Two identifiable prints became visible on the paper surrounding the can. Kamble always loved this part of the job, getting latent fingerprints from a case and trying to identify the perpetrator. He completed dusting the rest of the can with no further results. Placing the powder and brush off to the side, he picked up the special transparent tape and placed it on the can, one piece of tape for each fingerprint. He then slowly lifted the "latent print" and carefully adhered the tape onto the thin, black cardboard, which accentuated the image much better than other surfaces. Placing his black magnifying glass over the cardboard, he moved his head down for a closer examination. "Excellent." The process was repeated for the other print and the same result was achieved. He smiled, knowing he had a couple samples for the AFIS machine. The images were scanned into the machine.

The Automated Fingerprint Identification System came into operation in the early 1990s and revolutionized the identification of fingerprints. In Milwaukee alone, literally hundreds of cold cases were cleared when AFIS came online, as hundreds of thousands of additional fingerprints from arrested suspects from around the state and country were able to be accessed. Prior to that, the department could only utilize the fingerprints they had on file that were stored in countless files in the office. State warrants were obtained on thousands of suspects nationwide for felony offenses based solely on fingerprints.

He carried the paper receipt and brown bag to the back room where they kept the "fumer." Kamble placed the items in the machine, turned it on, and watched as the chemicals circulated through the paper. Within fifteen minutes, he had two more identifiable fingerprints. He categorized one as a loop and one as a whirl. Upon classifying these additional prints, he returned to the AFIS machine and entered the second group. Within minutes, all four prints were positively identified. He logged on to the computer and looked his suspect up.

"Mike, check this out. Harold Sampson Carter Jr.: white male; DOB 05/15/1985; B of I# 302128; AKA, Junior. His last photo was taken June 23rd of this year. This guy's a real gem—four felony convictions within eight years. Guess putting him in prison for his crimes against society wasn't a good option. Looks like we positively identified another suspect for Tomczyk. That turkey owes us something."

"You missed it, Scott. He brought in two dozen donuts last week when you were off. Thanked us for helping him out on all his other cases."

"Story of my life, missing all the fun."

— — —

Standing in the conference room of the intelligence unit, Captain Steven Spinnola surveyed a couple dozen five-by-seven-inch photographs spread across the large table. Dressed in his Marco Carelli navy blue pinstriped suit, powder blue shirt, and multicolor designer tie, he looked ready to take on the business world instead of commanding a special unit of some of the department's best detectives and police officers. "What do you make of it, Declan?"

Tomczyk's mind was still on the seven o'clock briefing he attended in the "Dahmer Room." The attempted homicide of Detective John

Lemke had stuck in his head because there were so few leads to follow up on.

"It started out yesterday morning, with my original inclination being mischievous kids, Captain," Tomczyk answered. "You see some of the photographs. Nothing too crazy or out of the ordinary until I spotted the wires underneath the headstone of the one belonging to this Harold Schlundt guy." He pointed out the before and after pictures of the headstone and the wires underneath it. "The headstone had been placed in a strange position, was defaced the most, and had the IED underneath—the IED without the explosives, that is. Inside the pipe bomb is that note saying we'd be seeing them again. You see the pictures with the stones knocked over and the pentagrams spray painted in red? Why the one had an inverted cross spray painted on it and the word *PIG* etched into the cross is the mystery.

Schlundt died over thirty years ago. Did the suspects just randomly pick his headstone to deface and place a bomb under? Or, was he a law enforcement officer someone had a beef with—a criminal who thought he'd wait thirty years to deface Schlundt's headstone by putting a derogatory cop phrase on it and placing a fake bomb under it? I think they had that orange wire Lurch followed as a ruse to draw someone over to the tree where they could detonate the bomb. I saw the driver, but he was too far away to positively ID. I'd sure like to see that prick again on another day. At the briefing, they said Lurch is still in critical but stable condition in ICU. I was there until eleven last night. He was still unconscious."

"I have a little birdie there, Declan. As of five minutes ago, he was responsive and downgraded to serious but stable condition. Sweet news! Lieutenant Hedder filled me in on your 'sixth sense' when you saw the guy and the car."

"Too bad my sixth sense came too late to save Lurch from getting hit. Thanks for the update, Captain. That's the best news I've heard so far today. Here's another twist to this whole, strange thing. The suspects spray painted *REMHAD* and *REDRUM* on the entrance pillars. I still don't have a clue what that has to do with this—if anything at all. The identification division reported they got some latent prints off the receipt, the paper bag, and two off the spray paint cans we found. They're still running that stuff through AFIS. I'm going to send the can out to the crime lab, along with samples of the spray paint we pulled off a headstone and the pillars to see if the paint matches. No prints at all on the plastic container, any of the components, or the typed up letter. The copper who found the bag and the spray painting, Jerry Boyek, is one tenacious SOB. He's like a dog on steroids, looking for anything connecting evidence to a suspect."

"I've heard of him. He's recovered so many guns off the street by arrest that he could open up his own gun shop. Didn't Boyek get shot in the arm some years ago by a guy with an AK47 on Eleventh and Burleigh? That was my old squad area at District Five, partnered up with Crazy Charlie Bernard. How many nights did I think Charlie was going to either get us killed or make us Milwaukee cop legends?" Spinnola shook his head in a thankful way. "Boyek and his partner took care of business that night, as I remember."

"The same guy. They shot the bastard; however, he lived and is probably in prison showing off his war wound and how he survived it," Tomczyk responded. "Jerry's one of those 24/7 kind of cops who will go places if he wants to."

Getting back to the case, Tomczyk pulled out his notepad, paging back to his notes from yesterday. "Anyway, REMHAD is the obvious one. I'm sure there's still a following who think Jeffrey Dahmer is a hero in some sick and perverted way. Still trying to figure out how REDRUM fits into the equation. There are a number of references to it on the Internet. I remember watching a very old *Son of Dracula* movie years ago, starring the king of scary movies, Lon Chaney Jr. Dracula went to some party and introduced himself as Count Alucard. Later on that night, he ended up killing someone and sucking out his blood. Even back in the '40s, when the movie was made, they were spelling names and words backwards."

"You have to be a buff of scary movies to remember Lon Chaney Jr.," added Spinnola. "He also played the best Wolfman."

"You said it, Captain. Speaking of scary, some hits came up on a Milwaukee case from May 1989 that happened on the South Side regarding Redrum." Tomczyk went on to relate how two women lured a man to their apartment and tried to kill him in honor of Jack the Ripper, to bring Ripper back from the dead. "The guy goes to the bathroom to take a leak and while he's in there, peeks behind a shower curtain for some reason. He looked down and saw two sets of legs, then looked up and saw the two women in the shower. He heard what sounded like a child's voice saying, 'Redrum, redrum.' One of the women hit him in the head with an ax. Kind of the opposite of what happened in the movie *Psycho*. This is more from the movie that should be called *Bizarro*. The guy ran outside, and the women chased him around a car, still yelling 'Redrum!' Before the police arrived, an ambulance saw the guy bleeding in the street and took him to the hospital. The two women pled guilty to attempted first-degree intentional homicide and got five years in exchange for turning key state witnesses against the third woman. They found her not guilty by reason of insanity, and she was sent packing to the state mental hospital in Oshkosh."

"Here's the bizarre part. Just over four years after the offense occurred, the victim shot himself in the head. Turns out he had attempted suicide before. In January of 1994, one of the two women was found nude and dead in her room at a halfway house—an apparent overdose. According to an article, her head was in a box of cassette tapes and a crucifix was lying on the bed next to her. The article also said the third woman told investigators she had been Jack the Ripper's mother in a previous life. Man, you can't make some of this stuff up."

Tomczyk completed his thought on the matter. "What, if any, connection this whole scenario has to thirteen defaced and dumped-over headstones with a fake bomb and one that almost killed a detective friend of ours, I have no idea. Guess we'll get the answers when we find the perps who did it."

Captain Spinnola shook his head. "Like they say, 'Milwaukee, a great place on a great lake'—except for some of the crazy things that happen in this city that we have to deal with on a daily basis."

Just then, FBI Special Agent Dvorak walked into the conference room. "I'm so sorry, Captain Spinnola, Declan. I had to brief my assistant special agent in charge on another case I have going. He wouldn't let me leave the office until I did."

"No problem, Anne. Declan can fill you in with everything after we're done here. Can you tell us what possible interest or knowledge the FBI might have regarding this since you showed up at our cemetery scene?" Spinnola didn't expect much of an answer, but thought he'd throw it out there anyway.

"Well, Captain, we've had some cult investigations with defaced headstones and dug-up graves in various cities around the country. That's why I responded since my squad supervisor has me as the local cult expert in our office. We've even had some conviction success and a couple related interstate offenses where we've taken two of them federal. The pentagrams and inverted cross are similar to some of the other crimes. However, the fake bomb and threatening letter are completely new to us, and the IED that blew up really has us perplexed. I don't think they're related to any of the other crimes we've had. I saw the words spray painted on the pillars as I was leaving the cemetery, but that could've just been adding some local flavor to it. How's the bomb tech doing? I saw Kevin Cleary this morning, and he's definitely not doing well. He told me that he and Detective Lemke go back a ways."

"I'll vouch for that. I've been out a couple times with them. Just so you know," Tomczyk said as he peered disturbingly into both of their eyes, "we still have a great cast of a size eleven Doc Martin boot that is the only one of its kind because of some strange marking when it hooked on something. If we find that boot and the person wearing it, we find a connection to this whole thing. At least it's a great start until we can connect a couple more of the dots. The homicide detectives found next of kin information on the thirteen headstones that were involved. I was way too tied up to take care of it yesterday. My main focus will be Harold Schlundt, but we need to cover all the bases. After thirty years, hopefully we will still find some useful info."

"I'm with you, Declan. Keep me posted. Since these turds tried to kill one of our own, it becomes very personal to all of us." Captain Spinnola walked back toward his office.

Tomczyk and Dvorak walked out of the room together. When they reached his desk out in the assembly area, he spoke up in a deadly serious tone. "Anne, you can blow smoke up the Captain's ass, but I know there's more to it than that. If you're going to throw out some BS story, cover your tracks. I spoke to my buddy who's our rep on the Joint Terrorism Task Force. He told me you're assigned to the domestic terrorism squad with him. You'll have to fill me in on why an FBI special agent on the JTTF DT squad would give a crap about defaced headstones in a cemetery. If you want to drop the FBI persona and talk 'cop to cop,' I'll give you 110 percent of all I have. If not, you can stick it because I won't give you a damn thing unless you throw a subpoena in my face. Lurch is like a very close uncle to me, and I want the guys who almost killed him."

Anne thought for a moment and a smile slowly came over her lovely face. "Let's start over. Detective Declan Tomczyk, I'm Special

Agent Anne Dvorak, FBI. I'd love to buy you some coffee." She warmly extended her right hand.

He reached his out in return, and they met in the middle. "Fair enough. I know of a great place. I'll even drive." They laughed and walked out of the office.

Chapter 5

MILWAUKEE

They conversed as Tomczyk drove the navy blue unmarked Dodge Charger east on Wisconsin Avenue in the direction of the lake. It was another beautiful, sunny fall day. As he reached the end of the "Avenue"—long considered Milwaukee's main drag—he passed the large, white, open wings of the Calatrava artwork that showcased the Milwaukee Art Center.

"Now that has got to be one of the more spectacular sites in Milwaukee," Dvorak remarked. "Especially when the wings are open. Santiago Calatrava is definitely one of the best architects in the world."

"Agree, 100 percent. Nothing prettier than that. I'm not sure if you know this, but the Calatrava sail was his first project in the United States, so we're lucky to have such a treasure. When they flew the wings in from Europe, they had to use that monster Russian cargo plane because no other plane could fit them."

"Really?"

Tomczyk followed the road as it veered north past the War Memorial Center and turned into North Lincoln Memorial Drive along the sparkling waters of Lake Michigan. A number of skaters, bikers, and walkers were taking advantage of one of the last warm days before winter. A minute later, he pulled into the parking lot of Colectivo at the Lake, his favorite coffee shop. Built in 1888, the grand old building, constructed of typical-cream city brick, was originally the Milwaukee River flushing station. Large turbines beneath the building pumped water from the lake through an elaborate piping system several miles north up the river to the North Avenue Dam. An engineering feat in its day, the dam was removed in the '80s, and the once-proud river assumed the appearance of a large creek.

They parked in the lot and got out. Anne asked, "What would you like?"

"A large iced mocha latte, please. That's what we chocolate addicts drink. I'll grab a table for us outside if it's okay with you. It'll give us a little more privacy, plus we can take advantage of November's rays."

"Excellent. A big strong brute who drinks lattes—now I've heard it all."

"Consider me a man of the twenty-first century. Just don't tell my dad. He flips when I tell him I drink lattes. Calls me a sally boy!"

"I love your father already."

She joined him on the patio a couple minutes later, holding two drinks in her hands. "I want to apologize. You know what they always tell us. Don't divulge anything to the locals because you can't trust them. Hope you don't mind, but I'm going to call you Declan. I've always loved that name."

"That works. I totally get the trust issue. We 'locals' always get a kick out of that since law enforcement is a lifetime commitment for most of us as well. Just a matter of perspective. There's a few 'bad apples' in every police agency in this country, whether local, county, state, or fed. By the way, would this be a good time to tell you about the Top Secret and other clearances I held as a captain in the United States Marine Corps and that I still hold as a major in the Marine Corps reserves? Except now I'm just an intel wienie, not a recon ranger. Life goes on, I guess. You remember what Maverick said to Kelly McGillis' character in *Top Gun*? 'I can tell you, but then I'd have to kill you.'"

"Haha. Great movie, loved the action." She settled into her chair, taking a sip of her coffee. "Ahh. Excellent."

"Great location, great coffee, and present company I am hoping will also turn out to be great. It's only ten o'clock, and my day is made already." He looked into her eyes. "I'm a big team player, Anne. Don't mind co-investigating anything, but I really don't have a clue what I'm stepping into yet—only that a good friend of mine was seriously hurt and nearly killed. What can you tell me?"

"Okay, and I apologize. I respect your clearances and your commitment to our country. Let me give you what we have. We received information several months ago from an anonymous source who contacted our Chicago field office. They spoke of a partial conversation they overheard in a North Side Chicago restaurant between four or five bald white men. Said they were wearing black leather jackets and had tattoos on their necks, but kept the jackets on during their meal. The men spoke of causing explosions at public buildings in Chicago and Milwaukee. Called themselves TMB."

"Never heard of them. We definitely witnessed some of their handiwork. But how does a Milwaukee-area cemetery enter into the equation?"

"The guy reported hearing them talk about defacing headstones in a Milwaukee cemetery to make it look like cult stuff, but their main purpose was getting back at 'the pigs, dead or alive.' Those were the exact words, whatever and whomever they meant by that. The report mentioned nothing about causing an explosion or leaving that bogus bomb. If they had, I would have had Kevin Cleary's butt in front of mine checking for it. Can't tell you how sorry I am to hear about Detective

Lemke. We just didn't expect this. I'm figuring Harold Schlundt was the target since his headstone was defaced and damaged the most. Do you have any idea who he was?"

"Not yet. My follow-up is to contact his daughter out in Brookfield. I'm calling her when we're through here to see if we can connect this."

"I'd like to go if that's okay. Definitely domestic terrorism related as I see it. We both know this is just the beginning of what could be a nightmare. I'll notify Jimmy Hill I'm going with you."

"You know he'll go insane if he can't be in the lead on this. He knew when he was assigned to the JTTF he wouldn't be as busy, but wanted to make a difference in other ways."

"Jimmy's treated me the best of all the task force officers who work there. I love the guy—in a professional kind of way, of course." She had to laugh, knowing that many crazy street cops were full of testosterone and aware of the endless array of connotations that might be construed with the word *love*.

"Okay then. Hope you've told his fiancé, Meg. She might have some say in the matter."

"You know what I mean," blushing at the thought of even opening the door for him to comment. "Have you set up a time to interview the daughter?"

"I'll make the call right now." Tomczyk dialed the number he had been given by Detective Roblewski.

"Hello," an older, male voice answered.

"Good morning, sir. I'm Detective Tomczyk from the Milwaukee Police Department. I'm trying to reach Fay Pavalko concerning an investigation."

"Oh, a detective you say?" said the man. "And what investigation would that be? Fay is my wife."

"It has something to do with her father's headstone at Holy Cross Cemetery."

"Not again," Erv Pavalko responded with genuine concern registering in his voice. "Hang on for just a minute. Fay, a Milwaukee police detective wants to talk to you."

Again? Tomczyk appreciated the man not telling her the reason before he had a chance to speak to her. *This doesn't sound good already.*

A few seconds passed, and a woman answered. "Hello, this is Fay Pavalko. Can I help you?"

Tomczyk sensed the nervousness in her voice. "Good morning, ma'am, I'm Detective Declan Tomczyk. I'm following up on a criminal damage investigation that occurred at Holy Cross Cemetery in Milwaukee. Headstones were damaged, and one belonged to a Harold Schlundt. I understand he was your father?"

"Yes, he was. This is very disturbing to me. My father died over thirty years ago. Why would someone do this to his headstone? This is the third time, and I'm at my wit's end."

Tomczyk's ears perked up. "Mrs. Pavalko, this is very important. Can I come out to talk with you today?"

"Sometime this morning would be fine. I just can't think of how or why this is happening. It makes no sense . . . no sense at all. Everyone knew him and liked him. He was well respected. I just don't know how I can help you. My father worked for the Milwaukee Police Department for forty years and retired over fifty years ago."

"He was on the Milwaukee Police Department?" Tomczyk asked with obvious surprise. The word *PIG* flashed into his brain in black block letters.

"Yes. He retired as a captain in 1962. He died in 1982."

"Mrs. Pavalko, I can be there within the hour. The cemetery provided me with an address of 18710 Capone Court in Brookfield. Is that still current?"

"Yes. Will you be able to find it?"

"My closest friend is a GPS. I can find anything."

"Thank you, Detective."

"Fantastic, see you soon."

Tomczyk looked over at Anne and smiled. "Perfect. She's home and expecting us. Are you ready to go? This is getting just slightly convoluted. An investigation of defaced headstones, an attempted homicide of a detective from an explosion in a cemetery, and I'm going with an FBI agent to interview the daughter of a dead police captain who lives on Capone Court. Anything just a little ironic going on here? You okay if we take one car? I'll drop you off when we're done."

"No worries. And no, nothing ironic to me." She rolled her eyes at him while climbing into the passenger seat. "If the moon isn't full tonight, it should be."

Chapter 6

BROOKFIELD, WISCONSIN

I t was eleven fifteen in the morning when they pulled up in front of a modest brick and beige two story house set among other larger ones. Down the block was a much older, two story brick home that looked out of place. The city of Brookfield was a large and upscale suburb located west of Milwaukee in Waukesha County. During the 1960s, as in many major cities around the country, Milwaukee suffered "white flight" and other issues, causing a sizable constriction in population. From a high of 747,000 in 1960—then widely known as a blue-collar, industrial city—Milwaukee shrunk to a population just under 600,000. Meanwhile, Brookfield and the rest of Waukesha County recorded substantial increases. Waukesha County was also known as one of the more conservative, Republican strongholds in the country, unlike the more liberal oriented Milwaukee County.

Tomczyk rang the doorbell, and an older white male in a brown flannel shirt and blue jeans greeted him. The man carried himself well for someone in his seventies. "You must be Detective Tomczyk? Come in; I'll get my wife. Erv Pavalko," he said, politely reaching out his right hand.

They stepped into the foyer. "It's a pleasure to meet you, Mr. Pavalko. I'd like to introduce you to Special Agent Anne Dvorak from the FBI. We're working together on this." As he spoke, a large, brindle-colored Akita scampered down the staircase on his way to conduct his own investigation.

"Take a break, Rocky. Mess with these people, and they'll be hauling you out in paw cuffs to the dog pound. That's where you belong anyway," he joked.

"He's a beautiful dog, Mr. Pavalko. Helen Keller sure knew what she was doing when she brought this remarkable breed over from Japan—bear face and all."

"So, you know the history of the breed, Detective?"

"Yes, sir. Our family had one when I was a kid. My wife and I bought a black and brindle right after we were married. Unfortunately, he developed severe problems at seven years old, and we had to put him down. Broke our hearts. Maybe one day I'll get another."

"Sorry to hear that. We sure love our Rocky." He looked over at the female agent. "Glad to meet you, Special Agent Dvorak."

"Thanks. Please, call me Anne."

A minute later, Fay Pavalko stepped down the open staircase, grabbing on to the beautiful oak and black wrought iron railing.

"Pleasure to meet you, Mrs. Pavalko," Tomczyk responded. "This is FBI Special Agent Anne Dvorak. We've already been introduced to Rocky."

"An FBI agent! This must be important."

"We'd like to think so." Anne warmly shook her hand.

"Please, come into the living room and have a seat." Fay Pavalko ushered the two law enforcement officers into a large and ornately decorated room, with a floor to ceiling stone fireplace. "Thanks for driving out here. Other than someone scaring me half to death with what is happening to my father's gravestone, is there anything I can help you with? Pardon my manners. Can I get you something to drink?"

"Water, if it's not a problem, ma'am."

"None at all. Would you care for some water as well, Anne?"

"Please. We enjoyed the ride out here. Have to admit, I've never heard of Capone Court before."

"That goes for me too. I've lived in Milwaukee my whole life, except for my time at college and in the military."

Erv interrupted. "If you don't mind me asking, in which branch did you serve?"

"Marine Corps, sir; seven great years. I was born to be a jarhead, but complications in my life forced me to come back home."

"Semper Fi! I served from '53 to '76—tail end of Korea and a whole lot of Vietnam. Not a pretty ending to either story. Wars where politicians thought they were smarter than professional soldiers. Just a bad mix."

"Can't disagree with that. I was raised to kick ass and take names, pardon my French. My father pounded it into me."

"I certainly could tell that. I'll shut my mouth now, but happy birthday to you, Marine. It's been a long and glorious road from Tun Tavern in Philadelphia to here."

"Hoo-rah."

Every member of the United States Marine Corps, past and present, knows November 10, 1775, as the birthdate of their proud branch of service. It is implanted into the DNA of who they are.

"Oh, boy, here we go again. All that testosterone in one room. Erv, can we get to the matter at hand and why these people are here?"

"Sorry, honey." Erv waved off his wife's comment. She'd heard it for their fifty-two years of marriage and never tired of ribbing him about it. "And about Capone Court," he started, "you apparently weren't aware that Al Capone had a house built in the 1920s just down the block. It's that older brick house you might have seen on your way in. Capone supposedly used the property as a still, distillery, and hideout during Prohibition. At one time, this was one big chunk of land with just his house and a couple outbuildings. You could only access it from a long driveway off Brookfield Road. There's always been a rumor of a secret tunnel between the house and the barn so the gangsters could escape if the feds came snooping. We were inside the house some years ago. There's a terrazzo floor in one of the large rooms with rusty metal rings on the floor, supposedly to chain up the kegs of whiskey. Back then, Brookfield was a sleepy town way out in the sticks from Milwaukee and ninety miles from the rattle and hum of Chicago—a perfect getaway for the most famous gangster in the country. We've always been big Depression-era history buffs, so we bought a lot and built when they subdivided the land into lots. Not as big as the other houses here, but it fits our needs."

"That is some story." Tomczyk took a sip from the bottle of water. "Never knew Capone even lived here."

Fay gave her husband "the eye." "So, how can I help you with your investigation? And how can you help soothe my nerves?"

"Why don't you start by telling us about your father, Mrs. Pavalko?" Agent Dvorak was trying her best to put the obviously distressed woman at ease so she would open up to them.

Fay sat down on the love seat next to Erv, took in a deep breath, and grabbed a piece of tissue from the pocket of her knitted sweater. "My father became a police officer for the Milwaukee Police Department in 1922 when he was twenty-two-years-old. He spent the next forty years doing what he loved most. He finally retired in 1962. Always told us it was his lifelong dream. Dad worked out of the Fifth District Police Station when it was on Third and Hadley. He was promoted to detective sometime in the late '20s, after being 'lucky enough' to have a good ranking. His favorite term was 'lucky enough.' 'Lucky enough' to make this arrest, to complete this or that investigation, to get a promotion or be assigned with certain partners. He used to drive my two brothers and me around the city, showing us different places and telling us unbelievable stories of the investigations he was 'lucky enough' to be involved in. Boy, did he ever love telling us about the old times. We always laughed about how those were some of our best memories with him." She dabbed at the tears that occasionally trickled down her cheeks.

Fay opened the drawer of the antique wooden side table next to her and pulled out several items, placing them next to her on the chair. "I've been going to the cemetery for over thirty years, since Dad died, to talk to him and share what was going on in our lives. Strange maybe, I know, but I loved him so. Even though he worked nights and odd shifts, he spent as much time as he could with us in so many other ways. We feel so fortunate to have had a father like him. I'm sure Erv can tell you how 'lucky enough' he was to have a father-in-law like that."

Tomczyk glanced over at Erv who readily nodded. "You're right there, honey. Any man who would share his Packer season tickets with me, especially during the Vince Lombardi glory years and all those memories, will be my friend for life. That, along with so many other countless things he engaged our sons in."

"I'm there with you, sir." Tomczyk looked back over at Fay. "What do you have there, ma'am?"

She picked up a plastic envelope and removed a copy of a newspaper article showing a picture of three men. "When I went to the cemetery in August, a clear plastic bag containing a manila envelope with this clipping was attached to my father's headstone. There was some disturbing, derogatory language written on the envelope, so I told the police they could keep it. I refuse to keep any memory of something like that in my home."

"What police?" asked Tomczyk, as Fay passed the newspaper clipping over to him.

"I drove straight to the Seventh District police station when I left the cemetery and told them about it. They made copies of everything, gave me a copy of the article, and said they would have it fingerprinted. They took my fingerprints to match up since I touched everything. It was probably a dumb thing to do, but I was shocked someone would write something so vile on an envelope and attach it to my father's headstone." She handed Tomczyk a small, yellow Milwaukee Police Department Form PP33, property receipt, labeled with a police officer's name and property inventory number.

"May I keep this? I want to track this down and will mail it back to you in a day or so."

"Please do, if it will help you in some way."

Both investigators looked closely at the August 1, 1934, issue of the *Milwaukee Journal*. Agent Dvorak recognized one of the men immediately. "Your father got an award from Melvin Purvis?" she blurted in disbelief.

"Dad was always so proud of that. As I'm sure you know, Mr. Public Enemy Number One himself, John Dillinger, was committing bank robberies throughout the Midwest during 1933 and '34. He and his gang even robbed one in Racine. They took hostages, including the bank president, and later tied them to a tree out in the country. The gang also got the jump on responding police officers, wounding one and disarming the others. The 'Tommy Gun' that Dillinger took from one of the Racine officers, and later autographed, is still on display at the Racine Police Department. Here's a picture of it." She opened the black scrapbook to the page that contained her father's memorabilia.

"Unbelievable! But what did your Dad have to do with it since the robbery happened in Racine? Do you know who this other man is in the picture?"

"Remember when I told you he was 'lucky enough' for this and that? Turns out one of Dad's informants called him the morning of the robbery and said he saw Dillinger and one of the other gang members at a hotel in downtown Milwaukee. By the time my father and his partner got there, they were gone. Some things were left behind, verifying that they had stayed there, such as the address and drawing of the inside of the bank. When Dad called Racine PD to tell them about it, Dillinger had already hit the bank and fled. The other man was 'Big Stan,' as Dad always called him. They were best friends and squad partners for years. I could never remember his long last name, but it started with an 'S' and ended with 'ski.' How embarrassing is that? Dad loved the guy like a brother, and I can't even remember his last name."

"No worries, ma'am," said Tomczyk. "I can't pronounce half of the names I run across."

"Thanks for that. Dad and Stan were assigned to a small unit of Milwaukee and Racine detectives to look into other sightings of Dillinger in the area. He said they'd drive down to Chicago every week to attend meetings with the 'Dillinger Squad' the Chicago Police Department had formed. They'd receive updates and offer any information they had. They learned that Dillinger also spent time in Milwaukee after the Racine bank robbery. Dillinger's girlfriend at the time was Billie Frenchette, a Menominee Indian from northern Wisconsin. They were seen in a downtown restaurant on New Year's Day, something Frenchette verified after she was arrested and questioned. She and another woman who traveled with the Dillinger gang bought a car in Milwaukee in January, 1934. When Dillinger was arrested in Arizona later that month, Wisconsin license plates were on the car. Racine authorities were sent to Tucson to have Dillinger and the other arrested gang members brought back to Wisconsin to stand trial for the robbery, but Indiana authorities won out. You know the rest of the story. It's been in every Dillinger movie ever made. Believe it or not, Mark Harmon even played him in a movie filmed in Milwaukee."

She gathered her thoughts and continued, "Dillinger was taken to Indiana to stand trial and escaped from jail using the infamous, handmade wooden gun. If you saw the movie *Public Enemies*, starring Johnny Depp, the first bank robbery scene occurred in Racine. The movie also told a lot about Billie, the shooting up north at Little Bohemia in Manitowish Waters, and Dillinger's death in Chicago. The week after Dillinger was killed coming out of the theatre, Melvin Purvis called everyone involved in the investigation and presented them with personal awards. Even though Dad was upset at the way the feds screwed up at Little Bohemia by not having enough officers to cover the place, he still considered the award an honor for all their work. My older brother Jim still has the award in his house. Anne, I'm sure you probably learned the history between Hoover and Melvin Purvis at the FBI Academy and know more about it than us."

"Sure did. We also spent a great deal of time on Hogan's Alley, which is a mock- up street at Quantico where we conducted live training. They even have a Biograph Theatre there. It's so cool. I bet Director Hoover hated the idea of Purvis becoming known as the FBI agent who got Dillinger. He demoted Purvis and exiled him to a desk. Purvis ended up leaving the FBI and committing suicide years later. Hoover was someone you didn't cross. The abuses of power by the FBI in days past have hurt us today with some of the restrictions we now have."

Tomczyk decided to keep quiet. He wasn't always a fan of the FBI. He knew and liked some of the agents he dealt with, especially the ones who were former cops and had that "street sense."

"That's too bad," Fay sympathized. "I'm sure policing today is much different than it used to be."

"Sure is," Dvorak agreed. "Now we have to figure out why someone would obtain a copy of an eighty-year-old newspaper article and attach it your father's headstone. Do you have any idea at all?"

"Neither Erv nor I have any clue. None whatsoever."

"So what else you got there?"

"When I went back to the cemetery in late September, the things in this picture were glued to the top of the headstone." She picked up a photo depicting a bloody, dismembered plastic body and the word *kaboom* printed on a smooth rock next to it in red ink. "I'm afraid I lost it right there and then. I started shaking and called Erv from my cellphone. Not sure if he understood a word I said because I was crying and scared out of my mind. All I know is that a police squad came quickly, and the two fine police officers were able to calm me down. They took pictures and removed the objects from his headstone."

"Mrs. Pavalko, has anything like this happened before?"

"Never."

"Well then, we have to figure out the connection. It's got to be here. Can you tell us about any other investigations in your father's career that could have triggered this so many years later? It has to be some friend or relative. Someone with intimate knowledge of somebody your father dealt with who is bringing up the past in this macabre fashion." Agent Dvorak felt a shiver run down her spine.

Fay Pavalko thought for a few long seconds, trying to collect her thoughts on some of those long-ago memories of her father regaling her with stories of his career.

"I know Dad was involved in investigations of the mafia in Milwaukee. Before Frank Balistreri took over in the early '60s and put Milwaukee on the map as a mob city, his father-in-law ran things here. Besides the nickname Frankie Bal, they also dubbed him The Mad Bomber. There was a good chance your demise would come by way of some type of explosion if you crossed him. Dad was in failing health in the early '80s when Balistreri and his two sons were facing federal charges and prison."

Dvorak and Tomczyk looked at each other. The Mad Bomber– TMB. "The Mad Bomber!" Tomczyk almost yelled. "I never heard of Frank Balistreri being called that one before."

"It was mainly after some of the explosions that occurred in the '70s. He wasn't the only Milwaukee Mad Bomber, though. Dad also talked about he and Stan being lead detectives on a case in the mid-'30s when someone set off explosions at Shorewood City Hall, a couple banks, and several Milwaukee police stations. He said the two young men blew themselves up in a garage on the South Side while trying to make another bomb. A little girl was also killed in the explosion. I don't recall anything else about it."

"Now this is getting interesting. Can you remember anything else?"

She went on to relate Harold Schlundt's undercover work on a German sympathizer group called *Die Bund*, which translates to "The Alliance." At one time, Milwaukee had the largest German population of any American city. Several riots broke out before World War II during some of the rallies that were held in Milwaukee and a number of other cities. The group faded away when Germany declared war.

"Let's see, what else? Dad said he was sent to Plainfield, Wisconsin, sometime in 1957 after Ed Gein was arrested. Their small department was completely overwhelmed with the investigation and requested expert help. He was a detective sergeant then and used to train other departments on evidence collection and investigation techniques for violent crimes and homicides. I'm sure you've heard of Ed Gein? He killed two women whose heads were found in his house and one of the bodies in his shed. Gein also exhumed bodies from graves and made trophies and keepsakes out of the skin and bones. A lampshade found in his living room was from human skin. That's sick enough, but Hollywood created characters based off him, like Norman Bates in

Psycho, and even the guy from *Silence of the Lambs*. I'm sure both Dad and Stan were involved in a ton of other investigations, but those are the main ones. This whole thing is starting to drive me nuts. My father was a very honorable man. He dedicated his life to doing what was right with an organization he loved, protecting a city he was ready to die for at any minute."

"You have my word. I'm going to track these items down and read the reports to see what I can come up with. Considering all the robberies, shootings, and other things going on in the city, I can see how something like this can get lost in the shuffle. However, with this most recent desecration of your father's and the other headstones, along with the attempted homicide of a detective, I assure you it's important."

Tomczyk decided to describe only what happened to the headstone and about the explosion, not the fake bomb and note found underneath it. Maybe another day. They stood up, shook hands, and said goodbye. Mrs. Pavalko kissed Tomczyk on the cheek. "Thank you for what you do. I know my father would be proud of your service to your country and the city of Milwaukee." She also hugged Dvorak and thanked her as well.

"You're very welcome, ma'am. Appreciate the exciting history you shared." Tomczyk and Agent Dvorak both handed their business cards to Mrs. Pavalko.

"I second that," said Dvorak.

Erv looked over his wife's shoulder to read the cards. "I KNEW IT! You're Declan 'O'ski/Bro-ski' Tomczyk! Young man, did I also mention I have Wisconsin Badgers season tickets?"

"O'ski/Bro-ski?" Anne looked over at Tomczyk in a surprising fashion. "What am I missing in this conversation?"

"Agent Dvorak, not only is this guy a detective, but he has a history in the annals of Wisconsin college football. Second Team All-American middle linebacker for the Wisconsin Badgers and Co-MVP of the 1999

Rose Bowl game against the Washington Huskies. Eighteen solo tackles, two sacks, and an interception, if I remember right. Was a second-round NFL draft choice, but decided to become a Marine instead. Now I REALLY admire you! I bet Coach Alaveres was pissed at you not going to the NFL."

Tomczyk's face flushed. "Thank you, Mr. Pavalko. I'm flattered. I told you becoming a Marine was in my DNA. Something I've wanted more than anything else. Even though my father served two tours in South Vietnam with the Army's 'Big Red One,' courtesy of Uncle Sam and the draft, my love was the Marine Corps. Going to Madison on a scholarship and playing under Coach for four years has been one of my greatest honors. There are only two men who have walked this earth I have more respect for than him: my father and Jesus Christ himself. That's saying a lot considering the wonderful men who've mentored me over the years. They've helped make me the man I am—good and bad. Now, how did you know about those nicknames? We always tried to keep those on the down-low, for obvious reasons."

Declan Tomczyk grew up in Milwaukee and graduated from Alexander Hamilton High School. He attended the University of Wisconsin on a football scholarship, a linebacker with 4.4 speed in the forty—highly unusual for a 6'2", 245-pound "white boy." In addition, he bench pressed over five hundred pounds. One of his nicknames had always been "O'ski" because of his Irish/Polish heritage. The black players on the team labeled him "Bro-ski" as a compliment to his unusual ability. They used to kid him that he must have black genes to be that big and fast. The Badgers played in the Rose Bowl his senior year, handily beating the Huskies from the University of Washington. He was named co-MVP with his close friend, Anthony Thomas, the big Badger fullback who had broken the Rose Bowl rushing record with 252 yards. Tomczyk also excelled academically once he realized the importance of study, becoming a

Scholastic All-American as well. He was drafted by the San Francisco 49ers, one of his favorite pro teams.

His father was a Distinguished Service Cross and Silver Star recipient, United States Army. Declan loved everything about the military. He dreamed of going to the Naval Academy and becoming an officer, but his grades were too low his senior year of high school, thereby ruining his chances for making any of the military academies. His dream did not die. After college, he joined the Marines instead of going into pro football. To him, it was a more important life mission, with no greater honor than to serve both the military branch and the country he loved. He reported to Marine Corps Recruit Depot in San Diego, then faced the usual screaming and harassment by overzealous drill sergeants who were born with serious "'tude." Tomczyk made squad leader because of his college degree, intense physical prowess, and desire.

After completing basic training, the Marine Corps sent him to Officer Candidate School and advanced training for Marine Force Recon. Tomczyk was living the dream, and a career as a Marine was in the offing. It was during his second tour in Iraq when his life took a dramatic turn. His wife was diagnosed with cancer and was given one to two years to live. There was no other decision he could make. He would leave the Marine Corps. On a one-month leave in Milwaukee to be with his wife, he was able to complete all the testing and was notified he would be entering the police academy in several months. He went back to Camp Lejeune, filled out his separation papers, and drove back home with all his belongings and a heavy heart. Even though some of his "jarhead" friends tried talking him out of leaving, they knew and understood the circumstances.

After his graduation from the Milwaukee Police Training Academy, Tomczyk was assigned to District Five, a very diverse district. Before redistricting in the mid-2000s, it encompassed the richest and poorest neighborhoods in the city, along with probably the largest concentration of local bars anywhere in the city.

Marie Tomczyk miraculously survived nearly five years before succumbing to her deadly sickness. Declan had no regrets for any of his decisions, such as passing up pro football or leaving the Marine Corps to be with her. He found being a cop, and then a detective, additional privileges in his life of service.

Erv Pavalko continued his story. "One of my closest friends and golf partners is Reginald Jenkins, proud uncle of a former teammate of yours. We still laugh about what you guys used to call each other."

"You mean 'Chardass'?"

"Chardass?" said Fay Pavalko, a little confused at the name.

"That's right, honey. Al Jenkins is 6'4" and 335 pounds. They originally called him Lardass, but since he's black . . . get it?" Erv Pavalko was beaming at his new discovery.

"Al played on the line in front of me for the three years I played varsity. He's always been like a brother to me. Talk about road clearing a line and making me look good. Some people may consider us 'non-PC' or racist by using those nicknames, but to me, they're terms of endearment. To be called 'Bro-ski' by my black teammates was an honor. Some remain my closest friends and I still get together with them. God gave me the gift of speed and strength, along with other things I'm extremely grateful for.

I went to Al's parents' house in Glendale about ten times when we were in college. My Mom is a great cook, but 'Ma' Jenkins takes cooking to a whole other level. Her chicken casserole and pecan pie are to die for. Told her I'd be 350 pounds if I lived under her roof. Talk about great people. Al still plays starting defensive tackle for the Jets. This past May, he took about eight of us out to eat at the Steakhouse, right around the corner from where Jeffrey Dahmer lived. If you've ever been there, you're familiar with the massive size of the steaks. Al ate two filets with all the salad and fixings. He was eyeing mine up because I was sitting next to him, and I had to threaten him with my fork," Tomczyk said jokingly.

"Reggie has told me on a number of occasions about the bond between many of you guys," Erv Pavalko remarked, laughing at the thought of what must have occurred at the restaurant.

"Even though Madison is a liberal campus in an interesting liberal city, I had a great experience there. For the record, I still have lunch with Coach when he comes to Milwaukee. He uses the word *crazy* when describing my road after college, but he totally respects my decisions. I'm sure you know he was a cop before becoming a football coach. He's like a second father to many of us. We all feel fortunate for that relationship."

"The University of Wisconsin has been more than blessed to be associated with Coach Alaveres and, for a couple of years, Declan Tomczyk. Thank you for coming and reassuring us about these incidents. Please stay in touch."

"I'll give you folks a call within the week for an update."

"Thank you," Fay Pavalko repeated. The sense of peace that flushed across her face after this most recent desecration of her father's headstone was evident.

As they walked out to the squad car, Anne looked over at Tomczyk with a newly found respect. "Bro-ski?"

They got into the squad car, and Tomczyk looked into her eyes. "Come on, Anne. With today's goofy climate, they would hang us for stuff like that. When I talk to any of my college buddies, I still refer to them by their nicknames. They do the same to me. People can talk all the racial things they want, but I'll tell you what. My wife, Marie, died three years ago after a six-year battle with cancer. Besides the love of my parents, 'Ma' Jenkins was probably the closest person in my life. She spent countless hours consoling me and had me over to their house for dinners too numerous to remember. Al called a couple times a week to ask how I was, no matter where he was during football season. I would do anything for either of them. I don't think Al's brother and sister even know my real name because all they've ever known me as was Bro-ski." Tears welled up in his eyes. "Boy, would the media ever have a field day with that one."

She took hold of his right hand. "I'm so very sorry about your wife. Cancer sure is a life snatcher. Maybe we can meet at that steak restaurant one night, and you can tell me all about her. I'm a great listener and would sure like to dig into one of their filets."

A smile came back to his face. "Thank you, Anne. It was a very long and sad road. I'll never forget Marie or our great times and sad times together. Nothing would make me happier than to share that with you. This sure was a very worthwhile interview. What wonderful people. We have some web surfing to do to find out about the connection, if any, to The Mad Bomber and TMB. And how does Saturday night look in your schedule for steak? Even though I'm still a big-time rookie in the dating game, I know enough that when a beautiful woman opens the door like that, I'm obliged to run through it."

They both laughed as Tomczyk drove past the old brick house where one of the most notorious criminals in the annals of United States history came and did some of his handiwork.

"Then it's a date. Pick me up at six thirty, and don't be late." She reflected on her own career. "To think Al Capone once rode up and down this road. Wow."

Chapter 7

MILWAUKEE'S RIVERWEST AREA

Squad 5151, meet the woman and her dog at the flagpole in Gordon Park regarding a man down. Additional info sent to your terminal."

"Copy." It was 8:10 a.m. and Officer Pat Heggins had just rolled through the fast food restaurant drive-thru at the intersection of Martin Luther King Drive and Locust Street. The order was placed for his usual king-size, hazelnut-flavored hot coffee to jump-start his shift. After receiving the cup, he was ready for anything the District Five dispatcher would give him. He pushed the button on his squad computer terminal and up popped the additional information on the fifteen-inch diagonal screen. *Gotta love modern technology,* he thought to himself.

"Let's see, caller's a Sheila Wentworth. Cell phone number, 414-265-5555. Came across a man with a gunshot wound to his forehead lying just off the walk path while she was walking her dog in Gordon Park."

Heggins made the mile drive to the park that sat at the southeast corner of Locust Street and Humboldt Boulevard. He drove onto the service road and observed an older white female wearing an open, brown, insulated nylon jacket over her navy blue jogging outfit. She had a chain leash in her right hand and was holding on to a large German shepherd.

"Good morning, Officer. I'm Sheila Wentworth."

"Morning, ma'am. Probably not a pleasant way to start your morning," Heggins said as he exited the squad. "Is that dog of yours friendly?"

"When I tell him to be," she mused. "Prince, you be a good dog now. This police officer is our friend." The shepherd gave his owner the "I understand" look. "The body is several blocks away toward the river, right along the path. Do you want to walk or follow me in your squad car?"

"I'll follow you in case I need to get something once I'm there. That way I can direct additional units on my radio if I need to."

The woman walked south along the path through the small park that abutted the west bank of the Milwaukee River, with Officer Heggins driving slowly behind her. Ahead of her, he noticed what looked like a white male lying on his back on the grass just off the path. He shifted the marked, white-and-black Dodge Charger into park, turned off the ignition, and got out. When he walked over to the body, Heggins saw a large-caliber gunshot wound in the center of the forehead and what appeared to be a hole in the victim's black leather jacket. The grass and leaves under the head and chest were drenched in blood and the unmistakable scent of death was in the air, overpowering the usually intoxicating smells of fallen leaves of autumn. He could see that postmortem lividity had set in. The face and hands were ashen white.

"Looks like this guy won't need an ambulance." Heggins grabbed the radio microphone attached to his squad jacket collar. "Squad 5151, request several additional squads at my location, along with a sergeant. Advise responding squads to drive south along the bike path from the flagpole."

"10-4." Seconds later, the dispatcher came back over the police channel sending a sergeant and two marked squads to meet the officer at his location to assist.

All three squads acknowledged the assignment.

"My exact thoughts, Officer. I've been living in the Riverwest area my entire life and have witnessed my share of violence. Guess you get thick-skinned after a while. I remember walking a different dog back in September of 1975 when Auggie Maniaci was killed in the alley behind his house on the corner of Hadley and Humboldt by one of Frank Balistreri's gunmen. Even saw the shooter run from the scene but couldn't identify him. Guess the guy got whacked by some other gangster a couple years later. Live by the sword, die by the sword."

"You're right, ma'am. Let me get some information from you so I don't take up your whole day." Heggins took her statement.

"And no, Officer, I didn't hear any gunshots last night. When I fall asleep, I'm asleep. My husband's home. Maybe he heard something."

"Thanks, ma'am. Tell you what. Detectives are probably going to want to talk to you again. Why don't you go home and spend some time with your husband? I'll send the detectives over to your house."

"You're funny. We've been married for forty years and you want me to go spend time WITH my husband? Maybe we'll be snuggling on the couch when the detectives come. Oh, almost forgot to tell you. Bill and I walked by here last night with Prince at about six o'clock when it was still light, and no one was around. Good luck with the investigation, Officer. These things are always bad. Very sad about the young man. I'm sure somebody still cared about him, and now he's gone." Sheila walked away while Prince was already looking for the next object he could attach his nose to.

Heggins went to the trunk of his squad and pulled out a roll of yellow police tape. Although it wasn't a high-traffic area for pedestrians, he wanted to be ready when the media came slithering up to the scene. No doubt they put two and two together that something was going on while monitoring the police radio and hearing his additional squad request.

After the experienced officer secured the scene with police tape, he looked around a little more. All the Miller beer empties were lying in the fire pit except one, which was in the grass less than ten feet from the casings. The can was visibly dented. To the right of the body, he saw something reflecting light in the grass, near a clump of bushes. As he stepped closer and knelt down to get a better look, he noticed it was a small, brass shell casing, probably a nine millimeter. Two feet away he saw another one, then a third. They were nearly obscured in the grass. *The plot thickens. Looks like we had a little shootout going on. Must have been at least three people here, and one of them got away,* he thought to himself as he stood back up.

He pulled the cell phone out of his uniformed shirt pocket and dialed the shift commander.

"District Five, Lieutenant Bernard."

"Lieut, this is Heggins."

"What you got, Wild Man?" buzzed the all-too-familiar voice of one of his favorite supervisors. You either loved or hated Lieutenant Charles Z. Bernard who, after thirty-eight years on the job and in his late sixties, was still ready to stand up against anyone in the department or on the street. That included captains and above in the hierarchy pecking order who thought they could intimidate him. His mold had been shelved years ago when police work became more of an occupation for sensitive types.

"I was sent at 8:10 a.m. to a man down in Gordon Park and was met by the caller. She directed me to a white male who looks to be in his early to mid-twenties. He was lying on his back in the grass, just off the path three blocks south of the flagpole, with a big-caliber hole in the middle of his forehead and one round to his left chest. He's been here for hours, Boss, and is definitely DOA. I found five .40 caliber spent casings on the ground within fifteen feet of the body, along with three 9mm casings in the grass closer to the body. No gun anywhere. So either it grew wings or there was at least a third person here. Looks like they had a little party sometime late last night. There's close to twenty empty beer cans by a fire pit the kids around here have been using for years. I bet someone got pissed off, and now we have homicide number eighty-five for the year. Sergeant Gomez and two uniformed squads are on the way to assist. This guy's wearing a black leather jacket with stuff hand-written on the front, blue jeans, and Doc Marten Boots. Some sort of skinhead or anarchist offshoot. He's got no ID on him, so I don't have a name for you yet."

"Roger that, Pat. I'll call you back after I contact the Bureau."

"Yes, sir" he responded and disconnected the call just as Sergeant Ruben Gomez pulled up in his white Ford Explorer.

"Should'a guessed it, Heggins. You had to call the sergeant again because a simple crime like this is too difficult for you to handle. What ya got?"

"Just a good thing you're out here giving all of us 'rooks' direction, Sarge. White male in his twenties with a big hole in his head. Also took one to the left chest. Five .40 caliber casings here in the dirt by the fire pit and nearly a full case of empty beer cans. I should have it solved by the end of shift with arrest imminent. Just got off the phone with the Boss. He's on the wire to the Bureau. I may need a little help from the Detective Bureau 'suits,' but other than that, it's covered."

"That's the spirit, Pat. I'll tell the other squads to start hitting the houses on Humboldt. Someone may have heard the shots. Do you want any other squads here?"

"I'm good for now, Sarge." The theme song from *Hawaii Five-0* started playing, and the officer answered his cell phone. "This is Heggins."

"Two Bureau squads on the way, Pat."

"Thanks, Lieut. Sergeant Gomez just arrived. The other responding squads will canvass for witnesses."

"Good. Have him give me a jingle if you find out who the guy is."

"You got it, boss," he replied, clicking the End button on the phone and placing it back in his shirt pocket.

"The high-priced help from homicide are on the way. Before you got here, I was checking this guy out. See the tats on his neck and right hand? Some sort of crossbones on the right side of his neck and an anarchist symbol on his hand. Never saw anything like that. What's on the other side of his neck that the jacket is blocking? 'Death by Bombing' or something. Guess he's an artist, too. See the bright red spray paint splatters on his pants and boots?"

"Yeah. Anarchist and skinhead. There's a combination." Sergeant Gomez looked at the tattoo written in navy blue on the victim's neck. "I'm reading, 'Death by Bombing,' with a stick of dynamite blowing off next to it. Maybe he should've had a .40 caliber pistol with a bullet coming out of the barrel. That'd be more accurate. Just sayin'."

"You're a sick man, Sergeant."

The Detective Bureau squads were on scene within twenty minutes. Officer Heggins briefed them as they busily copied notes down in their steno pads.

A short time later, one of the squads contacted Heggins. They told him they talked to four residents who heard five to ten shots at about three o'clock in the morning. "Two of them said they had called the police." As he was noting this in his memo book, a medical examiner investigator he knew pulled up. Now the real work would begin. He was always impressed when the ME investigators or the ME himself came to a crime scene. They were so thorough. As much as he tried to obtain the most information he could, they always asked him questions he didn't have answers to. *Damn brainiacs.*

Inside a small, dingy apartment in Milwaukee's Riverwest area, Spike created a text message on the cell phone using his tattooed fingers.

We left the 'bomb' and set the other one off at the cemetery. Too bad the pig didn't die. Will continue with the plan as discussed. Now it's ur turn to do the same. That explosive I cooked up worked like a charm. Use the ones I left and how I told you to do it. Btw, I put Squirt on ice in a park last night. Dude started talkin stupid and had to be taken out. Madman and I will tcb here. Also shot at his friend Elroy after he capped a couple at me and split. Not sure if I hit him or not.

Later, holmes

He hit the send button. Within minutes, he received the response he had looked forward to.

Set to go in the next day or two. Still workin on a couple details. I'll get back to u mañana. Chi-town's gonna lite up when all this shit goes down, dude. Let's hope they find Elroys body in a ditch.

"Fan-freakin'-tastic," he said aloud. He quickly thought about the guy who got away. That could bring them problems. *Hope the jerk died.* He rolled over in bed and began caressing the woman who was sound asleep beside him. He wasn't totally attracted to the large nose ring and two-inch ear gauges that expanded her ear lobes, but he could overlook those because of her excellent body. Her numerous body tattoos excited him even more, especially the large "tramp stamp" he knew was proudly displayed at the base of her back. As he gently continued down her body, she slowly rolled over. He began kissing her neck, and it was game on. She responded, and they had a twenty-minute interlude of fantastic sex.

"Yeah, baby, you sure know how to make a guy feel important. Wow, you are great in the sack."

"You know it, stud."

Spike got up from the bed and lit a reefer. "As long as we're high on life, we might as well continue the mood." He took a long hit off the marijuana cigarette, then handed it to her as she sat up in bed, the dirty, beige sheets falling off from around her.

"Now you're talkin', baby," she said as she inhaled two long puffs from the hand-rolled joint, savored the flavor, and slowly exhaled the smoke. "What's on for today, Spike?"

"Just hangin'. Nothin' planned. Met up with a couple guys last night and shot the breeze for a while. You work tonight at the bar, don't ya?"

"Yeah, I start at six and close up. When I get home, I expect the same treatment you just gave me. A girl can get used to that."

"Count on it." He took the final puffs from the joint and snuffed it out in the ashtray on the nightstand by the bed. "You hungry? I'll see what we have in the fridge."

"Just some munchies and a Miller Lite, if we got it."

"Anything for the princess." He went into the kitchen and returned a couple minutes later with a cold beer and a bag of kettle popcorn.

"Now that'll work. Thanks."

Chapter 8

OFF DUTY GET TOGETHER

The digital clock in his car displayed 6:22 p.m. as Tomczyk pulled into the common driveway of the Juneau Village Tower apartment complex on Milwaukee's Lower East Side, a couple blocks north of downtown. He walked into the lobby just as Anne came off the elevator.

"Five minutes early, Detective. I'm rather impressed. And you dress up well. Blue jeans and polo shirts during the day, suit after six."

"Just don't let my bosses know. They don't believe I own a watch or a suit," a broad smile coming over his face as he stroked the left lapel of his navy blue Vino Cabela athletic-cut suit. Tomczyk couldn't help notice how radiant Anne looked in her soft, green cashmere sweater, navy blue pants, and waist-length black leather jacket. Her brown hair glistened as the curls bounced gently off her shoulders. "You look fantastic, Anne. I didn't think you could improve on your usual beauty, but I stand corrected."

"Flattery will get you everywhere," she responded as Tomczyk opened the glass door and escorted her to his midnight black car parked in the ten-minute parking area. "Ford Mustang, and a convertible to boot. Now you're talking."

"I'm a retro guy, and the new Mustangs remind me of the '60s model my old man used to have back in the day. Besides, I made the command decision that it might be a little brisk to pick you up on my Road King."

"And a great decision it was."

He opened the passenger door, and Anne slid into the seat. As Tomczyk got into the driver's side, he turned the ignition, and the 5.0 liter V8 engine roared to life. "If you're going to do it, you might as well do it right. This car rocks, so I have to be careful."

"Still has the new car smell. It must have recently been taken off the car lot."

"My F-150 has miles on it. So I took the plunge and bought me a 'fair-weather vehicle.' The truck will come out when the snow and cold return to the Midwest in a month."

Tomczyk drove along the city streets as they made conversation. He pulled into the parking lot at the iconic Steakhouse on State Street. As they approached the front door, a middle-aged security guard dressed in his brown uniform approached. "Yo' Ski. How's my favorite vanilla brotha' doing tonight? You still tryin' to keep the lid on this city?"

"Always trying, Ty. I'm fantastic. How about you?" They shook hands and hugged each other.

The restaurant was ranked as one of the best in the city, but was located in a neighborhood wallowing in a fair amount of blight. Several housing projects and vacant houses were within eyeshot of the well-known establishment.

"Luckier than a man should be, my friend. Feels like you stopped lifting, Ski. Your arms are getting a little soft." His mouth opened to a wide grin, showing yellow-stained teeth.

"Too much overtime lately, so I haven't hit the gym much." He and Ty always exchanged friendly jabs when they saw each other. "I want you to meet a friend of mine. This is Anne. Anne, this is Tyrone. Just don't get too close to him. Thinks he's some sort of AARP card-carrying playa' and will try to hit on you."

"Pleased to meet you, ma'am." He took her right hand in a warm embrace and placed his left hand over it. "You're with one of Milwaukee's best sons, but if he doesn't treat you right, you come and talk to Tyrone. I'll square him up right."

"It's a plan, Ty. An honor to meet you also."

"That's a great lookin' suit, by the way. Looks just like the one I donated two weeks ago. Well, time to get back on the J.O.B. Good to see you, Ski, and to meet you, Anne." He winked at both of them and slowly walked over to another arriving car.

They walked to the front door, and Tomczyk opened it. "This place will definitely take you back in time—like about forty years." The bar was nearly full, but they were able to find two empty stools at the far end.

A short and stocky, sixty-something bartender came over and asked for their order. His pressed, long-sleeved white shirt and Rush Limbaugh tie fit in well with the décor.

"Excuse me, sir. I thought we kicked you out of here two weeks ago, along with that gang of thugs you were with. I told you to never come back here," the man stated with a stone-cold face.

Anne glanced over at Tomczyk.

"Decided I'm addicted to these crummy steaks, so I thought I'd come back."

"You still drinking that Nancy-boy rum and cranberry juice, with a lime, or have you started drinking brandy and a beer like a man? Ma'am, what can I get you? Sorry for you having won 'the loser-date-of-the-night contest.'"

"I'm surprised a man of your advanced age can still remember that much. Yes, that's my drink. And the lady would like a white zinfandel—if you stock any wine costing more than two dollars a bottle."

"I turn sixty-five next week, but still young enough to show you what for. You weightlifters may be strong, but you can't think fast enough, and I'd wallop you." He extended his hand. "Damn good to see you again, Ski. It's been a while. How ya doing?"

"Doing great, Whitey. Anne, this is Whitey Anderson, bartender extraordinaire at the Steakhouse."

"Fantastic to meet you, Whitey . . . I think," she smiled. "I wasn't too sure at first."

"Only 'cause I love him, Anne." A serious look came over his leathery face as he looked over at Tomczyk. "I heard the terrible news about Lurch. Our prayers are with him. You let us know when we can send a complete steak dinner or two for him at the hospital. It's pure entertainment to watch a man shovel so much food down his throat."

"Thanks, Whitey, it means a lot."

They continued their conversation for several minutes as an attractive, petite waitress approached. "Good evening. I was told you're Declan, party of two. Please come with me. Your table is ready."

"Lead the way."

"Great meeting you, Anne. Hope you enjoy your meal. Ski, don't be a stranger."

"You can count on it. Talk to you later, Whitey."

They were directed to a table in a corner of the medium-sized dining area. Pictures hung on the walls and the décor reminded Anne of some of the old black and white movies she watched on late-night TV while in college. The waitress handed them menus and came back several minutes later with a woven straw basket of warm bread.

"Okay, Anne. Now that you know everything about my life, you have to tell me about yours. Schools, dreams, and how you ever wound up in Milwaukee."

"Fair enough. I'm originally from Texas, but we moved around because of my father's job. Like yours, he's a Vietnam vet—Special Forces for five years and two tours in Vietnam. He finished out at Fort Lewis in Washington State, fell in love with the area, and attended the University of Washington in Seattle on the GI Bill. A football jock like you, he met my mother at school, and they got married. He then grabbed a job with DEA and spent the next twenty-eight-plus years as a narc. He retired at the mandatory age of fifty-seven as an assistant director, and they moved back to a small community called Issaquah. It's in the foothills of the Cascade Mountains, just east of Seattle. I spent my high school years around there and went to college at UW also. My parents have UW purple and gold running through their veins. They're season ticket holders, and the Husky is their favorite animal."

The waitress returned to their table. "Hope you're doing well tonight. Have you decided?"

"I was told the filet ranks on the top ten in the world list. I'll go with the lady's cut—medium, please—and a potato with everything on it."

"Excellent choice, ma'am. You obviously have a great source."

"I'll take the king's cut, medium also. And another Captain Morgan and cranberry juice, please. Anne, would you like another Zin?"

"Sure."

"And another white zinfandel, please."

The waitress thanked them, and a porter came with a large bowl of mixed salad and a dressing tray.

"So you're big Husky fans? Wonderful." Tomczyk squirmed in his seat.

"During the interview with the Pavalkos the other day, it struck me who you were. My parents were at the Rose Bowl game you played in. I watched the game from my sorority house on campus. You really seem like a nice guy, Declan, but my family doesn't like you very much. My father came home from Pasadena with fire in his eyes and hatred for some guy named Tomczyk, the one-man wrecking crew. If he knew I was out on a date with you, he would disown me." She shook her head and smiled. "Talk about small worlds. Maybe the fifteen-plus years since that game has softened his heart for you as a human being. If that wasn't bad enough, after you beat the poor Huskies, you became a Marine. How do I even approach my father and tell him that one? My parents are still both mother hens and will be calling me tomorrow night."

"Tell him you had a date with the water boy, maybe?"

Anne was enjoying the company. She found Declan to be an even more amazing person than she originally thought. "After college, I became a school teacher for a couple years, but realized I wanted more. My father's love for government service called me, and I joined the FBI eight years ago. They sent me to LA as my first office. LA is, as we say, an interesting office. I was originally White Collar Crimes and lateraled over to the JTTF. Six years of crazy California living was enough for me. I'm not looking forward to the Wisconsin winter, but it sure will be nice to have four seasons again."

They were finishing up their plate of salad when the steaks arrived. Anne cut off a piece of the steaming, tantalizing steak and placed it in her mouth. "Wow, this is really fantastic. Great choice of restaurants."

"Glad you like it."

"There's something I need to tell you, Declan. I was married for about five years and went through a nasty divorce several years ago. Guess my ex didn't like his wife being a 'pistol packin' Momma.' I have a six-year-old daughter named Krista who is the light of my life."

He looked at her with understanding and sympathy. "I'm sorry to hear about your divorce. Things don't always work out. Marie and I always wanted children, but the cancer ended all that. You've been blessed with one of God's truly beautiful creations. I love to hear she is the light of your life."

"Thank you so much for that. I've been lucky to find a wonderful woman in the apartment complex that takes care of her. Krista loves her almost as much as she does her grandmother. My Dad was on a mission to take my ex out, and I mean out of the living realm. I had to take a two-week vacation to calm him down. It's just my brother and me, so my parents are extremely protective."

"As well they should be."

They finished their meal, and the waitress asked if they wanted an after-dinner drink.

"Could I maybe have a glass of Baileys?"

"I'm good, thanks," Tomczyk said with a wave of his hand.

"Coming right up."

"Did I tell you John Lemke was my partner on a task force for about a year? He's a great friend and a super guy. He's been upgraded to stable and should be out of the hospital in a couple days. Thank God he made it."

"Rumor control has it you saved his life with your battlefield meatball surgery."

"No man left behind, and no one dies on my watch—if I can help it. It's a creed that was hammered into me in jarhead land."

"Oh, yeah, I know all about that from my dad! You know, Declan, maybe he could like you after all," she smiled.

"That's great to know. I'd hate to be dating the beautiful daughter of a father who couldn't like me." He raised his glass in a "salute."

"I'll drink to that."

"Going back to Lemke. He's been a bomb tech for over twenty years and still has all his fingers. He's not the smartest guy, but he 'aced' every test at the six-week bomb training at Redstone Arsenal in Alabama. That's quite an accomplishment."

"I'll say. Nearly every bomb tech I've spoken with said the course was a real beast. If you flunk any tests, they send you straight home."

Tomczyk paid the bill, and they stepped out of the front door. He glanced over to his right and noticed four teenagers walking toward them. "Anne, are you armed?"

She glanced at him with a surprised expression. "Never leave home without it, why?"

"Good. Don't look now, but four guys are walking our way. The guy on my right has the barrel of a shotgun or rifle sticking out slightly from underneath his jacket. They high-signed each other, and I think they're going to try to rob us. I'll take out the three guys on my right. You cover the one on the far left in case he's armed. If he tries anything stupid, show him how good you FBI agents shoot. This'll be interesting. You ready?"

"Not really."

"It will be okay; just follow my lead and cover that guy."

Several seconds later, as the group was within ten feet of them, Tomczyk calmly glanced over as if to say something to Anne. As he did, the peripheral vision in his left eye picked up the young black male on the right opening up the navy blue nylon jacket he was wearing and reaching for the weapon underneath it.

Chapter 9

ON THE STREETS OF MILWAUKEE

omczyk gently pushed Anne to her left and pivoted around on his left foot, swinging his right leg around in a roundhouse move. His foot struck its mark at the solar plexus. There was a loud grunt from the young man's diaphragm as the force of the blow sent him reeling onto his back with a thud. The sawed-off shotgun fell to the side, causing a loud noise as the metal hit the sidewalk. Tomczyk swung back around to his right and thrust his left fist into the upper chest area of the second man with such a powerful force that it caused the unprepared subject to be sent back about five feet, flailing onto his back. In the same lightning motion, he delivered a straight left-leg kick into the lower stomach area of the third person, buckling him over. His finishing touch was a "tomahawk chop," a right arm to the back of the neck, causing a now extremely sore body to be thrust straight onto the sidewalk. Tomczyk instinctively moved into a fighting stance to take on the last subject.

"Police, freeze!"

He looked over and saw Anne with both arms outstretched, with her FBI-issued Glock 22, .40 caliber pistol pointed directly at the young male. The subject's mouth was wide open as he stared in horror at Tomczyk, immediately laying down on the sidewalk and stretching his trembling arms out to the side.

"Please don't hit me, Officer, I told 'em not to."

Anne surveyed the scene. The first guy Tomczyk hit was gasping for air. She saw the short-barreled shotgun on the sidewalk next to him and watched as Tomczyk picked it up and told the suspect to calm down and slowly breathe. The other two subjects were out cold. Tomczyk did a quick pat down and recovered a blue steel-barreled .357 revolver from the waistband of the third suspect. From one of the pants pockets of the second suspect, he seized a large folding knife.

By this time, Tyrone, the security officer, approached and handed his friend two sets of handcuffs. "Here, in case you don't have any. Damn, brotha.' I ain't never seen nothin' like that before! Sure am glad you're my friend."

"Thanks, Ty. You mind calling the police so we can get some help over here?"

"Already called 9-1-1. They's on the way. Hate to break this to ya, Ski, but I don't think you need any help."

Tomczyk winked at Ty as he handcuffed the unharmed male. "Don't do anything foolish, young man. Just chill until the police get here and nothing will happen to you." He checked the pulse of the two unconscious subjects and used the second set of handcuffs to cuff them together. "They'll be sore tomorrow, but they're both still breathing."

They heard several sets of sirens blaring and saw the red and blue lights of the marked squads as they screamed up to the scene. Tomczyk pulled out his badge and identification, showing it to the first-responding officers. He also pointed out the weapons he obtained from the subjects and the circumstances regarding their recovery.

"You may want to have the EMTs take a look at the three I hit, just to make sure. I didn't go 100 percent."

"Well, that's reassuring, Detective."

A second police officer approached. "Some detectives and a lieutenant are on the way since it's a significant incident."

"Copy that. Thanks for making the call. By the way, my beautiful date tonight is an FBI agent who was Top Gun at her academy class. I was never worried."

All four suspects were taken to the city jail in separate squads after assessment by ambulance personnel. The EMTs were impressed with the precision of the strikes to the more vulnerable areas of the body and more impressed the person who delivered the blows didn't permanently debilitate them.

One of the officers walked over to Tomczyk. "Detective, we did record checks on all four guys. The three you took out all had extensive juvenile records. The two with guns are convicted felons. Surprise, surprise!"

"Good news for us, bad news for them."

Tomczyk and Dvorak were released about an hour later after their statements were taken. He walked over to the uniformed security guard and shook hands.

"Thanks for being around tonight, Ty. I appreciate the help."

"You know ya coulda' shot those fools, and I'd a backed you up on it. Dang kids. They messed with the wrong guy tonight."

They both smiled. "I know, man, but that local paper of ours would've been calling me racist, shooting innocent kids who just happened to be carrying weapons but were trying to turn their lives around." He put his arm around Tyrone's right shoulder.

"I owe you one, Ty. You have my cell number. Give me a call, and we'll go out, my treat. Just don't feed me all that Blue Label like last time. I still feel that hangover."

Tyrone Jackson shook his head at the activities of the night and went back to guarding the parking lot with a little more bounce in his step. "And don't forget to bring that pretty lady with you so I can make some time with her."

"Then it's a date. Later."

Tomczyk walked back over to Anne, who was still conversing with several of the police officers.

"Ma'am, your chariot awaits." They walked the short distance over to his car and climbed in.

Anne looked at her watch and saw it was coming up on eleven o'clock. "Now that was a wonderful dinner, but what a finish! I can't believe this whole thing happened. I'm still a little shaky."

"Sorry this had to happen. I guess you never expect to get robbed when going out for dinner. You did a great job out there."

"Unbelievable how fast you moved to take those guys out. Scary."

"Uncle Sam spent tens of thousands of dollars over the years to train me. Let's just say it paid off, and no one had to be killed. These guys can sit in their prison cells for a while and think about it."

"Ya know, Declan, on second thought, I know my Dad is really going to like you. They're flying out here in a couple weeks to visit us. I'd really love for you to meet them."

"As long as he doesn't hold grudges. I already have a couple strikes against me."

"Very true, but you picked up a couple points tonight showing what you can do."

Tomczyk drove through the streets he swore to protect and thought of the old *Prince of the City* theme song. He loved being a detective, almost as much as he loved being a marine. Different missions, different lifestyles, but both about serving his country. He drove into the driveway of the Juneau Towers. Just as he unbuckled his seat belt, Anne reached across the seat, placed her right arm around his neck, and planted a three-second kiss on his lips. He melted in the seat. It had been a while.

She looked squarely into his eyes. He could smell the exotic perfume and the cinnamon of a long-ago-dissolved breath mint.

"Declan, I had a remarkable time, and you are a remarkable person. Thank you very much. I'd really enjoy seeing you again off duty."

"There's nothing I'd like more." He gave her a kiss back.

"Don't bother walking me to my door. You know I'm packin' heat and can take care of myself."

"Boy, do I ever! Don't mess with the feds, that's what I always say." He watched as she entered the lobby. Through the large plate glass windows, he could see her get into one of the elevators.

Tomczyk was on cloud nine as he drove away. *What a woman.* He drove through the downtown streets and onto the entrance ramp of the expressway for the twenty-minute drive home.

Chapter 10

MPD HEADQUARTERS

How'd the search warrant go, Ski?" Detective Cary Jones asked, looking up from his computer.

"Great day, C.J. Two arrests, three kilos of cocaine, $53,000 and change in cash, and three handguns. Looks like Snake Eye Sammy is going back to prison. Bad career move to be on parole for selling cocaine after spending five years in prison and then get popped for having that much dope and guns in your house when you're a felon. Another condition of parole was to not associate with current biker members. Maybe Snake Eye didn't think being in the illegal pharmaceutical business with a current outlaw motorcycle gang member was the same as hangin' with them. Oops! The drug task force has him in a really big crack—no pun intended. Now that was definitely worth the oh-dark-thirty wake-up call to hit that house at six. Even though I was in the rear with the gear guarding the back door, it's still fun to be part of the team."

"I hear ya, man. Then they pay you. Can't get better than that."

Samuel "Snake Eye Sammy" Howard had been a member of the Milwaukee biker club for the past fifteen years. He was vice president of the chapter until about seven years ago when he was arrested by Milwaukee Police for possession of five ounces of cocaine, some meth, and a large .45 caliber handgun. Because of several prior arrests, he was sentenced to eight years in the Wisconsin prison system. Howard served just over five years and was paroled with a number of conditions; no illegal drugs or guns and no associating with current members were two of them.

The Milwaukee chapter had one of the largest in the country. Its clubhouse at the end of a dead-end street had been there for over thirty years. The unmistakable black background and white artwork logo was painted on the front of the old building. For several years, they were able to boast about having the national presidency in Milwaukee. Unfortunately for them, the president was convicted on federal charges and sentenced to prison, and the national chapter honor was moved. The Milwaukee High Intensity Drug Trafficking Area task force reached out and requested Tomczyk assist them on the search and arrest warrant because of his familiarity with outlaw motorcycle gangs. He also had a related investigation on another member. During the search warrant, a number of records and other evidence were confiscated having to do with Howard's continued association with the club and some of its members.

Tomczyk also had great familiarity with the black street gangs that plagued Milwaukee and had a number of current investigations on members. Vice Lords, Black Gangster Disciples and the Murder Mob were some of the main ones. There were also a number of offshoots from the five- and six-pointed star nations that he enjoyed staying on top of. Gangs, guns, and drugs have been going hand-in-hand for multiple decades, even though Milwaukee started having its main gang problems starting in the early 1980s.

Tomczyk removed a nutrition bar from his desk drawer and grabbed a manila folder with his name on it sitting in the center of his desk. "TMB" was marked in bold letters. He opened it and looked at the stack of papers inside. Andrew Reed, the new police aide assigned to the intelligence division, was a whiz on the computer and had copied different websites and articles related to TMB and The Mad Bomber. Reed had typed a note that was placed inside the folder.

Detective Tomczyk, this is what I grabbed off the computer re: what you told me to look for. I found nothing at all for TMB. When I googled The Mad Bomber, several different hits came up. The main one refers to a guy named George Metesky of New York who set off thirty-something explosions over a twenty-year period. You'll see what I got off Wikipedia and some other articles about him. There were two hits referring to Frank Balistreri, so I copied those. The last one is for a Hugh 'Idzi' Rutkowski who blew up himself and some sixteen-year-old kid named Paul 'Shrimp' Chovanec in a garage off Twenty-second and Mitchell in November 1935 while making a bomb. A nine-year-old girl in a house next to the garage also died. I copied a couple articles for you. There's a ton of stuff if you archive the Milwaukee Journal and Sentinel from that period. If you need anything else, I'll be back to work in a couple days. Taking some time off to hang out with my buds.

Later, Andy

"Andy Reed, you're a stud." Tomczyk looked through the paperwork and read briefly from some of the articles. *What do all these guys have in common? It's gotta be this Idzi and Shrimp deal. But they're dead. What's the connection to the current stuff going on?* He set the folder next to his computer and logged in. He had an email message from Scott Kamble of the identification division.

Great news, Ski. Positive ID on the spray paint can and the receipt found in the bag from the cemetery case. Kim said there were no fingerprints on any of the headstones or anything else. We're guessing they were using gloves at that point. The prints we identified belong to a Harold Sampson Carter Jr.: B OF I# 302128; AKA, Squirt. You can grab all his info off the computer.

Happy hunting!
Scott

"Excellent! This is starting out to be a great day," he said aloud. Tomczyk plugged the Bureau of Identification (B OF I) number assigned to Carter into the computer. An extensive criminal record dating back to Carter's juvenile days popped up on the screen. Everyone arrested by the Milwaukee Police Department was assigned an identification number, which stays with him for life. Whenever one is re-arrested, that number is accessed, a new photo is taken, and the new charge or charges are added. "A wonderful court system we maintain," he complained to Jones. "This punk has five felony convictions and only spent four years in prison. Doesn't felony mean a little time in prison?"

"C'mon, Ski. Where's your heart? Rehabilitation is the key to success, not re-incarceration." Jones loved pushing Tomczyk's buttons.

"Of course. And that's why I didn't become a social engineer or whatever they call the do-gooders who think everyone deserves a chance—and a chance—and a chance. I'm okay with cutting slack on first offenders, but over and over again? Drives me batty."

"What do you got?"

"A positive ID on fingerprints from the cemetery case. Lifted from left-behind items. Some guy named Harold Sampson Carter Jr., with a nickname of Squirt. Another ne'er-do-well roaming the streets."

"Harold Carter? Hang on a minute." Jones walked over to the roll-call board hanging on the wall outside the lieutenant's office and brought it back to his desk. He paged through it and showed the report to Tomczyk. "Knew the name sounded familiar. They read this off at roll call this morning. You obviously didn't see it because of that early police work you were doing."

Tomczyk looked at the typed report of a vehicle wanted in connection with a crime. "You've got to be kidding me! He was the victim of a homicide in a park yesterday? Sorry about what happened to you, Squirt. Bad for you, good for us."

He dialed the number to the homicide squad.

"Homicide, Detective Bernems…"

"Rickey, this is Ski. Talk to me about Harold Carter Jr. His prints were positively ID'd on some items in the Holy Cross Cemetery case where Lurch was injured. I was just told Carter was the victim of a homicide yesterday."

"You're right. I was sent to investigate. Junior had a big hole in the center of his coconut and one to the chest. We recovered a number of .40 caliber and 9mm casings. Sent those to the crime lab. Looks like they were partying by a fire pit off the asphalt walkway south of the flagpole. Must've got into an argument with an acquaintance or something. It didn't end very well for him."

"I know the spot. Used to drive through when I patrolled that area. Can you give me some info on clothing or anything?"

"He had on a black jacket, blue t-shirt, black pants, and a pair of Doc Marten boots with red spray paint splatters on them. Guess that makes some sense now. The ME's office also found a cell phone in a pants pocket and a thumb drive in his right boot. Now that's an interesting place to put something. The phone was password protected and the thumb drive was encrypted. We sent them out to the experts at Secret Service to analyze."

"Fantastic. I'll be down in less than five," he said as he hung up the phone. "Jonesboy, that's why you're the star detective around here. Even though the bosses think you're useless, I respect you."

"Makes my day, buddy. We're here to help you high-profile detectives."

"And we appreciate it. This is a big break, my brother. Thanks."

Tomczyk scaled the stairs two at a time to reach the fourth floor detective assembly. He buzzed through the security door and found Detective Bernems at his desk.

As Bernems stood up, the dress shirt and pants hugged his chiseled build. He was no stranger to a gym and shook hands with his fellow weightlifting coworker. "Here are some of the photos and the inventory listing his clothing. Most of the reports are still on the machines being typed up."

Tomczyk examined the photos. He noted the red spray paint splatters on the black pants and boots—*the* boots. He was especially hoping the bottom of the right boot design matched the cast they got from the cemetery. "Somebody musta' really got pissed off at Junior."

"I'll say. Had to be a close shot. Look at how centered that round is in his forehead. Cops did a good job canvassing the neighborhood and found some guy who said he was out jogging at about three in the morning. Said he was coming up Humboldt when he heard about ten gunshots from what sounded like somewhere northeast of where he was. As he approached Hadley, he saw an older green, Toyota four-door with two white males in it come over the bridge from the park, squeal off the curb, and continue west. Didn't get much of a description of them; however, he did get a partial plate on the car. Said it was partly covered with mud or something and couldn't read the numbers."

"Excellent, Rickey. I'd sure love to get a look at this guy's boots. We made a cast of the right one, which had a very distinctive mark on the sole."

"No worries. All his clothing is still hanging in the drying room. I was going to package it this afternoon and take it over to property. Follow me. Got some other good news for you. The fingerprint gurus lifted prints off a couple beer cans and a 9mm casing. We're going on an early morning search warrant tomorrow morning."

"Great. Mind if I tag along?"

"The more the merrier."

The "drying room" was temperature controlled with continual air flow and was located in the back of the Criminal Investigation Division assembly. It could only be accessed by personnel assigned to the division. The room had a number of open storage compartments so clothing from criminal offenses could be dried before packaging. A white paper sheet was placed at the base of each storage area to collect any trace evidence that fell from the clothing during the drying process.

Detective Bernems directed Tomczyk to storage area number twenty-two. They took note of the clothing and boots. Tomczyk donned a pair of rubber gloves from one of the boxes located on a shelf and carefully lifted the boot, turning it upside down, and examining the sole carefully. With his cell phone, he took several pictures. "Looks like a perfect match to me. I'll grab an ID tech from downstairs to take some photos for the case file. Did you see any bomb techs at roll call this morning?"

"Yeah, Kenny Schmidt's here. He was just in the assembly ten minutes ago talking to a lieutenant."

"Great. I'll be right back. Hold that thought." Tomczyk walked back to the assembly and saw Detective Schmidt coming out from Lieutenant Bill Gram's cubicle. "Yo, Schmidty. Can I talk to you a second?"

"Oh, boy. If it isn't one of our precious intel wienies. Whadya need, Ski?"

"I was wondering if you could grab your chemical testing kit. I need you to check a pair of boots for explosive residue. They're in the drying room."

"Sure can. I'll meet you back there in five."

"Excellent, thanks."

Less than five minutes later, Schmidt walked into the drying room where the other two detectives were waiting for him.

Schmidt opened his black leather briefcase and pulled out the Thermo Scientific chemical tester. "We just got these two weeks ago. This is the 'FirstDefender RM' that's replacing the older model we used to use—much smaller, lighter, with a quicker analysis. Check this out." He pointed the one-and-a-half-pound piece of equipment at the boots and pushed the button. "This is the amazing part." Within a minute, a readout appeared on the small, digital screen. "Nitrates, methanol, and sulfuric acid." He repeated the process for the pants.

"In layman's terms, what do you think it is?"

"My best guess is methyl nitrate. Hope no one was using this stuff to blow anything up. It blows like a banshee, but it's like trying to drive a dump truck across a lake in winter on two-inch-thick ice. Too damn dangerous."

"Methyl nitrate! Matches what the bombers used at the cemetery when Lurch got hit."

Schmidt flashed Tomczyk a shocked look. "This is connected to Lurch's case?"

Chapter II

RIVER HILLS NURSING HOME

It was a quarter of one when Demetrius walked through the front door of the nursing home for the start of his one o'clock shift. He was off school and thought he would earn some extra cash working the partial shift. The computer tablet he wanted would be within financial reach with the money he made this week.

"D, you're gracing our presence awfully early today. Did you skip out of school again?" joked one of the nurses.

"Naw, the principal sent all the smartest students home early. He said there was nothing else they could teach us since we already knew everything."

"You got me on that one! Great to see you. What do they have you doing today?"

"Tim said we'll be waxing some floors. I love operating that wax machine. My new life's goal: Demetrius Simms, Wax Master."

"Okay, Mr. Wax Master. Let's get a move on."

Demetrius turned around and saw the familiar, older, large man wearing a dark green shirt and matching work trousers. "You got me, Tim. I-I was just having some fun with the nurses."

Tim grabbed Demetrius by the collar and playfully pulled him toward the maintenance room. "I'll get him out of your hair so he doesn't bother you, ladies." Tim put his arm around Demetrius and hugged him close, whispering in his right ear. "D, you're a piece of work. You ready for the big game tomorrow? Helen and I will be there cheering you on."

"Sure am. Thanks for asking."

"Excellent. They want us to wash and wax the rooms on the third floor. Equipment's already up there. Let's see what we can knock out by five. They have good eats tonight. I already talked to the cooks."

"Great."

Demetrius went into the locker room, quickly changed into his uniform, and joined his supervisor on the targeted floor. They attacked the rooms and hallway with mops in hand. After finishing the rooms, he grabbed the large waxing machine and filled the liquid wax solution to the top. "Now the fun begins," he said to Tim, smiling from ear to ear.

"You're a sick young man."

Demetrius turned on iTunes and placed the earphones in, then set about his work. When he finished waxing half of the floors, he looked over at the clock on the wall—4:35 p.m.

Tim came down the hallway and nodded his head approvingly. "Great job, kid. Go take a break. I'll meet you in the cafeteria at five."

"Okay." Demetrius strolled down the hallway and went to the TV room on the main level where he saw George sitting in a corner reading a book.

"How you doin', George? You have time to tell me more of the story you started the other night?"

George looked up and smiled. "Of course I do. Nothing but the best for my bud. Sit down and take a load off. Where'd I leave off?"

"You guys just drove away from the store after Idzi tried to rob it with the shotgun."

"Good memory." George collected his thoughts and continued where he'd left off. "A week or two went by, and Idzi's gettin' antsy again. It's now around the latter part of October. Me, Idzi, and Shrimp were out driving around in a stolen car when Idzi decided he wants to steal a police car. Can you imagine that? Said it'd be easy enough. So he had me drive over to the West Milwaukee Police Department. Idzi broke into the station, took the keys, and drove off in one of the two squads parked there. Started racing down the street, with me trying to keep up with him. He turned on the red light and siren once or twice, then pulled into an alley and stopped the squad. Then he yanked the police radio and siren out and turned off the red light. Threw the stuff in our car and got in laughing his head off. He opened his hand and showed me two sets of car keys, saying West Milwaukee Police was out of business since we had the keys to both their squads. We drove back to our garage. That was one wild night."

George adjusted his position in the chair. "Here's where it starts getting crazy. I should've got off the merry-go-round about then, but didn't, so I deserved the prison time I got. It was a couple days later when Idzi pulled out a bomb he made with three or four sticks of dynamite. We drove over to Shorewood City Hall. I remember it being a clear, bright night. Idzi stuffed the bomb in a drainpipe on the side of the building and lit the fuse. We ran like hell. When we reached the car, we barely had enough time to turn around and see the explosion. It was really loud. He was laughing the whole time we drove back to our neighborhood. Kept sayin' how these rich folks over here need some excitement on a Saturday night."

"Why'd you stay with them, George?"

"I got caught up in the whole gangster thing myself. They took down John Dillinger in '34 in Chicago. We all idolized Dillinger and thought we could do our own thing in Milwaukee. So every time Idzi suggested something crazy, me and Shrimp would be right on board with it."

"I'm with you on that one. Peer pressure can be intense. I had some buddies who started selling dope down the block from me. I stopped hangin' with 'em. My dad was a Milwaukee cop and was killed in the line of duty a couple years ago. Can't even think about what my Mom would do to me if I ever did something like that. I couldn't tarnish the memory of my pops. He meant the world to me, and I still miss him a lot." Demetrius teared up, and George put his hand on his knee and patted it a couple times.

"You're a good kid. I was one of nine children. It was the middle of the Depression; there was no money and no jobs. Those were tough times, and I got stupid. Don't want that to happen to you."

"Sorry, George." He wiped away the tears falling down his cheeks. "It's been real tough with Dad gone. Please, go on with the story. I only have ten more minutes, then I have to meet Tim in the cafeteria for supper."

"This'll be short. I had this part-time job at a pharmacy on Mitchell Street. On Sunday afternoon, we got into another stolen car and drove back up to the North Side. Idzi said he was going to 'light it up,' which sounded kind of crazy and exciting all at the same time. He had me stop the car at the back of a First Wisconsin Bank. Idzi and Shrimp got out for a couple minutes, then ran back to the car and told me to hit it. As I drove out of the alley, I heard the explosion. Them guys were in the back seat, giggling like school girls."

"They bombed the bank! You gotta' be kiddin' me."

"Ain't half the story, kid. Idzi had me go back to that pharmacy in Shorewood again. Said he was going to rob them and finish what he started the week before. I parked the car on the street a couple doors away. They got out of the car and put sunglasses and handkerchiefs on.

Idzi grabbed the shotgun, hid it under his coat, and they went into the store. I stayed in the car with the engine running. Less than five minutes went by; they jumped in, and we hightailed it out of there. Said they robbed them this time and got some money. Then he told me to keep driving down the street for about five blocks and pull over to the curb. They got out and did the same thing with the sunglasses, handkerchiefs, and shotgun—robbing another drugstore! *Not again,* I'm thinking. They came out a couple minutes later, and we sped away. Idzi told me we had one more stop to make before we were finished for the night."

"Let me guess, another robbery or bombing?"

"Now you're catching on. He was a definite adrenaline junkie. We headed over to another First Wisconsin Bank on East North Avenue. They got out and walked to the back. There were a number of people walking down the street because the Oriental Theatre was down the block, and they had some popular movie playing—big, beautiful place. Some of the big names used to play on the stage. So anyway, Shrimp and Idzi got back into that car and another loud explosion goes off. They both started cheering and laughing. I got the heck out of there. What a rush. We parked the car on the street and hoofed it back to the clubhouse. We took the money, but left the weapons and disguises in the car. Idzi pulled out a bottle of brandy. Think we finished the bottle that night."

Demetrius looked at his watch. "Unbelievable, George. Hate to leave you, but I have to meet Tim for dinner. He hooked us up. Great story."

"Good luck with the game tomorrow night, kid. And knock 'em dead."

"Thanks." Demetrius shook George's frail hand and pulled a chocolate bar out of his pocket. "Brought you a little something. Can you have it?"

"Me, chocolate? Hey, my false teeth let me eat almost anything. I can't tell you how much I enjoy having you around. Always loved chocolate bars. Thanks. See ya when I see ya."

Chapter I2

SEARCH WARRANT: MILWAUKEE

The four marked squad cars pulled into the District Two police parking lot on Milwaukee's South Side neighborhood at five for the early briefing scheduled at five fifteen. The markings on the squads said TEU, which stood for tactical enforcement unit. Having gone through a number of changes since its inception by then Police Chief Harold A. Breier during the Milwaukee riots in August 1967, the full-time unit was still an integral part of the department. Many police departments and agencies called theirs SWAT; Milwaukee had the TEU.

The ten police officers entered the assembly room and were readily noticed by several district uniform officers writing reports or drinking their morning coffees. The unmistakable TACTICAL ENFORCEMENT UNIT patch bearing a helmet with crossed shotgun and baton on the right shoulder of their navy blue uniform shirts and jackets was easily identifiable. The two TEU sergeants were already in the large room, speaking with several homicide detectives. Tomczyk walked in a minute or two later.

"I'm always surprised when the department knuckle draggers can get up so early on their own and be here on time."

A tall and lean officer in his early thirties with close-cropped blonde hair smiled at Tomczyk. "C'mon, Ski, if it wasn't for you teaching us how to set an alarm clock when you were on the squad with us, we'd still be catching our beauty sleep." The comment was enjoyed by all.

At promptly five fifteen, Homicide Detective Rickey Bernems stood in front of the group and asked for their attention. "Thanks for coming, men. I know it's a little early, but we have information that our subject shacks up with his girlfriend, so we wanted to hit it early while they're still lyin' in bed. This case stems from a homicide in Gordon Park where the victim was found with one gunshot wound to the forehead and one to the chest. Evidence at the scene shows our suspect was there. His name is Matthew Elroy Wallk, with a birthday of April 15, 1991. He has a prior record for a couple burglary convictions and one carrying-concealed-gun arrest. He also has an outstanding felony warrant for reckless endangerment with a weapon. Wallk is 5'10", 195 pounds with brown hair." Bernems held up a large booking photo of a white male in standard orange coveralls.

"His girlfriend is Amber Solie. They live at 2437B South California Avenue in Bay View. It's a dark green and white-trim bungalow that sits along the alley behind a green duplex. We don't have any info on dogs or fortification. As of a half-hour ago, Wallk's beat-up, brown Chevy pickup truck was parked on a concrete slab in the alley. He may be in possession of a 9mm pistol, one of the guns used in the homicide. The sergeants will give you your assignment. We want to hit this place as close to six as we can. Finally, Detective Tomczyk's here because Wallk may be connected to the bombing at Holy Cross Cemetery where Detective John Lemke was severely injured. If you see evidence of explosive materials during your room clearing, we have a bomb tech on standby. Any questions? Good. Thanks."

Bay View was one of the oldest neighborhoods in Milwaukee. It included large, old brick and wooden homes with remarkable views of Lake Michigan, along with a number of duplexes, bungalows, and businesses. Its lifeblood was South Kinnickinnic Avenue, or South KK, as it was known. Kinnickinnic ran diagonally from northwest to southeast, less than a mile west of the lake and on a similar angle.

Sergeant Jim Olevo stood up from his chair. "Okay, here's the lineup: Heine, hammerman; Novak, Halligan tool; Kotch, ballistic shield; King, MP5, behind Kotch; followed by Heinamann, Marcheesy, and Orlowske. Heine and Novak, you guys become rear guard and assist in prisoner control. Don't forget, this is a no-knock search warrant because of the severity of the crime and high probability of a gun in the house. Treat anyone we find as armed until verified otherwise. Lindsey and Ryan, you're outside perimeter. Suit up and be by the van in the parking lot by a quarter of six, and we'll roll out from here. Questions?"

It was five-fifty-eight when the navy blue, windowless van pulled up in the alley four houses south of the target. The team piled out of the rear doors and moved in precision formation as they walked quickly in single file toward the house. The coolness of the still-dark morning and the adrenaline rush caused each member to shiver slightly as he moved. The "human snake" walked along the target house and came alive upon reaching the front door. Police Officer Les "The Black Adonis" Heine, at 6'4" and 240 pounds, quietly but quickly walked the four steps leading up to the porch. He was followed closely behind by Ted Novak, tightly holding the Halligan, a large pry bar used to forcibly open doors that pulled out instead of pushing in. Once in position, Heine swung back on the 80-pound "ram" and mightily struck the door just above the door handle. The wooden doorjamb splintered under the force of the strike, and the door burst open. "Milwaukee Police, search warrant, police, search warrant," was heard as the loud voices split the silence of the quiet neighborhood. The officers methodically and swiftly entered the home behind the "shield-man" as they peeled off in teams of two, thoroughly searching each room and looking for the target, ready to take out any armed threat.

"All clear," echoed from several rooms. "Police! Put it down and get your hands up, now!" boomed a loud voice from a back bedroom.

Heinamann had his loaded Remington 870 pistol-gripped, twelve-gauge shotgun with sensor flashlight fixed on the white male whose picture he had viewed a half-hour earlier. The suspect had a Bryco brand 9mm pistol in his hand, but quickly realized it wasn't worth a large hole and immediately dropped the black semi-automatic to the floor. The Remington shotgun still remained a valuable weapon in the law enforcement arsenal because of the sheer power and damage the weapon sent out from its "business end."

Bob Marcheesy continued with his arrest procedures. "Now, slowly turn around. Place your hands behind your back and move two steps to your right. Do anything stupid and my partner will aerate your body." The sure-footed officer approached the suspect and handcuffed him. "Very foolish. At least you wised up before you got yourself a free trip to the morgue."

"Screw you. What are you doing in my house?"

"We have a search warrant. Are you deaf? Plus, there's a warrant out for your arrest. My advice is to shut your mouth before you put your foot in even further."

"Give me a break, pig!"

Police Officer Marcheesy placed a firm grip on Wallk's right hand and twisted it upward, creating intense pain to the wrist. "Stop resisting." People in similar positions appear to be able to nearly walk on air to avoid the excruciating pain.

"Ow, let go of me! Police brutality."

The stocky, well-built officer put his face close to the suspect's left ear. "First off, Mr. Wallk, I'm not a pig or any other farm animal. Second, if you want me to release my grip on you, you better drop the attitude. You're lucky as hell you're not bleeding out right now with several holes in you."

"All right, all right. Just let me talk to whoever I need to talk to."

"Hang tight with that. Where's your girlfriend?"

"She's at work. Starts at five at The Coffee Joint on KK."

"Okay, anyone else here?"

"No."

Just then they heard the final "all clear" signal coming from the officers who searched the basement.

Bernems and Tomczyk walked into the room and looked at the suspect, who was maneuvering his feet to place a tennis shoe on his right foot, a challenging task with handcuffs on. Matthew Wallk looked over at the black detective. It was the micro expression of shock he showed upon seeing Tomczyk that told the story. Like they had seen each other before under different circumstances, probably in a cemetery. Tomczyk made a mental note to visit that subject when they spoke to him later at police headquarters.

Bernems pulled the booking photo out of a folder he was carrying and placed it close to Wallk's head. "Not much change in a year-and-a-half."

"What the hell's going on? I didn't do anything. These cops are violating my rights."

Both detectives noticed the handgun on the floor in the corner of the room. "We'll explain everything to you downtown. There was enough probable cause to get a search warrant for your house. Looks like we found what we were looking for. There's also a felony warrant out for your arrest. For everyone's safety, are there any other firearms in this house?"

"How would I know? I just moved here a couple days ago."

"Okay, but if we find any others, you'll be charged with additional counts of felon in possession of a firearm. That would be bad for you."

— — —

"Spike called last night and said he wants us to pick out two police stations to set off explosives at—kind of a little tandem of two in Milwaukee and two in Chicago. Already checked the web to see if Dillinger was ever held in any Chicago police stations, but couldn't connect anything. Too bad. We'll have to get back to him with locations. Let me do a little more research so we can make a statement here. He's bringing up his history, so we might as well bring up ours. Now's our chance to bring Dillinger back from the dead."

"You and that Dillinger craze. Could be kind of fun blowin' up police stations, though."

"C'mon, little brother. You know he was a rock star in his day. What's wrong with having a little fun?"

"Okay. Let me think about it. We'll talk some more when I get home from work, but I already have a couple ideas. Later."

— — —

The next time Detectives Bernems and Tomczyk saw Matthew Elroy Wallk was in an interview room on the fifth floor of the Police Administration Building. There are several ways to interrogate prisoners. Because of the read they got from Wallk at the house, along with his prior, non-violent criminal record, they chose to stack the deck and put many of their cards on the table by laying out the evidence against him before reading Miranda rights. The rules of the Miranda decision state that the warnings against self-incrimination must be given to a person in custody before asking any questions about a crime.

They explicitly told Wallk to remain silent until they fully explained all the evidence against him. He was informed of the two additional firearms and six ounces of marijuana located in the house during the search. Each count of felon in possession of a firearm carried a five-year prison term. Tomczyk went extensively into the psychological importance of micro expressions. He went into how the brief look Wallk gave upon seeing Tomczyk at the house was because they had seen each other before. Tomczyk related how Wallk was in the stolen car at the cemetery when Detective John Lemke was hurt. He spoke of the ramifications and maximum prison terms for attempted homicide of a police officer and manufacturing improvised explosive devices. Finally, Bernems laid out the homicide scenario in Gordon Park where Harold "Squirt" Carter was killed. He explained how Wallk's fingerprints were on four beer cans and, most important, the dented one found in the grass by the .40 caliber casings. Bernems closed the scenario with Wallk's fingerprint being found on one of the three 9mm casings, but stressed how .40 caliber bullets were removed from Squirt's dead body, so Wallk obviously didn't fire the murder weapon.

Using this approach can be problematic. If the suspect lawyered up, he would know the evidence against him right away. The detectives were convinced Wallk would waive his right to a lawyer and speak to them. Wallk was visibly shaken and gave up his Miranda rights when they were read to him. He admitted the handgun was his and contemplated getting into a gun battle with the officers during the search warrant, but realized it would have been suicidal. The other two guns belonged to friends, whom he declined to name. He related how the marijuana was for him and his girlfriend's personal use, even though six ounces was a significant amount. He admitted they smoked marijuana multiple times daily and had gotten a great price for the big bag. Wallk confessed to the shooting he was wanted for on the warrant, saying it was more of a misunderstanding between two former friends who took it to a potentially deadly level. He expressed remorse, but held they were both at fault to varying degrees.

Wallk hesitantly confessed to being in the back seat of the SUV at the cemetery when Madman detonated the bomb from a cell phone he was carrying. He revealed the mastermind as some "genius crazy dude" with the nickname of Spike who drove the SUV. Wallk was good friends with Carter and had joined TMB, or "The Mad Bombers" as Spike referred to them, a week or two earlier. The only thing he could say about either Spike or Madman was that they lived somewhere in the Riverwest area near the Milwaukee River. No other names were ever mentioned. He gave the detectives a detailed physical description of both suspects.

Finally, Wallk delved into the events at the park. He related how he and Squirt picked up Madman and Spike at a bar over in that area in Squirt's car at about eleven o'clock. Spike told them he would give them money for a case of beer, which they bought and placed in a cooler in the car. They all drove over to the park and were drinking and partying around by the campfire pit. Squirt was slamming down beers along with smoking marijuana, then started stammering stupidly about how he was going to tell his girlfriend they "effed up the detective" in the cemetery with the explosive device. Squirt mentioned how he couldn't wait to blow up more stuff and tell his girlfriend about it. Wallk looked over at Spike and saw him getting really pissed off. Suddenly Spike pulled out a gun, started swearing at Squirt, then shot him twice. Wallk told the detectives he got freaked out thinking Spike might shoot him next since he and Squirt were friends. He threw his full can of beer at Spike, pulled out his gun, and started shooting as he ran toward the trees. He heard a couple more shots being fired as he ran, but wasn't hit. Finally, Wallk summarized that he followed a trail leading straight down to the river, walked home, arriving at about five in the morning. Spike and Madman only knew him as Elroy, and they always referred to Carter as Squirt, so he was sure they wouldn't be able to track him down.

Bernems told Wallk about a witness seeing two guys drive out of the park in a green Toyota after hearing shots fired. He looked over at both detectives, tears slipping down his face. "Them son-of-a-bitches killed my best friend and stole his car."

Chapter I3

PULASKI FOOTBALL STADIUM, MILWAUKEE

Tomcyzk arrived at about four-thirty for the five o'clock start of the game. The early morning wake-up call for the search warrant was wearing on him, but he promised himself he would make it. He paid his five dollars and entered the stadium. It had been nearly twenty years since he played here, and his mind flooded with memories. This was his home stadium when he played high school football for his alma mater, the Hamilton Wildcats. He started at both running back and linebacker, earning All-City and All-State nominations. Located in the heart of Milwaukee's South Side, Pulaski High School and Pulaski Stadium were named after Casimir Pulaski, who emigrated from Poland to fight in the Revolutionary War. He was credited with saving George Washington's life and appointed a general in the Continental Army.

"Take a break, you old superstar-has-been. You don't own this place anymore. Let the younger generation have their time in the lights."

105

He turned around to a familiar face. "Thanks for the invite, Bobby. Looking forward to seeing Junior play," Tomczyk said as they shook hands.

Bobby Heard was a police officer in the intelligence squad and a friend of Tomczyk's. They had been squad partners for two years at District Five when both were police officers. Whenever they saw each other at work, football was the first subject discussed. They also bounced work-related information off each other. Bobby possessed an encyclopedic mind for the names and faces of Milwaukee's North Side gang members. Bobby's son, Junior, was the star running back in his senior year at Rufus King High School. Bobby tugged on Tomczyk's jacket.

"They're nine and one, Ski. A win today takes them into regionals against Cudahy High School. They're no joke."

"Nothing's changed then. The Cudahy Packers were always a thorn in our side when we got into tournament play."

"Ada and James are already up in the stands. Both my boys are gonna freak when they see you."

"Come on, Bobby, I went to two of Junior's games last year—and two of Little Man's soccer games. My schedule screwed me up this year. I couldn't make any games. Bummed me out."

"You're right. And no hitting on Ada like you did last time. Just because you're a studly detective who's been on the cover of *GQ* three times doesn't land you a date with my wife."

A big grin rushed over Tomczyk's face. "So you subscribe to the magazine, too?" he kidded. Tomczyk ran his hand through Bobby's wavy perm. "She just wants a guy who uses real hair shampoo and not all that gel and chemical crap."

"You're lucky I feel sorry for you, or I'd sick my homeboys on you."

"I know, I know." Declan put his arm around Bobby's huge shoulder, and they walked up the stadium's concrete steps together.

"Uncle Ski, you made it!" Bobby's ten-year-old son, James, ran over to Tomczyk and wrapped his arms around his waist.

"Great to see you, little buddy. Make a muscle and let me see if those exercises I gave you are making a difference. I want to see you get as big and strong as your old man."

James put both arms up in a bodybuilder pose. "I did twenty-six pushups yesterday," he told him.

"Fantastic! I'm proud of you. Keep it up. How's your big brother playing this year? Is he going to tear up the football field again today?"

"You said it! He's leading the conference in rushing, just like last year. Sure's great, ain't it?"

"It's *isn't* James, not *ain't*."

"Sorry, Mom."

Tomczyk walked over to the strikingly beautiful, early forties black woman ten feet away and gave her a kiss on the lips. "How's it going, Ada? Great to see you again. Wish I could see you at work instead of your hubby. You'd brighten up my day more."

"Thanks, Declan. So Bobby tells me you're hooking up with a hot-lookin' FBI agent. Tell me all about it."

"One date doesn't make a relationship, but she's a fantastic person—even if an FBI agent. You're off the market, Ada, so I had to review my options and figure something else out. Bobby's not the smartest, but I realized he latched on to one of the finest women around and won't let you go. The best we can do is envy him." Looking over at Bobby, Tomczyk winked.

"Always the charmer. Bobby keeps telling me you're one of the best interviewers he's ever worked with. Is it because of your fine line of BS?"

"Who, me?" Tomczyk innocently declared, pointing his finger at his chest.

Bobby sat down next to his wife. James grabbed onto Tomczyk's arm. "Uncle Ski, can you sit next to me?"

"Nobody else I'd rather sit next to in this whole stadium than you, kiddo."

They spent the next twenty minutes talking about what had been going on in their lives. The announcer spoke into the loud speaker, and it crackled to life.

"Welcome to the divisional playoff game between the Alexander Hamilton Wildcats and Rufus King Generals. Please rise and remove your hats. Janie Marking, a senior music student at King, will be singing the National Anthem."

The thousands of fans in attendance rose and waited for the music to begin. Tomczyk placed his right hand over his chest and looked over at the large American flag located at one of the end zones of the stadium, marveling at how it waved in the breeze. The view brought memories of his days in Iraq, fighting for that beautiful red, white, and blue cloth. Tears welled up in his eyes as he listened to the talented, young female belt out the song he'd heard so many hundreds of times before.

He saw a couple of teenage boys wearing their baseball caps, talking, and being disrespectful several rows away. His first thought was to go over, remove their hats, squeeze them by their necks, and point their heads in the direction of the flag. He decided it would be better to stand down. *Not my fight—they obviously have parents who don't know any better*, he thought to himself. *Let a child of mine EVER act like that during the playing of the Star Spangled Banner. Guaranteed he wouldn't be able to sit for a week.*

"Hamilton won the coin toss and has elected to defer," the announcer intoned.

"Great, we get the ball first," James said gleefully.

"You're right. We'll get a chance to see what your big brother can do."

The kickoff landed deep into the end zone for a touchback. The referee placed the ball on the twenty-yard line.

"Ski, the QB is a junior named Ken Downing. Heck of an arm." Bobby pointed to the player wearing the number four blue jersey with gold lettering. Downing took the snap and handed the ball off to Junior, who slammed up the middle for a twelve-yard gain. "That's what I'm talkin' about!" Bobby yelled at his talented son. "Keep it going!"

Downing took the snap on the second play, stepped up into the pocket, and threw a bullet spiral twenty-five yards downfield to number eighty-eight. The receiver, making some amazing jukes to avoid two defenders, shook off two additional tacklers and ran into the end zone for a sixty-eight-yard touchdown.

"Oh, my gosh, who are these guys?" Tomczyk excitedly proclaimed, high-fiving James. "Go, Generals! Can't believe I'm cheering against my alma mater."

"That's Junior's best friend, Demetrius Simms. They made First Team All-Conference together. As you can see, he's got game. Has several scholarship offers, but is still undecided. Remember Willie Simms from District Seven? That's his kid."

Declan recalled the shooting several years ago at a gas station in the inner city where Police Officer Willie Simms was killed trying to stop a robbery in progress that he happened upon while stopping for a soda. Simms shot and killed one of the robbers and wounded the other, but not before one of them shot him in the chest. He died the next morning. "That was a terrible day. I remember it well. Only had one dealing with him. A heck of a cop was the impression I got."

"I hear ya, brotha'. He was good peeps. Yeah, this will be an interesting game—as long as King wins," Bobby added, reaching over to give Ada a kiss on the cheek.

The game went back and forth for the next two hours, with the Generals coming out on top, 45-24, and moving onto the next playoff game. Bobby Heard Jr. finished with over two hundred yards rushing, and his friend Demetrius Simms finished with eight receptions for 184 yards.

"Very impressive win, Bobby. Thanks again for the invite. Makes me feel bad I missed this season, but I'll clear my schedule for the next game. Keep me posted when and where."

"You got it, buddy. C'mon. Let's catch up with Junior. I know he'll want to see you."

"That'd be great."

They strolled out of the stadium and stood outside the visitors' locker room doors for the next fifteen minutes. Some of the players emerged from the locker room, carrying blue and gold Rufus King gym bags and wearing sport coats, ties, and dress shirts.

"Still a dress code. Gotta love it. Builds character."

Junior walked out of the locker room, speaking with several other players. When he saw Tomczyk, his eyes lit up. "Uncle Ski, you made the game!" He walked over and hugged the longtime family friend. "Great to see ya."

"Don't make me feel bad, Junior. I've been slacking. See you haven't stopped growing yet," as he looked at the handsome young man who was nearly as tall as he was. "Man, you guys rocked it. Tore it up, man, tore it up."

Junior gave Ada and Bobby a hug, then a double high five with his biggest fan, James.

"Thanks for coming. Hey, I'd like to introduce you to two of my buddies. This is Ken Downing, our QB, and this is Demetrius Simms, split end. We call them Thunder and Lightning."

"Boy, I'll say," said Tomczyk. "Think I saw that quote in the *Milwaukee Journal Sentinel* sports section once or twice. It's an honor to meet you guys. Just stay on track; study hard, and train harder."

James chimed in. "C'mon, you guys. You have to do your thing."

"Okay, okay, James. Always for you, Little Man."

"Thunder," said Ken as he did a left arm curl bodybuilding pose.

"Lightning," said Demetrius as he did the same with his right arm.

"Booyah!" they said in unison as they struck a double arm trapezius pose.

"Oh, boy. Now I've seen it all," Tomczyk said bursting out in laughter. "Fantastic!"

"Thunder, Lightning, this is my Uncle Ski, uh, Declan Tomczyk. You may see the family resemblance," Junior smiled as he positioned his ebony face next to Tomczyk's Caucasian face. "Former All-American middle linebacker for the Wisconsin Badgers and Rose Bowl wrecking ball against the Washington Huskies. He works with my dad at the PD."

"Nice intro, Junior. I'll give you that twenty bucks later for the kind words."

"Pleasure to meet you, sir," they both said as the young men shook hands with a fellow gridiron lover. "Then you played for Coach Alaveres, right?"

"One of the greatest men I've ever known. You know what a difference a coach can make in your life. Coach A had the uncanny ability to make you the best you could be, both here and here," he said pointing to his head and heart. "Truly, a man among men."

"Well said. We're going to check out Applebee's for a little celebration and late dinner. You want to join us?" Bobby asked his good friend. "By the way, did I tell you Junior accepted the scholarship at Stanford?"

"Good thing he has his mother's brains and will do well there. Would love to, brotha' Bobby. I have no plans for tonight. Can't tell you how much I appreciate you including me in your celebration." Tomczyk walked up behind Junior and James and placed his arms around them. "Let's do it, guys. Your Dad is letting me tag around with two of my best buds. Plus, he said he's going to buy, which is a rare treat in itself. Congrats on the scholarship, Junior. I'm so proud of both of you!" How he wished he could have had kids with Marie before she died of that terrible illness.

"Big shot detec and he wants *me* to buy!"

Declan's mind shot back to reality when he felt the cell phone on the left side of his waist start to vibrate. He grabbed it from the black leather case on his belt and looked at the familiar number on the screen. "This is Tomczyk."

"Ski, this is Bill. Lieutenant Vohl told me to give you a call. He just received a call from Chicago PD intel. Appears there was a bombing in their city with the same MO as our cemetery bombing. Two cops were conveyed to the hospital. No details on their conditions. They want you and Agent Dvorak down at CPD HQ first thing tomorrow to discuss the similarity of the cases. We notified the FBI. Dvorak just called back to say she'll be here at oh-five-thirty to pick you up. You need her cell number to square things up?"

"I have it, Bill. Thanks. I'll call her right now."

William Howe was the sergeant assigned to the intel squad for the early shift, which ran from four o'clock in the afternoon to midnight. He was the supervisor for the police officers who worked there and occasionally partnered up with the detectives when they went on the street. He had fifteen years with the department, twelve of those being one of the most active cops in the city. Sergeant Howe worked some of the specialized units because of his knack for solving crimes and tracking down "bad boys." He was a wealth of information for the unit and a mentor for the officers assigned there.

Tomczyk touched the screen next to Anne's name, which dialed her work cell number.

"Declan, I just saw you last night. You miss me already?"

"You're a funny girl. Thought about you all day, and I realize after our short time together that I can't live without you."

"Now that's what I like to hear. Ha-ha. Just spoke to my supervisor about the trip in the morning, so he's on board. I'll pick you up in front of the PD at five-thirty. They want us down there at eight, and traffic to Chi-town is always a wall around rush hour. Is that cool with you? I probably know as much about this meeting as you do, so it should be interesting."

"I hear ya. Heading out to get some chow with a good friend and his family for a little high school football victory celebration, but I'll cut it short for the oh-dark-thirty wake up. See you mañana."

"Looking forward to it. 'Night." She placed the light blue-colored cellphone back on the nightstand. She hated getting up that early—for work or any other reason.

A text crossed over his phone from Sergeant Howe. *"CPD just called back. Bad news. One cop just died at the hospital. The other is in critical but stable condition."*

"Damn!"

Chapter 14

CHICAGO TRIP

omczyk maneuvered his truck into the public parking garage. He placed his key fob next to the gray plastic reader, and the wooden gate came to life and lifted up. *All right,* he thought to himself. *Got one of the premium parking spots for a change.* He grabbed his backpack and walked across a quiet State Street. He pulled the lanyard containing his ID card out of his jacket and buzzed himself in. Above the double doors, the sign read EMPLOYEES ONLY. The numbers 749 were attached to the concrete wall above the door. Police Headquarters, built in 1970, was located next to the Milwaukee County Safety Building. Behind both buildings was MacArthur Square, a plaza named after an infamous Milwaukee native, General Douglas MacArthur. Also attached to the square was the old and dramatic-looking County Courthouse, with its newer addition, the Criminal Justice Facility.

Tomczyk ran the stairs up to the second floor and keyed his way into the squad. He grabbed his assigned department radio from the rack, along with a spare battery just in case. No one was there yet. He removed the case file he had amassed from a locked drawer in his desk.

He also snatched a couple power bars from a box he stored in another drawer. His watch showed five-twenty-five. *Five minutes—I better hit it.* As he walked out into the hallway, Lieutenant Fred Hetzer happened to be waiting for an elevator. Hetzer was a new lieutenant on the midnight-to-eight shift. Tomczyk was never a fan of Hetzer's, whom he considered a lazy coward from their time together as police officers. Hetzer made one of his usual sarcastic remarks about Tomczyk being at work early. "Always trying to beat the other detectives for the big headline, huh, Tomczyk?" he said with an irritating smirk. Declan was in no mood for the comment as the dead and wounded officers in Chicago weighed heavy on him.

He positioned himself directly in the man's face. "Lieu-TEN-ant, you wouldn't know what an arrest was if it kicked you in the face. Your years at Number Five were spent hiding from work, just like at the Bureau, so you could study your ass off and get promoted. I have no use for any person who refuses to do his share of the work and not back up fellow cops when they call for help. I have more respect for some of the people I arrest than a do-nothing like you. I'd love to discuss your uselessness further, but I have a very important place to be right now!" Before the lieutenant could say anything, Tomczyk took the stairs down to the exit and climbed the concrete steps to the sidewalk level. The now-familiar Dodge Intrepid pulled up, and he saw the smiling face of Anne Dvorak behind the wheel. He would deal with the repercussions of what he had said when he returned to the building.

"Morning, sunshine," he said, climbing into the front seat.

"Back at ya, Detective. You ready for a hopefully informative and productive day? Did they tell you about the one cop dying?"

"Yes. Absolutely terrible news. Let's hope the other officer pulls through and we can figure out what's going on with these cases."

"I second that. I'm NOT a morning person, so nudge me if I nod off at all today." She caught the nearest entrance to the expressway taking them to I-94 and Chicago. "You ready for some coffee or can you hold off until we cross into Illinois?"

"I can wait until we hit the oasis. No sense me waking up quite yet as long as you're driving."

"Oh, sure. This is what I get for volunteering to drive."

"That's how it is, kid. You're the fed. I'm just the local boy, remember?"

Tomczyk told her about his activities the day before at the game and what a great time he had with Bobby and his family. "Junior is a heck of a fullback. He's getting to be built like a brick crap house, just like his old man. You should've seen his buddy Demetrius play. I swear the kid had glue on his hands. He made some amazing catches that would've challenged many pro players. It was unbelievable."

"Looks like you'll need to invite me for the next game. I love football, except for Badger and Packer football, of course. Go Huskies and Hawks."

"We'll have to work on that," he joked. They broke into laughter. "C'mon, Anne. Hate the game, not the playa." He thought for a second. "Let's see, I filled you in on everything with the Gordon Park homicide and his connection to the cemetery bombing. We caught a break on the search warrant of the guy in Bay View. He laid much of it out for us during the interview. It was very productive."

"Only question I had was who's doing the forensics on the cell phone and thumb drive?"

"We took the items over to the Secret Service. They have a couple wizards who live to figure that stuff out. Our contact there guaranteed results within the week."

Anne pulled off the Illinois State Tollway into the Lake Forest Oasis parking lot spanning I-94. "Starbucks okay?"

"That'll work. Not too bad; it's six-twenty. It'll be a little slower as we head south from here."

"You can count on it."

Within ten minutes they were in the car with full cups of coffee and back on the tollway toward the Windy City. The traffic turned out to be lighter than usual, and they made good time. They merged from the Kennedy to the Eden's Expressway as they wound through Chicago's Loop. It was a clear day. The Chicago skyline, with 1,451-foot Willis Tower, formerly the Sears Tower, as well as some of the other iconic buildings, loomed high over the city.

"Well, Mr. Navigator, I've never been to CPD Headquarters, so you'll have to direct me."

"No worries." The Dan Ryan Expressway was also running smoothly. "This is great. Take the Thirty-fifth Street exit here by U.S. Cellular Field—old Comiskey Park." They found a rare parking spot on Michigan Avenue down the block from the building. "This neighborhood sure has changed over the last twenty years. Used to be 'housing project central' on the east side of the x-way. What do you call that—gentrification?"

"Very good." Upon entering the building, they showed their badges and credentials to the uniformed police officers and were directed around the magnetometers. Declan pointed out to Anne all the plaques with badges honoring slain officers along both sides of the walls in the main lobby. "A number of cops have been killed in this city. One of the more storied histories of any city in the country."

"I'll say. Unbelievable." She took it all in. "Where are we heading to?"

"Their intel squad is on the fifth floor. I've only been there once before."

When they got off the elevator, they walked over to a large, wooden door with black letters—INTELLIGENCE SQUAD. He knocked, and a buzzer sounded within seconds, allowing them entry.

They identified themselves and were directed to a conference room where about twenty people were milling about, waiting for the meeting to begin.

A tall, well-dressed man of about fifty walked up to them and shook hands. "Captain Tim Kocur, pleased to meet you. You must be Special Agent Dvorak and Detective Tomczyk. Welcome to Chicago."

"Thank you, Captain. We're sorry to hear about the officers and are here to assist in any way we can."

"Appreciate it." Captain Kocur addressed the group. "How about we begin this meeting? John, why don't you start it off?"

"Yes, sir. Good morning, everyone. I'm Lieutenant John Davis, Chicago PD bomb squad. This is Lieutenant Ray Mehls from Calumet City PD. We were at the scene last night and would like to walk you through what we have right now. Go ahead, Ray."

"Hello, everyone. One of our squads was sent to Holy Cross Catholic Cemetery and Mausoleum in Cal City at about four fifteen last night for a vandalism and suspicious persons complaint."

Tomczyk's ears perked up when he heard the name of the cemetery being the same as the one in Milwaukee.

"When the one-person squad arrived, he spoke to the maintenance supervisor, who informed the officer about three white males congregating around an area on the northern end of the cemetery. The supervisor said he went about his work, and when he passed the area again, he saw the same three males leaving in a dark blue Trailblazer. He noticed that about ten headstones were knocked over, and one had some sort of design carved into it. He took a couple pictures with his phone and called the police. Said he wasn't able to read the license plate number on the SUV as it was leaving. Another one-person squad responded, and they drove over by the headstones. The supervisor said he showed the officers where the headstones were and walked back over to his truck to get some equipment. He was just finishing up when the explosion went off. He was about one hundred feet away, and the loud cracking sound shook his truck; some of the marble from the headstones struck it. Said he got on his radio, telling them to call 9-1-1 for some help. He ran over to the officers and tried to perform first aid. The ambulances arrived within minutes and transported both officers to Ingalls Memorial Hospital in nearby Harvey. Peter Richards, the officer who was originally dispatched, died of blood loss and severe burns at a quarter of seven. Officer Amy Zarembas is listed in critical but stable condition and is expected to survive. The hospital called this morning and reported she was being upgraded. She's being interviewed as we speak. We don't have much to go on right now and are looking for some help."

"Thanks, Ray." Lieutenant Davis stood up. "Here's what we have in the way of explosives. We received a positive reading for methyl nitrate and an unknown substance. We found parts of a small, blue cooler, bits of green wires, and a sensor switch. One of the officers—we're guessing Richards because of the extent of his wounds—tripped a wire and set off the explosion. The use of methyl nitrate confuses the heck out of me. Just so all of you know, methyl nitrate is a powerful but very unstable compound. The unknown chemical we're not identifying may be used to make it more stable. What other purpose it would have, we don't know. It has an extremely high detonation power, but is a nightmare to deal with. That's just a guess from an old techie who's been playing with bombs for twenty years."

Lieutenant Mehls gave a brief PowerPoint showing pictures taken at the scene. One was a close-up of the area. "Do you all see the green wire leading out from under that headstone? It would have been tough to see because of how it blended in with the grass."

Tomczyk shook his head. He could really appreciate that comment.

"Here's the list of names on the headstones and a picture of the headstone with the anarchy logo cut into it. The name on the headstone is Martin Zarkowich, born in 1895 and died in 1969. Have any of you ever heard of him?"

One of the Chicago detectives spoke up. "Martin Zarkowich was the East Chicago PD sergeant who gave up Anna Sage, the famous 'Woman in Red.' She was with John Dillinger and his girlfriend the night Dillinger was killed as he came out of the Biograph."

"Correct. Depending on what source you read, Zarkowich was dirty as mud or white as the windblown snow. He either knew Anna Sage in his professional position, or he was getting some on the side from her. She was a known madam and was busted a couple times for keeping a disorderly house. Zarkowich became the chief for East Chicago Police, but was removed and indicted on other crimes. Years later, it was determined that he fired one of the final shots at Dillinger. The $64,000 question would be why someone would desecrate Zarkowich's headstone so many years later and place a bomb underneath? Because of it, we have a dead cop and a severely injured one. Finally, there was a note left at the scene. You can see the picture here. The note didn't survive the blast very well, and we only have bits of it. Detective Declan Tomczyk is here from Milwaukee Police. They had a very similar incident in their city. Could you give us a synopsis of your cemetery explosion, Detective?"

A chill went down Declan's spine. At the bottom of the note, clear as day, were the initials TMB. "I sure will." He pulled out some paperwork from his brown manila file and stood up. He went through the scenario of what happened, described how he luckily saw the green wire in the grass and the bomb with no explosives, and discussed the near-deadly second one. He reviewed the positive ID of methyl nitrate as the explosive, the homicide of Harold Carter, his tattoos and affiliations, and the explosive residue and spray paint found on Carter's clothes. He showed a picture of the note left at the scene, and finished with the results of the search warrant and arrest in Bay View, including several details from the Matthew Wallk interview.

"Declan, did you guys ever figure out what TMB stands for at the bottom of the note?"

"We're thinking, The Mad Bomber or Bombers but are still looking into it. There were a number of bombings that occurred in Milwaukee in the fall of 1935, but there is just no way to connect those with what's going on so far. Sure is eerie, though. I'd also like to introduce FBI Special Agent Anne Dvorak. She's helping us out on the investigation and has assured us we have the backing of the FBI and the Department of Justice."

Anne rose from her chair. "Thanks, Declan. Now that we've got a fairly good tracking of criminal activity going across state lines, there's no question the federal government is here to provide any assistance. We want these perpetrators behind bars as much as all of you. I would also like to offer my deepest condolences on the loss of the police officer."

"Thanks, Anne. It's great knowing we have the assistance of the FBI. You guys definitely have the resources to get this case solved." With that, Captain Kocur asked if there were any questions. A paper was passed around, and each person present put their name, agency, phone numbers, and emails down for future contact and easy accessibility. "We'll keep everyone up to date with further developments. Please do likewise if any of you get anything."

The meeting ended, and the participants stuck around engaged in conversation. The deceased officer and the condition of the other officer was foremost on everyone's mind.

Chapter 15

MILWAUKEE'S RIVERWEST AREA

nside a nondescript, old warehouse on North Gordon Place in Milwaukee's Riverwest area, Richard Zuber concocted his strange brew. He paid two hundred dollars per month rent for a small corner room on the main floor, with no questions asked. His makeshift laboratory was a clear plastic floor to ceiling, ten-by-ten-foot enclosure. A view from the partially painted over, metal-framed windows revealed a glimpse of the Milwaukee River and vacant land around it.

Zuber had completed three years at the University of Wisconsin-Milwaukee campus in the field of chemistry when he took a two-week sojourn to Olympia, Washington, that changed the course of his life. He met up with a couple of students from Evergreen State College who preached to him the notion that government and society were doing everything wrong. He joined a faction of the Puget Sound Anarchist movement. After communing with several members of the group for six months, he found the Great Northwest not to his liking and returned to the Milwaukee area. He promised them he would carry on the fight against society and the police. Two arrests by Milwaukee police officers for disorderly conduct during the 99 percenter protests and a recent conviction for possession of psilocybin mushrooms cost him his job at a River Hills nursing home and hardened his hatred for the police. He was going to get back at them and in a big way.

Zuber befriended ninety-eight-year-old George Kugawicz his second week at the nursing home. He was intrigued by George's stories about an Idzi Rutkowski. Doing research on the Internet about Milwaukee's "Mad Bomber," who terrorized the city for several weeks in October and early November 1935, gave him the ideas he needed for revenge. He especially liked the idea of the extortion note Idzi sent demanding hundreds of thousands of dollars from the City of Milwaukee during the middle of the Depression. Zuber thought he would ask for upwards of ten million dollars. He was going to make them pay, or it would really cost them.

He adjusted the heavy-duty mask with hands covered by two sets of purple-colored rubber gloves. Once before, he received a severe headache from inhaling the toxic substance and didn't want to experience that again.

Germany first used methyl nitrate as a rocket fuel during World War II in a mixture that contained 25 percent methanol and was called "myrol." Zuber did his research and was impressed with its twenty thousand plus feet per second detonation factor. Not quite as fast as the military grade C4 compound of twenty-six thousand feet per second, but he had no way to steal C4. Making his own "explosive of choice" seemed like a logical alternative. Methyl nitrate was one of the simplest of the nitric esters to create.

He carefully mixed in the sulfuric and nitric acids, inducing the nitration of the methanol, then added the urea, which removed the last traces of nitrous acid. The process was almost identical to making nitroglycerin, except for being run at a higher temperature and stirred mechanically instead of with compressed air. The knock against methyl nitrate as an explosive had always been its instability. Zuber solved that problem with his secret concoction of an amyl alcohol stabilizer that somehow fortified it with even more detonation power. He decided to make methyl nitrate his "signature" explosive, as he knew it would make the investigating bomb technicians crazy trying to figure out why he would use such an unstable compound. He felt like he was following in the footsteps of Alfred Nobel, the famous Swedish chemist who invented dynamite in 1867. The difference was that Nobel established the Peace Prize to offset his discovery, while Zuber was using his creation to wreak havoc within the ranks of law enforcement and to injure or kill as many as he could.

After completing the steps needed to create the dangerous elixir, he carefully poured the clear liquid into eight separate pipe bomb containers and sealed them. He felt instant success while his brain processed the chemical formula he diligently committed to memory: CH_3NO_3—methyl nitrate.

He placed the vials of death inside a heavy, gray metal box in the corner and secured it with a large, bronze-colored Master Lock, patting his jeans pocket where he kept the key. He turned off the light switch and secured the door with another large lock.

Looking at his watch, he realized he still had ten minutes to make the three o'clock meeting with his partner. He drove his '98 maroon Buick Skylark over to the cafe a half-mile away on East Center Street. *Better get that damn muffler fixed, or the pigs'll stop me and give me a ticket. That's all I need.* He walked in the front door and joined his friend sitting at a booth in the corner.

"Holy shit, Madman. This has got to be the first time you've ever been on time. I see you didn't dress up at all on my account." The skinny white male was wearing the same faded, black Harley-Davidson t-shirt he always wore, along with the filthy blue jeans and well-worn, black leather work boots. "You still washing your hair with that Pennzoil

10W40 motor oil? Gotta' be easy for the chicks to slide their fingers through. Must leave a helluva residue on their hands, though."

"You know I ain't got no time for bitches. All they do is cost me money and be a pain."

"Yeah, but they keep your pipes clean and warm at night."

"If I want sex, I'll just hire one of them hookers over on North Avenue. They're cheaper than having a girlfriend and are very good at what they do. If I wanna stay warm at night, I'll get a freakin' dog."

"Just remember to wear a Trojan."

"Where you been, man? Ain't a hooker anywhere who doesn't bring along her own supply of condoms for the dudes."

"Sorry, I've been out of the mix." Spike pulled a piece of notebook paper out of his shirt pocket and unfolded it. He had a number of notes printed on it. "I just mixed up a batch and got eight of 'em out of it. I'll go back tomorrow and start getting 'em ready. Have a couple good ideas on a little variety of circuits and stuff to keep the pigs guessing when they do their post-blast investigation. Them ground-pounders are too stupid to figure out who's doing it."

"How can I help you out, dude?"

"No worries yet, man. It's all good. I'm in my element. Just call me the Mad Professor."

"I thought you wanted them to call you 'The Mad Bomber.'"

"WTF? Don't be broadcasting that around. Someone may hear you, and we'll be in deep." Spike shook his head and looked around the sparsely filled restaurant to make sure no one was within hearing distance.

"Speaking of deep crap, Spike. Why'd you have to cap Squirt? I'm still freaked out over that one."

"Squirt was an idiot and needed to be capped. Don't you remember him saying how he was going to tell his girlfriend about the explosion in the cemetery 'cause he thought it was so cool blowing that cop up?

And that was after only drinking a couple beers. What the hell else was he going to tell her?"

"I know, dude. But did you have to shoot him between the eyes? That was freaky as hell."

"Screw him. Dead men tell no lies. Bet that bullet rattled around in his empty brain for a while." Spike chuckled at that one. "The problem we have now is Elroy. I know I missed him. Do you know where he lives or anything else about him? We need to cap him so he doesn't start blabbin' about us."

"No clue, man. Sorry."

It was during this conversation that Madman realized he didn't want to cross Spike. They had been friends for years, but Madman didn't think Spike was this cold-blooded. The guy was strong, smart, and ruthless. Madman got his nickname years ago for doing crazy stuff but was nowhere near as crazy as Spike.

"You think the cops got anything on us?"

"Hell no. They're all about as smart as a box of rocks. The only thing they probably figured out was Squirt's real name. Big deal. No way they'll connect him to us. I bet they're still trying to figure out why there were no prints on any of the beer cans or bullet casings, except maybe for Squirt's or Elroy's. They're too stupid to realize anybody can wear gloves. Even when drinkin' a freakin' beer."

"I guess you're right there."

"Of course I am."

"I'm up with maimin' and killin' cops and blowing stuff up here in Milwaukee, but what's the deal with doing it in Chi-town, too?"

"'Cause Milwaukee's just a pissant town. Go big or go home. By doing crimes in Chicago, them schmucks won't know which way is up. It's only an hour-and-a-half away. No big thing. Besides, my cousin got popped by Chicago cops for burglary and a humbug robbery. He caught nine years at Joliet prison for it. He's as happy as hell to help us out. Payback's a bitch, and I know my cuz wants some big time payback."

"Won't the cops catch on that it's the same guys making the bombs?"

"That's the beauty of it, Madman. Just think how many more potential suspects they'll have to figure out now. Talk about multiplying the gene pool since we're also including Chi-town in the game. Thought that was a cool idea of yours to spray paint that backwards crap, *Dahmer* and *Murder*. That'll screw them guys up trying to come up with theories. Too funny. I know they're scratching their balls already, thinking about all that BS. Not only that. My cousin, Worm, has some sort of history fetish with John Dillinger. I know dude wants to somehow include a couple of Dillinger's crime scenes or haunts in one of the explosions and hopefully blow up another cop or two. Just like they did at that cemetery in Calumet City."

"You have one sick family," Madman said, shaking his head and grinning. "But how are we going to monetize this stuff and get some bread out of all this?"

"Did you ever hear of the word *extortion*? If they don't pay up, the bombings will continue, and the body count will rise. That's what my man Idzi did in 1935." Spike pulled out a couple pieces of paper with writing on them. "These are some articles I printed off the Internet from old area newspapers. Cool stuff. Wait till the cops get their next surprise." They both laughed and finished their beers.

Chapter 16

ST. ADALBERT'S CEMETERY: MILWAUKEE

eclan and Anne had traveled halfway through Racine County, past the acres of farmland dotted along the expressway. He turned his department portable police radio back on. The *Hawaii Five-O* theme song ringtone of his work cell phone broke the silence. "Tomcyzk."

"Whaddup, Stud? This is Howe. Who said lightning can't strike twice? Looks like your boys hit St. Adelbert's Cemetery last night. For some reason, no one discovered anything until an hour ago. Same MO as Holy Cross, but only seven headstones this time. They primarily defaced one headstone. Guy's name was Stanley Strychalewski. Ran him through our database. He retired from our department as a detective lieutenant in August 1967, just after the riots. Almost forty years on the job, and he had more commendations than space on a shirt or jacket to put them on. Bomb squad's on the scene, but haven't turned anything up yet. Enter off the main entrance and a cemetery employee will guide you in."

"We'll be there in twenty minutes. For the record, there's definitely a connection between Lurch and the police officer killed in Chicago. Thank God the other cop survived. Looks like she'll make it. Don't know what it is yet, but these scumbags are really starting to piss me off. I'll get back to you when I can, Bill." They hung up.

"Where we heading, Declan?" Anne looked visibly concerned. "Doesn't sound good."

"Another cemetery job. Looks like we found Big Stan, Schlundt's partner and friend. His headstone was desecrated, along with some others, at St. Adelbert's Cemetery. Seven headstones were defaced, but they concentrated on just one: a retired MPD lieutenant, Stanley Stryckalewski. No wonder Mrs. Pavalko couldn't remember his last name. Bomb squad is on the scene and haven't located anything yet, which is good news. Makes you wonder what these guys are thinking on this one."

"Think I passed that cemetery once or twice during my familiarization rides when I first got here."

"My dad used to take me to visit the graves of my grandparents and some great aunts and uncles. More names ending with 'ski' there than all the skis at Squaw Valley during prime season. The main entrance is off South Sixth Street. A worker will meet us there and guide us to the scene."

"Fair enough. A laugh a minute, aren't you?"

"Makes the job more interesting. They pay me well, so I strive to serve the citizens the best I can. Humor keeps you sane. You can only see so much sickness from the underbelly of society, and the tragedy it causes, before it starts to engulf you."

They pulled into the cemetery and were met by a service employee in a green truck. They followed him to where a marked squad and the big blue Milwaukee PD bomb squad truck were parked. An eerie feeling went through Declan's body. The last time he saw that truck, his good friend was hanging on by a thread. He shook off the thought and "zeroed in" on his assignment. "Okay, partner. Let's get down to business."

"Partner? Now you're talking. I'm honored."

They walked over to the truck where another familiar face was standing.

"How you doing, Phil?" Declan introduced him to Anne. "We're working together on this case. What do we have?"

"Nothing yet, Ski. Searched the area thoroughly, and it checked neg-res for any signs of explosives or residue. There was a standard-size white business envelope attached to the back of one headstone. I was just coming back to the truck to grab my scintillation counter. I'm just not taking any chances on this one. No sense touching anything unless we know what it may contain. I don't trust people who like trying to kill friends of mine. These guys put Lurch out of commission for a couple months."

"Amen to that, brother." Even though Tomczyk concentrated on explosive devices in the Marine Corps, he had some knowledge of scintillation counters. They were used to detect radiation.

Phil grabbed the handheld Delta Epsilon brand SC-133 device off the shelf in the truck and showed it to Declan and Anne. The SC-133 was a sodium-iodine-based radiation detector.

"This baby here will tell me if there's any radioactive material in that there envelope. Can also be used as a BS detector." Phil pointed it toward Declan. "Beep, beep, beep, beep. Anne, you should have been warned to stay away from this guy."

They broke out laughing.

"Somebody sure had a thing for Mr. Strychalewski. Yanked his headstone out, then etched some design into it. Come over and take a look." Randall walked them over to where the headstones had been disturbed.

Six of the stones had been spray painted with an anarchy symbol. The seventh was completely pulled out of the ground and left leaning on an angle against one of the other headstones. The front of the tan, marble stone had been spray painted in red with an upside down cross, the same as Harold Schlundt's. The word *PIG* was also spray painted at the base of it.

Tomczyk stared at the configuration of damage. "Did you get the word about Stanley? He was a retired MPD detective lieutenant with nearly forty years. Sounds like the guy had a stellar career."

"Didn't know anything about him. I told the lieutenant his name when I called it in so they could check things out."

"You're a peach, Phil. That's what connects this case with Lurch's. Now we concentrate on how." In the back of Declan's mind, it was becoming more obvious that the common thread was in some strange way related to Idzi "The Mad Bomber" Rutkowski.

"Let me check the envelope to see if our creative souls placed something in it that can subject us to anything."

Phil flipped the ON switch for the SC-133 to warm up, then turned the instrument in the opposite direction of his target to obtain a background reading. He started moving toward the angled headstone, got down on his knees, and pointed it in the direction of the taped, white envelope to take measurements. The machine started clicking like a Geiger counter, telling the operator that radiation was nearby. He took a reading off the gauge on top of the device.

"Looks like there is some form of cesium in that envelope. My guess is cesium chloride. What rock did these dirt bags crawl out of? They know explosives, and they also know radioactive materials. This is some bad stuff!"

Chapter 17

ST. ADALBERT'S CEMETERY

Declan didn't like the sound of that. Cesium chloride was a salve for cancer patients, but also had nefarious uses. "Oh, wonderful. Just what we need. Bombers, murderers, and now mass destruction knowledgeable."

Cesium (caesium) chloride: a highly radioactive material made with cesium 137. In September 1987, one of the world's worst radiological disasters occurred in Goiania, Brazil. Illegal scrap collectors burglarized an abandoned hospital and absconded with almost three ounces of the compound. The thieves were able to breach the container and observed a blue-colored, glowing material inside. They brought it home and showed a number of people. Four people died from exposure. Hundreds were seriously exposed, and over one hundred and ten thousand others flooded area hospitals with symptoms.

"Well, this changes everything. Instead of placing the envelope inside an evidence bag, now I have to send in the robot to retrieve and put it into a lead pig. I wanted to show you the envelope, but you'll just have to wait to see for yourself."

"Lead pig?" inquired Anne.

"Just a term we use for a container to store radiative material in. The problem is that I'm the only bomb tech working today. I could sure use someone else with the expertise to do this."

"No worries," Anne cut in. "One of my FBI buds is the WMD coordinator for southeast Wisconsin. He lives a couple miles from here and lives for this."

"You gotta be talking about 'The Doctor.'"

She dialed Brett Plover's cell number. "Yeah, it's for real, Brett. We're at St. Adalbert's right now ready to send in the robot." Anne ended the call. "The Doctor will be here in fifteen."

Dr. Brett Plover was an anomaly in law enforcement. He received his doctoral degree in chemistry from Harvard University and entered the research field. One day he decided he wanted to be an FBI agent. A special agent with a doctorate in chemistry was a natural for being the FBI weapons of mass destruction coordinator. Plover could probably manufacture most of the "ethyl-methyl" bad stuff in his basement if he wanted to. It was only right for a person of that caliber to be one of the good guys.

Phil and Declan pulled the robot out of the truck and prepared it for the mission. Phil attached the "long arm" to the robot's mechanical right arm for longer reach. He looked over at his fellow detective.

"Obviously, we can't expose the robot to radiation. With the use of the long arm, we reduce or eliminate the chance of the robot touching the envelope. If it does, all we'll have is an expensive piece of radioactive junk to get rid of. A mechanical attachment is easier and cheaper to send off to the radioactive graveyard."

"No argument from me," Tomczyk agreed. "I love the color blue, just not when it's glowing by itself and emitting radioactivity."

"It's all about time, distance, and shielding. We'll have you stand back a safe distance.

Within ten minutes, a dark gray Chevrolet Impala parked behind the bomb truck. Out stepped the mid-thirties, brown-haired, bearded FBI WMD coordinator.

"Dr. Plover, I presume," Phil said with a smile.

"Thanks for coming, Brett. Phil said he could use the help. Meet Detective Declan Tomczyk. I'm working with him on these explosions."

"Heard about you, Declan. Nice to finally meet you."

"Thanks, likewise."

"Here's what we have, Brett." The two experts stepped off to the side where Phil explained the situation so they could discuss strategy.

Brett nodded his head with approval. "Sounds like a plan." They walked back over to the other two investigators.

"Here's what we'll do," Phil said calmly. "Anne, you go dig a hole over there about five—no, make it six-feet-deep. Ski, make believe that headstone is one of those running backs you used to trounce in college and throw it into the hole Anne dug so she can fill it in. The shelf life for that stuff's only about fifty years."

Brett looked over at Phil and shrugged his shoulders. "I thought it was a great idea and much easier than what we're going to have to do. On second thought, we probably can't do that. Your boss would go ballistic since we aren't following ALARA protocol."

Tomczyk looked over at Plover and Randall in complete ignorance. "What's an ALARA?"

"Total flat foot, Phil. How can a twenty-first century detective not know what that stands for?"

"Give him a break, Brett. He's a former Marine."

"That explains it." They gave each other a fist bump. "Got ya, jarhead. ALARA stands for 'As Low as Reasonably Achievable.' Exposing yourself to the bad stuff the minimum amount of time to keep the possibility of contracting radiation lower."

"Thanks for the Cliff Notes explanation."

"We're here for you." Randall went back to the truck and pulled out what appeared to be a heavy container about the size of a one-gallon paint can. "This lead pig is going to be our savior today—theoretically speaking, of course." Phil placed the container in the desired spot, leaving the lid next to it.

Another unmarked car pulled up. Out stepped Lieutenant Tony Stilger, one of the Criminal Investigation Bureau's shift supervisors.

"Well, there goes the party."

"When the captain sends me out here to check up on the bomb tech, it's never a good thing. What's the plan, Phil? Good to see you again, Doctor Brett. Tomczyk, what the heck you doing here?" He glanced over at Anne, nodded his head, and smiled.

Randall looked over at the supervisor. "How's it going, Lieut?" He introduced Dvorak and laid out their plan. "The Geiger counter showed that an envelope taped to the back of that angled, tan headstone contains cesium chloride. I was going to send the robot to retrieve the envelope and place it in the container. We'll figure out who wants to be brave and place the cover on it."

"Just pull straws and make sure Ski loses," Lieutenant Stilger quipped. "Nothing will penetrate that thick head of his."

"I'm good with that." Phil turned on the remote control for the robot and tested it to make sure all parts were good to go. The robot responded fluidly as the detective operated the joystick. They watched the robot move in place.

"Okay, we're ready. Any final thoughts?"

Everyone shook heads in unison.

"We need a hero today, Phil. So you and 'Johnny Five' have to do it." The lieutenant smiled.

"You got it, boss man. We're up with that." Phil guided the joystick, and the robot lurched forward from the asphalt drive onto the slope of the grass. "Go get 'em, Robot-buddy!"

When the robot had advanced about ten feet from the headstone, Phil lowered the long arm and attempted to move it into place. He slowly positioned the robot closer and the arm began going under the angled marble. "Here's the problem. I can't see the envelope from this location for the robot to latch onto."

Special Agent Plover burst into action. "Let me grab one of those powerful flashlights you have in the truck. I'll be able to illuminate that sucker like the Wrigley Building at night."

"That'll help."

When Plover clicked on the flashlight, the space behind the headstone lit up completely, allowing Phil total visibility of the envelope. The robot inched forward as Phil readied the pinchers. It would be tricky as there was only a slight clearance between the envelope and the headstone. The pinchers on the one side of the long arm slid along the marble, but missed going behind the object and brushed over it.

"Damn! I'll have to try it again from a different angle. Too tight at that spot." He again looked through his binoculars for any opening. "Why didn't I see that the first time?" Phil brought the robot back about three feet and readjusted the angle of the long arm. "Okay, let's do this again."

Phil zoned in. The expert controller moved the robot in slowly toward the headstone as he gently turned the joystick, like a surgeon performing brain surgery. *No more screw ups*, he thought. He guided the long arm to the back of the headstone, sliding it along the marble. He watched it go behind the envelope and slowed down the movement to nearly a stop. "All right, you're mine now." When Phil observed the envelope completely in the grasp of the pincher on the long arm, he paused.

"You latched onto it!" Brett exclaimed. "Great job. Now ease it off and 'git ur dun.'" Plover shined the flashlight in the darker area behind the headstone to give Phil maximum light.

"Feels good, Brett. Okay, let's finish this."

Declan glanced over at Anne, who looked relieved. "C'mon, Phil, don't fail us now."

"No worries; I got her." He expertly touched the joystick on the remote controller, and the robot responded in kind. They could see the envelope slowly break away from the headstone and watched as the tape separated from the stone surface. In another second, the envelope was completely in the grasp of the robot's extended arm. Phil slowly moved the robot away from the headstone. "Okay, phase one is finito."

"How you doin'?" asked Lieutenant Stilger.

"Like I just got lucky with my once-a-month roll in the hay with my wife."

"You guys are just plain sick," Anne said, shaking her head in feigned disgust. "Way beyond help."

"Sorry, Anne," Phil responded, laughing. He steadied his grip on the controller. The robot backed up about ten feet and completed a ninety-degree turn, moving slowly toward the lead pig. When it reached striking distance, Randall touched the joystick and the robot's long arm extended to a point just above the lead container. The envelope released from the grasp of the mechanical device and fell harmlessly into it. "All right!"

Brett already had on the stage-four rubber gloves and a respirator. He walked over to the container, picked up the cover, and carefully secured it in place.

"Done," he exhaled, giving the "thumbs-up" sign.

"Crazy fool!" shouted Randall.

"C'mon, Phil," Brett countered as he walked back over to the truck with the container firmly in his hands, placing it inside a holding box specially made to reduce motion during transit. "You saw the same thing I did. You slipped that envelope straight into the pig without even striking the side, clean as a three-point 'swish shot' by Ray Allen."

Phil walked back over to the headstone with the radiation device in tow and checked the levels of the area and the back of the headstone. No residue had transferred from the envelope to the marble or anything else as the gauge registered low-normal amounts. He was relieved.

"See how good you can get at this stuff by watching a couple episodes of TV cop shows?" Phil quipped to all who were watching him.

"You're right," Declan responded. "They would be darn proud of you."

"I'll get this sent out to Savannah River first thing in the morning. It's farther away than Oak Ridge, but they're geared up better to identify these materials. Plus, I'll put in a rush to find out the contents of the letter I bet is inside the envelope." Randall thought for a second. "I wonder if there's ever been a study on the average number of brain cells per person employed in those places. Bet it's REALLY, REALLY high!"

Savannah River National Laboratory in Jackson, South Carolina, was part of the Department of Energy. Founded in 1951 and certified as a national laboratory in 2004, they specialized in the handling, identifying, and disposing of hazardous materials.

"Ski, did I mention the envelope was addressed to you?" Phil said as he casually looked over at Brett, winking to clue his friend in to go along with the story.

"I saw that and thought it was strange," Brett joined in. "Didn't know you had a relationship with the bad guys."

"What are you talking about, addressed to me?"

"I'm not hosing you, Ski. It was addressed to you."

Both Tomczyk and Anne gave Phil a shocked look.

"How can it be addressed to me? These dirt bags don't know who I am. They only saw me from a distance."

"What can I tell you? There's only one word on the envelope, and it's written in all capitals with your name—*P-I-G*."

"You got me!" said Declan, definitely relieved. "They could have at least called me *Mr.* Pig."

"All in a day's work, Mr. Pig." Phil started laughing heartily.

"And these guys are your friends?" Anne had to chuckle at that one.

"Garth Brooks said it best about having friends in low places."

Lieutenant Stilger walked up to Declan and put his arm tightly around his shoulder. "You're like our favorite little dog, you musclebound turd. We'll deal with your outburst to Hetzer on another day. He's pissed and wants to push the issue."

"Just wasn't in the mood for his crap this morning, boss. If I get a couple days on the beach for disrespect, it will have been worth it. Hetzer and I will NEVER see eye-to-eye."

"I hear ya. He doesn't have many fans anywhere. Later." Stilger walked back to his squad and drove away.

"Our work here is done," Randall commented. "Nice meeting you, Anne. Please watch over him. He's not that intelligent, but we keep him around for humor value."

"I'll keep that in mind. Likewise, and in a cemetery—such an interesting setting. Brett, see you at the office."

Declan looked at the main damaged headstone. "So, Lieutenant Stanley Strychalewski, this deep fog just lifted a little on what role you had in this strange web of weirdness."

The ID tech who responded to the scene took digital photos of the headstones and checked for fingerprints, which turned out to be negative. "Do you need anything else?"

"No, we're good. Thanks."

Tomczyk looked over at the uniformed officers. "Do me a favor, guys. File a short report with the who, when, and where's. I'll send you the complaint number. Thanks for your help. We can turn this little piece of real estate back over to the cemetery and call it a day." He looked over at Anne. "How about a quick meal before heading back downtown to finish up?"

"Wouldn't miss it. So which high-class, fast-food restaurant would you like to visit and partake of? My treat."

"Gotta love a woman with culinary class."

She gently pushed him and smiled. "Another day, big fella. We're crunched for time. Don't you keep telling me how the job isn't done until the paperwork is done? Me thinks you have some paperwork to do."

Chapter 18

CHICAGO'S NORTH SIDE

T he old dirty blue Chevrolet Malibu turned right onto North Lincoln Avenue and into the alley in the 2400 block of the Lincoln Park neighborhood on Chicago's North Side. The driver stopped and peered at the passenger next to him.

"You know what you have to do. Let's move." The tall, white male stepped out from the passenger side wearing a black denim jacket and blue jeans. He was carrying a dark green plastic bag as he emerged from the alley and walked along the sidewalk past several buildings. The tattoos on his neck were still visible under the illumination of the street lights. It was three in the morning, and there was no one on the street. The famous theatre sign became larger as he got closer. *Windy City—I'll say,* he thought as he shivered in the cold and windy early November morning.

He walked over to the double-glass doors in front of the old movie theatre and looked at the large, white sign in the glass window above the doors. "Victory" was spelled out in large, black capital letters. *Fitting,* he thought to himself. He set the bag in the concrete entranceway next to

141

the glass doors, obviously out of place so it would be readily noticed as something that didn't belong.

Just before going back into the alley, he briefly looked back at the large theatre marquis. Some of the light bulbs were off for the evening. The iconic name still stood out like a beacon—Victory Gardens Biograph. *Lots of history there. We'll make our own history tonight.* He saw a marked Chicago Police Department squad driving down the street toward him. *Too close for comfort. Hopefully that cop sees it—unless he's blind and dumb like the rest of them.* He continued down the alley and climbed back into the car.

"Let's get the hell out of here. There's a squad coming down Lincoln Ave."

The driver sped away with his lights out and rounded the corner of the alley in seconds.

River Hills Nursing Home - River Hills, WI

Demetrius pulled into the nursing home parking lot for his eight o'clock start. He walked into the lobby and was greeted by the receptionist.

"Saw the prep scores in the paper this morning. You're a stud. Great job."

"Thanks, Penny. We really clicked last night."

"Clicked? Sounds more like you rocked the house."

"Oh, yeah? There was a little bit of that going on too. Our fans sure got into it. Man, it was a great experience." He walked down to the maintenance office and opened the unlocked door.

"So, which one are you, Thunder or Lightning?" Tim said as he laid the local newspaper down on the desk.

"Man, I can't believe they printed that—again. A couple of guys on the team mentioned it to the reporter, and she was all over it. That was just a private joke we had. Don't need everyone razzing us about it and thinking we're showboating."

"Get used to it, kid. Everyone wants a hero. Right now, you're the superheroes."

"Yeah, but I just don't want to be the super-duds. Someone is always out there trying to bring you down. I just wanted to go out on the field and give 100 percent to my game. Don't need no broadcasting so our opponents can jump on us about it."

"Makes sense. Well, let's get on it. I'll take the third floor. You have the second, and we'll meet on the first and knock it out as a team."

"Got it. Between us, I'm Lightning," he said sheepishly.

"I'm proud of you, D. Take it all in stride. I know you won't get a big head about it 'cause I'll knock it off your shoulders." He grabbed Demetrius in a bear hug, rubbing his head with a closed fist, and pretending to swing at it.

"You can count on it. Thanks for your confidence in me. Your guidance and friendship mean a lot."

"No problem. I have this strong feeling you won't be moppin' floors for a living like me. We have to prepare you for the big leagues."

For the next couple of hours, they went about sweeping and cleaning rooms.

"Okay, break time. I know, I know. Go find George and let him bend your ear. Don't think he's said ten words to me since I've been here. It's good to see you've grown on him."

"He's a great old guy."

Demetrius found his friend sitting at the usual spot on the leather chair in the large gathering room on the first floor. The TV was on, and others were watching it. George was reading the current issue of *Sports Illustrated*.

"So, what good article you reading, George?"

"I was looking for the results of your game from last night," he smiled. "Can't find it."

"Mr. Comedian. We won, and I can guarantee you won't find it in there. I had a pretty good game, but dropped two easy balls, one that woulda gone."

"Watch the ball fall into your hands, then run with it."

"Boy, I'll say. I took a lotta ribbing for that. Always said if I can touch it, I can catch it. Sometimes, not always so easy."

"The pros can't always do that, D. Don't be so hard on yourself."

"You're right. I'll just do better next week. We continue division play. Don't know who we play yet."

"How much time you have so we can get back to my story?"

Demetrius thought about it. "About twenty minutes. You guys just finished robbing the pharmacies and blowing up the banks."

"That really sounds bad, doesn't it? I didn't tell the detectives I drove the car for those crimes because I was too scared they would throw me in prison for a lifetime. They only charged me for being in a stolen car and involved in a hit and run. No sense telling them everything."

"I hear ya on that one."

"Okay, so it's Halloween, and Idzi planned something crazy. We took one of the stolen cars we had in that garage and drove over to the old police station on Third and Hadley. All the way, Idzi kept sayin' how he wanted to hurt and kill some cops. It was plenty dark out, so I parked the car on the street and turned off the lights. Idzi and Shrimp took one of the bombs from the car and walked down the alley. They were back in a couple minutes. The explosion went off just as I was pulling away from the curb. It was loud as hell. Idzi told me to drive over to the other police station on Twelfth and Vine. They got out with one of the bombs and did the same thing there. When they got back into the car, I drove off and *kaboom!* I bet all them cops were freaked out when the place exploded. I parked the car on the street a couple blocks from our clubhouse, and we finished off another bottle of brandy that night. I used to get some hangover headaches from those nights."

"Nutso. So how much damage and stuff did you do?"

"We read in the paper there was damage to both police stations and some officers got hurt, but none were killed. Idzi was really mad the bombs didn't do as much damage as he wanted them to, especially not killing any cops. He said he was going to build a big bomb and take out some people with the next one. I think he was planning on doing either city hall or the safety building next. That was police headquarters back then."

"Boy, I bet the cops were really ticked off."

"You bet. The FBI came into the city in force after the bank bombings, and there seemed to be blue suits and G-Men everywhere. I know the city was in a frenzy about the whole thing. The local paper even started referring to us as 'The Mad Bombers.' Idzi fed off of that."

"D, come on. We have to go."

Demetrius turned around and saw Tim motioning for him to come over.

"I have to go, George. See you next time."

"Okay."

Demetrius walked over to Tim. "What do we got?"

"A resident in Room 243 threw up all over her room and in the hallway. Ambulance just took her to the hospital."

"I'll get the mop bucket and meet you over there."

"Good. I roped it off so no one does the slide until we can clean it up."

Wisconsin Crime Lab: Milwaukee

Sitting at his desk in the ballistic section of the Wisconsin Crime Lab on Eleventh and Lapham in Milwaukee, Forensic Program Technician Walter Ferio grabbed scissors off his desk and cut open the top of the sealed plastic bag. He removed the two small, white cardboard matchbox-size boxes, using his knife to break through the white adhesive tape. He noticed the initials "RHB," indicating the law enforcement officer who sealed the bag, along with the date of sealing, on the tape as he did so.

Some of the red wax used to seal the tape endings fell onto his desk. He opened the box and removed a Remington-Peters brand .40 caliber brass casing from the first box. Ferio etched his initials, the date, and item number onto the casing to complete the chain of custody requirements. He then placed the casing into the IBIS computer and ran a standard correlation on it.

Ballistic matching on the bullet was performed using a program called BULLETPROOF. Another program, BRASSCATCHER, ran the correlations of cartridge casings with similar markings. The IBIS computer took two photographs of the casing: one that the computer searched by shades of blacks and grays for comparisons, while the second photograph was more examiner friendly for searching.

IBIS stands for Integrated Ballistic Identification System. It is an automated computer system developed in 2003 by Forensic Technology Manufacturing, linking firearms-related evidence. The specific markings left behind on the back of the cartridge casing firing pin is where IBIS searches. The marks created are like fingerprints to the technician. The circles, parallels, crosshatch marks, and arches have their own identification when the breach face of the weapon is machined.

The IBIS computer works much the same as AFIS and CODIS, which are identification systems used for fingerprints and DNA. The images are entered into the system to search from multiple databases of current and past crime scenes. It then kicks out nearly exact matches, leaving the investigator to compare between the images of the evidence and the database to achieve a perfect match.

Ferio carefully lifted the casing out of the IBIS holder, placed it back into the pillbox, and duplicated the process with the next four casings. Under the microscope, there was no question the weapon used in the homicide was a Glock brand .40 caliber. The imprint from a

Glock firing pin nearly always leaves a unique elliptical imprint on the primer that is observable to the trained eye, compared to the hemispherical mark left by other .40 caliber guns. That meant either a model 22, 23 or 27.

He had already pulled several comparison brands of semi-auto lab weapons from the gun vault and fired them through the "beer mug." This part of the job was a "gunlick's" dream. Ferio enjoyed working the firearms section, but to be able to fire weapons on the job was a bonus. The beer mug was a 3/16th-inch thick, heavy-duty steel pipe. One end of the pipe had a flat, metal welded plate that sat solidly on the floor, leaving the other end open. It was packed tightly with cotton threads and the rounds were fired into the cotton and retrieved. The pristine bullet had all the lands and groove imprints from the inside of the barrel and could be matched with the recovered bullets. His two-dimensional computer confirmed that the bullet taken from Harold Carter's head was fired from a Glock .40 caliber pistol. He noted this conclusion in his report, which would be sent back to the police department in the morning, hand-delivered mail.

In another lifetime, Ferio was a member of the US Navy in Vietnam, assigned to a boat patrol in the Mekong Delta. He was often at the ready with a fully automatic M-16 and within close proximity of the twin-mounted .50 caliber machine guns. The names of some of his buddies were etched into the granite walls of the Vietnam Wall Memorial in Washington, DC. Upon returning to the States in 1970, he switched to the Coast Guard and spent the next twenty-two years at a number of small boat stations along the West Coast. While at his final assignment at Station Sturgeon Bay, he fell in love with Wisconsin. He married a Milwaukee girl and decided to plant his roots there.

"What do you have, Walt?"

"Just matched the recovered casings and bullet from the homicide in Gordon Park from a week or so ago. For some reason, this case was flagged for an immediate. Definitely a Glock. My guess is a model 22, but the examiner will have to verify with his machine."

"I remember reading about it."

"Always love it when we get a positive identification. Now the cops will know what to look for. It's the least we can do for them, for now."

Chapter 19

DISTRICT FIVE POLICE STATION: MILWAUKEE

I t was ten fifteen in the evening when Police Officer John Birke parked his marked Dodge Charger "police package" squad in the south parking lot at District Five. He had two reports to file before his four-to-midnight shift ended, with no desire for a late assignment tonight. Three full days of court for an armed robbery jury trial and five straight work nights had sapped his strength. As he exited the squad, he noticed an older, green Toyota four door containing two bald white males going southbound through the alley. The men gave him a "fisheye" look, which he knew was a sure telltale sign of trouble.

Birke noted the rear Wisconsin license plate. The car turned eastbound out of the alley and caught the green light at Martin Luther King Drive, heading back north. Just as Birke was about to get back into the squad to catch up to them, he heard a loud explosion and saw a bright flash from the back of the station. Instinctively, he knelt down between his squad and another parked next to it, to protect himself from flying debris or shrapnel. Instantly, he was faced with a dilemma: get back into his squad and chase after the car or stay at the scene to assist those who had been injured or worse.

He reached for the microphone on his nylon squad jacket. Calmly, he keyed the mike and spoke into it. "Squad 5258 to dispatch for the air!"

One long second passed. "All squads standby. Go ahead, you have the air."

"5258 to all squads. Explosion just occurred at the northeast corner of District Five. Damage and casualties not immediately known. Involved is an older-model, green Toyota four door, Wisconsin plates ADF673. Wanted are two bald, white males in their twenties. Both suspects appeared to be wearing black leather jackets and the passenger had a dark beard. Vehicle last seen northbound on MLK Drive from the scene. Dispatch, I need a listing. Fire department units requested. At least two vehicles on fire, east side of the building along the alley."

"10-4, squad 5258, get back to us with any additional, KSA536."

"Shit, that pig saw us!" screamed Spike, turning right onto a side street. The loaded Glock 22, .40 caliber handgun sat next to him on the seat.

"We need to ditch this bitch," Madman yelled, scanning the road for any signs of squad cars. "I thought you said no one would be around the station now."

"Nothing's 100 percent!"

Spike drove the car into an alley west of the Milwaukee River and parked it behind a garage. There was no movement up or down the alley. "Okay, let's go."

"What are we gonna do with these other bombs?"

"Hide it behind one of the garbage cans, and we'll get it later."

Madman grabbed the red plastic bag from the trunk, and they ran halfway down the alley. He set it behind one of the large, green garbage carts in front of a garage. They threw their blue latex gloves into a cart and cut through one of the yards, walking down the street to a corner bar.

"Let's have a coupla brewskis to celebrate."

"Now you're talkin'."

"Doubt if we hurt anyone in the initial blast. I know we wrecked some of them pigs' rides. Would love to see their faces when the other one goes off."

Cautiously walking along the east side of the brown brick building, Birke tried to assess the damage. A newer-model Chevrolet 1500 parked next to the building was engulfed in flames. So was a car on either side of it. The explosion left a gaping hole in the wall he "guesstimated" to be ten feet in diameter. Birke could see straight into the garage and hoped no one had been inside when the bomb went off. Bricks and brick shards would have been high-speed projectiles flying at them.

"John, what happened?" Mark Sandick and two police officers came running toward him. Sergeant Sandick was the acting shift lieutenant.

Birke put his left index finger up for them to standby as he re-keyed the radio mike. "5258, dispatch, advise the fire department there are three vehicles in flames. Injuries unknown."

"10-4. Be advised the plate comes back to a Harold Sampson Carter Jr., on a 1999 Toyota Corolla four door listed as stolen. Taken in a homicide from a week ago. MFD notified on the status of the vehicles."

"Copy." He looked over at Sergeant Sandick. "Sarge, I had just parked my squad in the lot. When I exited, I saw a car with two white guys driving through the alley. They went east, then northbound on MLK when the explosion occurred. I immediately broadcast what I had, including the subject vehicle and license plate."

"We heard the broadcast in the station. Why didn't you pursue? Three squads just split from the station trying to locate it. Every squad within three miles of here is doing the same."

"When they first eye-balled me, they gave me that look like I was from Mars. I was getting back into my squad to see what they were up to, but that's all I had to go on until the explosion. By the time I got my bearings, they were gone. More important for me to be here and assist for possible casualties."

"Good answer. We think we have everyone accounted for who was working inside tonight. I saw the garage on the way out here, and there are bricks all over the place. We have people combing through to see if anyone was in there when it happened. I better give the captain a call and tell him what happened to his police station. This place will soon be a circus with all the brass and media response."

"Engine 30, ladder 10, respond to Number Five District on Fourth and Locust. An explosion just occurred in the alley behind the station. Received an update; three vehicles in flames at that location. Time out: 10:17."

"Copy that, fire dispatch." *So that's what the loud noise was,* Lieutenant William 'Buck' Bucholtz thought to himself as he responded to the radio call. He pushed the alarm button, and a loud, clanging bell sounded in the fire station. Within two minutes, ten firefighters mobilized in the garage, getting into their fire gear and preparing for a quick departure.

"Let's hit it, boys. Our brothers in blue need us. There was an explosion, and three cars are on fire in the alley behind the station." Buck raised his right hand and waved it in a circular motion, signifying the urgency of the situation. The two large garage doors opened, red lights were activated, and the siren blared as the big, red Pierce-brand fire engine lumbered out of the garage, turning eastbound. The large horsepower engine roared and arrived at the location in just over a minute. The motor pump operator veered left into the alley, following the hand directions of a uniformed police officer who was standing on the grass island of the boulevard.

"Jeffers, did you see the hydrant in front of the library? When this beast stops, it's yours. Hook us up, and we'll get this show rolling." Buck spoke into his headset as he looked over at the young firefighter in the backseat.

"Copy, Lieut. I'm all over it."

The truck stopped mid-alley, and the professionals in fire-retardant clothing jumped out and went about their assignments. One firefighter lifted the fire hose up from the concrete and felt the water pressure building. It came to life, with a full stream of water charging at the flames.

Two minutes later, the fires were extinguished. The hose bearer and his backup approached each vehicle and finished the job by dousing all remaining hot spots. They walked alongside each vehicle. Firefighter Norris winced as he sprayed water on the front of the beautiful Chevy 1500 4X4. *Whoever owns this is going to be really upset.* As he walked between the charred green Ford Fusion and blue Hyundai Elantra, the last thing Norris felt was a slight tugging at his left front calf. He didn't see the trip wire stretched between the two autos that set off the secondary explosion.

A blue plastic Igloo cooler, containing highly explosive methyl nitrate set inside of a lead pipe bomb, along with additional shrapnel, had been strategically placed just in front of the Hyundai's front tire. The firefighter didn't stand a chance and was dead instantly from the intense power of the blast and shrapnel that pierced his body. Firefighter Kubick stood a much better chance of survival at the rear of the cars as the back-up fire hose tender. He immediately fell to the ground as metal shrapnel struck his lower extremities and shredded his legs.

As Kubick writhed in pain, Norris lay completely motionless.

"First aid kit, now!" screamed Buck over the radio as he looked on in horror. "Get me two med units here!" He rushed over to Norris, knelt down and felt for a pulse on the carotid artery, glaring at the large puddles of blood forming under the man's lifeless body. Absolutely nothing. He forced the tears back as he maintained his composure and kept a cool, focused demeanor. *Just too many big holes to patch up.* Buck stood up and ordered one of the dual EMT-trained firefighters to perform the "ABCs" of survival in the very slim chance they could save him. Meanwhile, several firefighters were attending to Kubick, professionally working on controlling the bleeding from his legs.

Police Officer Birke surveyed the mangled scene in from of him. "Those two bastards are mine!" he seethed through the openings in his teeth. That's when he noticed it. On the undamaged section of brick wall in front of the red Hyundai, "TMB" was spray painted in large, red capital letters.

Chapter 20

TOMCZYK RESPONDS

Declan was finishing off the second Guinness when his work cell phone started ringing at 11:20 p.m. He set the intriguing Vince Flynn book down and noticed the intelligence office phone number on the screen. *Now what?* He touched the answer button. "This is Tomczyk."

"Ski, saddle up and report to District Five ASAP," Sergeant Howe commanded. "Your boys hit again. An explosion struck a corner of the building, ripped open a hole in the wall, and torched three private vehicles. One firefighter's DOA. One may lose his legs. A cop walking through the garage was hurt badly from a brick projectile. Not a good night. 'TMB' was sprayed on the alley side wall. Looks like it's going to be a long one."

"Those SOBs again! Thanks, Sarge. I'll head right over." He hung up the phone and went into the bathroom. After a one-minute "man shower," he got dressed. Grabbing his holster and department-issued black Smith and Wesson M & P (military and police) .40 caliber pistol, he attached it to his belt along with the black leather holder containing two loaded magazines and a set of handcuffs. He placed the navy blue nylon lanyard with his MPD detective badge around his neck. Within ten minutes, he was in his truck for the twenty-five-minute drive to his former workplace. A million thoughts raced through his head about what had happened. *Who had been injured? What else were these domestic terrorists planning?*

Exiting the expressway, he drove to the district, finding a parking spot in the library parking lot next door. Pandemonium prevailed. Media trucks with antennas raised, a swelling crowd, and squad cars of every color lined the area. He brushed past the plastic, yellow "POLICE LINE DO NOT CROSS" tape, identified himself to the uniformed police officer, and then walked into the station. Inside the large assembly, he heard his name called over the voices of the thirty-plus people present.

"Tomczyk, could you come over here?" He looked over and saw Lieutenant Tom Walsh, Homicide North Supervisor. "We need your help. I'm sure you heard that this 'TMB' group has struck again. Officer John Birke observed two white, bald males in a car coming out of the alley after he parked his squad at about ten fifteen. A minute later, there was an explosion along the building next to the alley. Birke got a license plate, which is listed to a Harold Carter Junior on East Clarke Street. We have a recent homicide victim with that name."

Tomczyk's eyes widened.

"MFD responded and extinguished the fire. Two firefighters were completing a final wash down. Matt Norris, twenty-seven-years-old, tripped a wire and set off a secondary explosion. It had been hidden under a car, which was one of three that were burned. He's DOA. The second firefighter, Tony Kubick, twenty-five, is at Froedtert with two mangled legs. Right now, it's touch and go to save one or both of his legs. Police Officer Robert Bahr was walking in the back door of the garage when he was hit with brick pieces. He sustained severe injuries to his chest and leg. Looks like he'll pull through, but they still have him listed in critical condition—a bad night. Give us a little history. All I know about this stuff is what I read from Lurch's incident at the cemetery."

"Not sure how much I can help you." Tomczyk felt uneasy. He wished he had more info on these guys, but he'd been hitting dead ends on nearly every lead he had pursued since the cemetery incident. "First off, the owner of the car *was* the homicide victim found in Gordon Park. Paint stains on his pants and boots, along with a boot-print cast, matched him up as one of the suspects in the cemetery explosion. We've run every database we have, along with the FBI's, but have turned up nothing as far as associates. Executed a search warrant with Bernems a couple days ago and arrested a Matthew Wallk. He confessed to being at the scene. Said he was Carter's friend. Could provide nicknames for only two other guys, maybe the two in the car tonight—Spike and Madman. Carter had one relative here in Milwaukee, who's been interviewed and proved uncooperative. His sister lives in South Milwaukee and said she hadn't had contact with him for over two years. All she could add was his nickname: 'Squirt.' We also did a search warrant on his apartment, but only found a couple things. He had anarchist literature, pamphlets, and books, along with some cult material. Strange bedfellows."

"Okay, anything else?"

"I went to Chicago PD with an FBI agent last week on a related incident. A Calumet City cop was killed and one severely injured in a cemetery when a bomb attached to a headstone was set off. Eerily similar to ours as far as the chemical used. Same MO on the defaced headstones, along with a note signed by TMB. We've performed Internet searches and pieced together a couple possibilities, but none of them make any sense. Were you aware of the words *Murder* and *Dahmer* spray painted backwards at the cemetery?"

"Oh, yeah. Anything on that yet?"

"No. We think it was a ruse to take us off track. Still open as a possibility. I just received a lab report on an envelope that was attached to a headstone at St. Adalbert's Cemetery the other day. Confirmed the substance as cesium chloride, some serious WMD stuff. Inside was a typewritten letter signed by TMB to the mayor, demanding ten million cash in exchange for ending the bombings. Gave us until this Friday at four o'clock to respond. Guess they wanted to show us they were serious. A meeting has been scheduled for ten tomorrow with the mayor's staff and our 'top dogs' to go over strategy."

"You think?! Why weren't we in the mix on this?"

Declan's typically calm demeanor vanished. "I spoke to Captain Spinnola right after I received the phone call at quarter of four this afternoon. He made the arrangements and contacts for the meeting. Why he didn't notify the homicide squad is above my pay grade, Lieutenant!"

"You're right, Ski. There would have been no reason to keep us in the loop at this juncture. But now these murderers detonated a bomb at one of our police stations; we have a dead firefighter, a couple injured brothers, and not a whole hell of a lot to go on."

Tomczyk thought for a second before responding. "The headstone where they found the fake bomb at Holy Cross was a retired MPD detective captain who died in the early '80s. The one at St. Adalbert's belonged to a retired MPD detective lieutenant. He was a good friend and former partner of the captain's. They worked together on some serious cases, including a task force hunting down John Dillinger. The headstone in Chicago where the cop was killed belonged to a former East Chicago police chief. He was connected to the famous 'Lady in Red' who ratted out Dillinger the night he was killed. I received a call from a CPD detective lieutenant two days ago. Said some district cops recovered a fake bomb in a shopping bag planted at the front door of the Biograph Theatre. There was an extortion letter demanding twenty million. The letter was signed 'TMB.' I didn't know that theatre still existed."

"I didn't either. Some crazy stuff."

"Well, to finish it off, old number Five District used to be located on the corner of Third and Hadley," Tomczyk said, pointing in the direction where the building had stood a block away. "Patterson Tires, if you remember, was there for years."

"Remember it well. I worked at Five for about six years."

"Knew we had something in common. We googled 'The Mad Bomber' and found a couple things. Most promising case is two guys who blew up bombs at some banks, Shorewood City Hall, and 'that' police station on Halloween night in 1935, along with the old station on Twelfth and Vine. A number of personnel were injured from glass and brick, but nothing serious. These two guys blew themselves up while making a big bomb in a garage off Twenty-second and Mitchell a couple days later. Over a dozen people were injured and a nine-year-old girl was killed. The *Journal* and *Sentinel* referred to them as 'The Mad Bomber.' How we connect the crimes that occurred all these years apart is a bit of a stretch—even for my normally warped mind."

"Holy balls. You're right . . . That's plain eerie. Anything else?"

"Nothing, Lieut. Wish I had more, but I'd be lying. I'm hoping for something that will break this case because the file on my desk is getting thicker by the day. All I have is slightly more than a goose egg. I can tell you one of these TMB bastards is packing a .40 caliber Glock. The State Crime Lab matched the bullet and casings from the homicide of Carter through the IBIS system with that make and caliber."

"I heard about that, just wasn't aware of the other connections."

"If there's anything else I can help you with, give me a shout."

"Lieutenant Walsh, can I talk to you a second?" The voice came from inside the sergeant's office located off the assembly room.

"What's up, Sarge?"

"One of our squads found the Toyota in an alley a mile east of here. I told them not to touch it and to stand by for your guys."

"Great news! Heads up on that one. These guys are cold-blooded killers. I wouldn't put anything past them." Lieutenant Walsh glanced at his watch and saw that it was two fifteen in the morning. "Finally, we've got something." He looked over at several detectives sitting at one of the squad tables. "Ron, Bill, see Sergeant Marshall and get the info about the location of the green Toyota. Head over there and get things going. I'll have a bomb tech meet you. Don't touch anything else until the bomb tech says it's clear. We'll tow it downtown and search it there. Also, get a couple squads to canvass the area and make sure they search under every rock. Maybe we'll catch a break with a neighbor who let their dog out for a walk or something."

"Okay, boss."

Tomczyk sat at one of the desks in the assembly room, going back and forth whether he should call her. He decided not to since it was so late. The case was as much hers as it was his since parts of it crossed state lines. *This whole thing has to connect to the Mad Bomber from 1935 somehow.* He just didn't know where to go from here. He instead texted Anne with all the necessary information so she would be informed when she woke up for work. He also pulled a business card out of his wallet: WILLIAM MACCARTHY, DETECTIVE, CHICAGO POLICE DEPARTMENT INTELLIGENCE DIVISION. He called the cell phone listed on the card, which was answered on the third ring. Declan and Detective 'Bill' MacCarthy had hit it off well at the meeting regarding the explosion at the Chicago-area cemetery.

"Area code 414? It's gotta be my favorite Mac-Pollock brother up in Brewtown. Who else would call me so damn late?"

"Bad news, Mac. We had an explosion at my old police station. One firefighter's DOA, one may lose a leg or two, and a cop's in bad shape. These TMB guys set off a secondary that did most of the damage."

"You're kiddin' me, Ski. What time did it happen?"

"About ten fifteen last night."

"Not good. We had two explosions hit separate police stations down here at about the same time. I'm at the scene of one of them now. Thankfully, only a couple minor injuries. Hey, John, what time did they happen?"

Tomczyk heard a voice in the background.

"The first was at ten thirty and the second at a quarter past eleven. We were very lucky. A firefighter triggered a trip wire for a secondary bomb, and it misfired. Coppers were on the ball and broadcasted the information. When the second bomb detonated, they found the tripwire and the bomb tech defused it after they put the fire out. The perps even spray painted TMB in red on the station walls."

"Same MO here, Mac. Unbelievable. I'll give you a call tomorrow, and we can compare notes."

"That'd be great. Talk at ya then."

CRAP.

Chapter 21

MILWAUKEE'S RIVERWEST

They walked out of the corner bar just after one thirty in the morning with a guy they met there. Spike realized the neighborhood would be infested with cops out looking for a couple of white males wearing black leather jackets. He struck up a conversation with a patron and gave him some bogus story about needing a ride home.

"No problem, dudes. I don't work until two in the afternoon. You're on the way to my crib."

"Thanks, man. My knee is still killing me from that operation. Car's on the 'fritz,' so we bummed a ride from my girlfriend, but she's gotta work till three." The slightly tinted windows, which Spike noticed as he slid into the front seat of the older model Chevy, made him that much more relieved. Madman hopped into the back seat. Spike saw three uniformed and one unmarked squad on the one-mile trip to the duplex. *Good thing we took the ride. Too bad, pigs . . . Ain't gettin' us tonight.*

"This'll work. Right here, dude . . . thanks."

The man dropped them off at the top of the alley. They got out and walked the half block to Spike's place.

"C'mon, Madman. You better stay with me tonight. All kinds of pigs roaming around looking for us. This was a close one. We'll go head-to-head on *our* schedule—not theirs."

"You're probably right. I saw a couple squads myself."

When they walked in, Angela was sitting on the sofa in the small living room drinking a beer and smoking a joint.

"Just got home from work, babe," she mentioned in a nonchalant manner. "Hey, dude," she continued, looking over at Madman.

"Angela, this is Madman, one of my homies. He's going to lay his head down for the night on the couch."

"No worries. Offer him a beer and a reefer. Picked some up tonight."

"Now you're talkin'," responded Madman. He couldn't help but notice her great body underneath the t-shirt and blue shorts. *No wonder Spike's always so happy.*

"I'll be right back. Gotta do a couple things in the basement." As Spike walked down the creaky stairs, he pushed the speed dial number for his cousin in Chicago.

"What's up?" said a voice on the other line.

"Good and bad news. We blew the shit out of the cop shop. Saw the news coverage at a local bar. Killed some hoser turd, injured another, along with a cop. Too bad we didn't have all three sleepin' in the morgue. The bad news is some uniformed pig saw us leaving just before the explosion, so we didn't do the other station. We dumped the car and went to a corner bar to lie low. Probably had half a million cops roaming the area for us, and I couldn't risk being in that car any longer. The bar was probably a punk idea in case any pigs walked in. I hid the two bombs we had stashed in the trunk. We'll go back and get 'em tomorrow. Way too dangerous walking down the street with them things, and I didn't want to leave 'em in the car. Thought about booby-trapping the car, but it was too hot to hang around."

"Too bad. We detonated ours at both cop stations like you said, and they were crap. Just saw the TV news. Not much damage, and only a couple pigs got minor injuries. These Windy City cops are too stupid to figure out who did it, though. I left that bogus bomb with the extortion note at the Biograph the other night. Funny as hell. Bet they shit when they saw the bomb. Twenty million bucks by five o'clock next Wednesday or Chicago will light up like the Fourth of July."

"Something's wrong. Did you do it exactly like I told you?"

"Yeah, Spike."

"And you placed the dummy bomb by the Biograph? Isn't that the theatre Dillinger came out of when the feds shot him up? You're trippin' man. You and your love affair with that dude."

"The master of his time. We need to be the masters of our time. Answer me this, Spike. Why we settin' bombs off if we're already demanding money?"

"A little more incentive for them bastards to pay up. Well, I gotta hit it. Talk to ya tomorrow."

Spike walked back up the stairs, joining Madman and Angela on separate chairs in the living room. They talked for the next hour and a half. After a couple beers and marijuana joints, Spike was done. "We're outta here, dude. Here's a pillow and blanket. Just chill for the night, and I'll see ya later. We'll have breakfast sometime, unless you're just gonna split."

"Thanks, man. I'll see how I feel."

"'Night, Madman. Great hooking up and sharing laughs," Angela said. She and Spike went into the bedroom and closed the door.

"Babe, I was going to rock your world, but not with some dude on a couch. You wrecked the mood."

"Sorry, but Madman needed a place."

"You got it." They laid down on the bed and embraced. Within ten minutes, they were both asleep.

Chapter 22

RIVER HILLS NURSING HOME

Demetrius walked down the hallway at the nursing home and peered into his elderly friend's room. He saw George sitting in a recliner by the window, reading the local newspaper.

"What's shakin,' George? How's my favorite super senior citizen doing?"

George lowered the paper and looked toward the door. "D! Haven't seen you in a couple days."

"Been busy with school." Demetrius sensed something. He noticed tiredness in George's eyes and a softening in his voice. "Run any marathons lately, or have you given it up for Lent?"

"Good one. To tell you the truth, I've been slowing down lately. Had a good thing going up into my late nineties, so I have no complaints. Pert near outlasted all my family and friends. My tank's been coming up on empty. You got a couple minutes? I want to finish my story, or you may never hear how it ends."

"Don't talk like that, George. I only did a four-hour shift today. You got all the time you need. Can I get you something to eat or drink before you start?"

George held up an unopened can of Dr. Pepper and smiled. "Just finished lunch, and here's dessert."

Demetrius shook his head and gently grabbed the can from George and flipped open the top. "You're a trip, you and that Dr. Pepper." He placed the can back in George's slightly shaking hand.

"Got the best doctor in town right here." He took a sip from his drink, along with a deep breath. "Let's see, where were we?"

"You stopped off talking about when you guys bombed those two police stations."

"Oh, yeah. Milwaukee got pretty wired the next couple days after that. I told ya the city was already crawling with police officers, but it got even worse. J. Edgar Hoover musta sent half the FBI agents to track us down. It didn't faze Idzi at all. Said he was making the 'king of all bombs' that would bring the city to a standstill. Think I told you about the extortion letter he typed up and left at some school, demanding over a hundred thousand dollars. You know how much money that was during Depression?" George went into a coughing jag, grabbing a white handkerchief from his left pants pocket to cover his mouth.

"You okay? Can I get something for you?" Demetrius was very concerned and not sure what to do.

George, waving his hand, shook his head no. "I've been having them occasionally." He placed his hand on Demetrius' knee to assure him. "The three of us got together at the clubhouse on Saturday night and had a great time. Think it was the first or second of November. We played some cards and Carrom board games for a couple hours. We used to pass the time playing Carrom games. Couldn't find a job, so you had to do something. No video games back then." He smiled. "I was dang good at it, too.

Anyway, we broke up at about midnight, and Idzi said to meet him and Shrimp at the garage at six on Sunday night. Before I left, he showed me all the fuse caps and the hundred sticks of dynamite they were going to use. My eyes about popped out of my head. I went home that night and kept thinking about what he was going to blow up. Didn't sleep very well."

"A hundred sticks of dynamite? Man, George, that would've blown up half the neighborhood!" Demetrius was on the end of his chair.

"Exactly. The next afternoon while I was in the house listening to the radio, I heard an explosion that shook the house. I knew right away what happened. Them guys did something wrong while making that bomb and blew themselves up. My old man and I walked down the block to where it happened. The garage was gone. It had a metal roof that landed a couple blocks away. We later found out the little girl who lived in the house next to the garage was killed and a number of people injured. I remember seeing her on the porch a couple times when I went over to the clubhouse. She always said hi to me. We heard all kinds of sirens within a couple minutes and walked back to our house. There were people all over the place, trying to help out."

"Wow!"

"They were still finding Idzi and Shrimp's body parts for the next couple days after that. Within a few hours of the explosion, the cops were knocking on my door and hauled me down to headquarters. Guys we hung out with at the pool hall were also brought in. I know a couple neighbors ratted me out as far as them seeing me going to and from the garage. The only good thing about my two buddies dying was that I lied my butt off about my involvement, and no one could say differently. I admitted driving with Idzi and Shrimp a couple times in stolen cars, but denied being with them when we stole the dynamite—or anything about the explosions and robberies. No sense going to prison for the rest of my life.

The cops couldn't prove anything more on me. About a month later, they found stolen cars in two garages Shrimp had rented. They were cars we used for the robberies and the police station bombings. One had a couple sets of stolen license plates, a shotgun, and a couple bombs still in it. The other just had plates, best as I remember. Detectives came back and questioned me about it again, but couldn't pin anything else on me. I'm so glad Idzi had us wearing black leather gloves, or my fingerprints would have been all over those cars. I'll never forget them two detectives' names. Even remembered how to spell them both all these years. Always promised myself I was going to go and pee on their graves. They were a couple of real hard noses. They knew I was lying, but couldn't break me. I was scared as hell and stayed with my story. That's why I got seven years at Green Bay Reformatory instead of seventy or a hundred years at Waupun State Prison."

"Now, that's a heck of a story, George."

"And if you don't believe me, jump on a computer and check out the 'Mad Bomber' or Idzi Rutkowski. Bet you'll find stuff on him. Somewhere buried in all those newspaper articles in the two local newspapers is my name. The whole thing really broke my parents' hearts. They came to see me a couple times when I was in prison, and I could see the hurt in their eyes. It took a toll on 'em. When I came back from Europe after the war, we sat down and had a long talk and put it all behind us. I promised them I was going to walk a different path instead of the foolish one I had been on. They both died in the 1970s and saw that I had stuck to my promise." George took another sip of the soda. "You know, I never did get around to pissing on those flat foots' graves. Guess I just tried to put it all in my past and realized they were just doing their jobs. Funny, though, I pretty much told this same story to Richie, and I could really see the anger building up inside him about cops and those detectives in particular. Kind of a weird deal."

"Did you tell him their names?"

"Yeah, but I didn't think it was a big deal since it was so long ago. Come to think of it, I never saw Richie after that. Don't know if he quit, got fired, or just didn't want to talk to me anymore. That's been about four or five months ago by now. I read about the bombing at the cemetery a couple weeks ago where the detective was injured, along with an explosion at the police station the other night where the fireman was killed. Seems like, what do you call that?"

"Deja vu?"

"Yeah, deja vu. Probably just the ramblings of an old man . . ."

"Amazing stuff, George. I'm just impressed you remember all the details."

"Ingrained in my head, kid. Had a ton of anger built up inside when I was younger. The Depression was tough, and we didn't have anything. Hanging around Idzi made it all come out. I hate to say it, but thank God that Idzi got killed in that explosion. He never did tell me what he was going to blow up, but it would've been a big one. I keep thinking city hall since the city never paid the money. We could've toppled a section of it, or that big, old beautiful building could've come down. I was definitely on a path to destruction. Going to prison for those years and then going into the military during WWII were by far the best things that ever happened to me." George opened the drawer on the table and pulled out a small box which he opened for Demetrius to see. Inside were about ten medals and ribbons.

"Man, where's the uniform that goes with all that?"

"I think the moths gorged themselves." George chuckled at the comment. "Spent six years in the army. Funny how they waived some of my criminal issues because they needed live bodies. I was as healthy as a horse when they signed me up. I needed a big change after prison, and the army was a godsend."

"So what are the medals for?"

"Believe it or not, I got two Bronze Stars for bravery, two Purple Hearts for injuries, and the rest for being in different areas of combat. Was at some great locations in Europe. Too bad it was for such a terrible reason. My wife and I went back for a couple weeks, and I showed her where we fought. Sure was a healing journey for me, and the places were even more beautiful than I remembered." Tears rolled down George's cheeks. "Demetrius, here's the bottom line. I had some great times with the men I fought beside, but I had many more that weren't. War is hell. I lost some good friends and made some great ones. Stayed in touch with a couple of 'em for years after the war. The whole experience changed my life for the better."

Demetrius wasn't sure how to respond. He enjoyed George's company and didn't want to say the wrong thing. All he could think of was to be a good listener.

George grabbed Demetrius' right hand with both of his frail ones. "What I'm trying to tell you is to just keep being the fine young man I've come to enjoy and admire. You're a good friend. No question, your parents raised you right, and your Mom's obviously still doing an excellent job. I'm so sorry for you having to lose your Dad at such a young age. Don't let ANYONE give you crap about being black or that you'll never be worth anything. The sky's your limit, son. Don't ever get entangled in the stuff I did. There's a college out there lucky enough to find this Demetrius Simms who is going to be a star student and athlete."

"Can't tell you how much that means to me. Well, better get going. I have a ton of things to do by tomorrow. You be good, and thanks for the stories and your friendship. Till next time." As Demetrius got up to leave, George began coughing heavily again. "I'll have a nurse come and check up on you."

"Thanks, D," he got out between coughs. "Remember what I told you."

"I'll never forget, dude. You're the best." He smiled, pointing both his arms at George in a "got you" gesture.

"Dude? I'll give ya dude," shaking his right fist in the air in a joking manner.

Demetrius walked straight over to the nurse's station. "Excuse me," he spoke up to the nurse on duty. "I just came from George's room, over in 126. I've been with him for almost an hour, and he's had four or five coughing spells. Could you check in on him to see if he's okay?"

"You're Demetrius, right? I'll go in right now and see how he's doing."

"He's a friend of mine and sure looks tired and weak since the last time I saw him." With that, Demetrius left and walked to his car. The brisk breezes sent a shiver through his body. As he drove out of the parking lot, he couldn't shake the feeling he had from something George had said—the way this Richie guy acted when George told him about the detectives and how George wanted to piss on their graves. *Why would Richie act like that if he had no skin in the game? What about that explosion a couple weeks ago in the cemetery? Oh, yeah—Holy Cross off Appleton Avenue. Who bombs a cemetery? And the explosion the other night at District Five where the firefighter was killed, along with the two others injured.* Demetrius knew the locations of all the police stations because his dad showed him around. He had to talk it over with his mom and see what she thought.

Chapter 23

DOWNTOWN MILWAUKEE

The maroon Buick pulled up and parked in front of the building. Madman glanced around and slid into the front seat as the vehicle pulled away from the curb. "What's the scoop, Spike? You sure sounded ticked off on the phone."

Spike's face turned red as he spoke. "Didn't you see the press conference? That idiot mayor and police chief were on. They refuse to pay us the ten million, saying they won't negotiate with terrorists. I'll show them we're not playing around."

"They didn't think blowing up a police station was enough to encourage them? What you got in mind, man?"

"We're headin' down to city hall. I'd like to shove a bomb down that mayor's throat, but that could be tough to do."

A bunch of scenarios flashed through Madman's mind, none of them being very positive. "You sure you want to just do this without a thorough plan? Not like you. Now's not the time to be screwin' this thing up. You know that; we gotta keep a cool head with this."

"I know." He gave his friend an icy stare. "They're gonna pay for their stupidity, though. I've got it figured out." Spike parked the car in a lot several blocks away and explained his plan.

Five minutes later, they emerged from the lot and headed downtown.

"Sounds good. You have everything we need?"

"Yeah. This'll be a special gift for them." Spike found a parking spot a block from Milwaukee City Hall. "Go into the entrance on Market Street and place it where I told you to. There's no security, so this will be a cakewalk."

"Famous last words."

"Just don't forget how I told you to arm it. The backpack has to be stationary or it won't set properly."

"Got it."

"You sure? If not, I'll handle the backpack."

"I got it, Spike. I'll be out in less than ten."

Police Officer Susan Bicker took the stairs from the mayor's office down to the lobby. As part of Mayor Smith's security detail, she also had the responsibility of occasionally patrolling around city hall. At the eight o'clock roll call, the bombing of the police station was mentioned, along with a description of the suspects. Bicker filed it away. She exited the staircase and casually glanced at a white male who entered the building. The navy blue backpack first alerted her, even though many people carry bags and packs of every description around the downtown area. Her eyes moved up to his bald head. She noticed a tattoo on his neck, just behind the right ear. *Is that an anarchy tattoo?*

Madman had entered the double doors off Market Street and walked over to where Spike told him to place the backpack. He set it on the floor by a heat register and was in the process of unzipping the top when he heard a female voice behind him.

"Get up slowly and keep your hands where I can see them."

Madman's heart rate spiked, and he could feel the blood pulse through his body. As he stood up, he turned around and observed a uniformed female officer less than ten feet away.

"Just getting my papers out so I can pay my tax bill."

"Okay. Let's see some ID."

As the officer cautiously closed in on him, he made a slow motion to reach into his rear pants pocket to remove his wallet. Instead, he came back around with his right arm and landed a punch to the officer's face, knocking her to the ground. He kicked her once to the chest and was turning around to start the bomb sequence.

"Dumb move." Bicker's former Air Force security forces training kicked in, and she was able to shake off the pain to her jaw and chest, scrambling quickly to her feet.

Madman didn't wait around. He raced out of the doors, leaving the backpack behind.

Bicker gave chase, but couldn't believe the evasive speed the man had. She got on her portable radio, notifying the dispatcher she was in foot pursuit. When she reached the sidewalk outside the building, she scanned both directions. He was already across the street, heading eastbound on Wells Street. By the time she got to the intersection of Market and Wells, the suspect was gone. She walked along the sidewalk, looking for any possible hiding spot he may have ducked in to. A maroon Buick Skylark pulled away from the curb fifty feet in front of her. She caught a glimpse of two white males wearing baseball caps. *Damn!*

She broadcast a description of the vehicle, license plate, and direction of travel. Having no squad to get into, it was all she could do. Bicker also advised the dispatcher of the suspicious backpack, requesting immediate bomb squad assistance. She returned to the building and secured the area around it.

Within fifteen minutes, Detective Schmidt from the bomb explosive detail, along with FBI Special Agent Kevin Cleary, arrived on the scene.

Inspecting the backpack, they could see the detonator had not been armed, and the attached black plastic Timex watch was still set for five minutes. There were seven large, metal pipe bombs inside.

"Does the word *lucky* mean anything to anybody today? That's what I would call this one. Sue, you saved lives here today. Nice work."

"Thanks. I copied the license plate wrong, though. The plate I had comes back to somebody in Eau Claire on a Toyota. Better run a couple variations of it. Thought for sure I had it right. Secondly, I wish I would have taken up track instead of volleyball. That guy flew out of the building. No way was I catching up to him."

"What do you mean you didn't arm it? Are you that brain-dead? All you had to do was set the switch." Spike smashed his fist into the dashboard.

"I didn't have a chance. As soon as I put the backpack down, that bitch cop told me to stand up and keep my hands in sight. Her hand was on her gun, ready to draw. I may be crazy, but not suicidal."

"Shit. Now what? I better hide this car in the garage when we get back to my place. Good thing I altered the plates a little to lead them on a snipe hunt. Damn it, Madman!"

"My bad, Spike. Sorry. We'll do it again tomorrow. She had me. Got two good licks on her, so I know that bitch is hurtin'. Still can't believe she was back on her feet so fast."

Declan had arrived home just before five thirty that morning and slept for a couple of hours. He changed his hours from eight to four to eleven to seven so he could finish paperwork on his case. He met Anne for coffee at two and briefed her on everything that had happened up until that point.

"Thanks for the text. I was able to get my squad supervisor and ASAC up to speed on the case this morning. Anything further on the attempted bombing at city hall?"

"Nothing yet. Has to be our boys, though. I didn't get a chance to call you until well after two in the morning. You'd be feeling as crummy as I feel about now if I had. Less than three hours of sleep just doesn't cut it."

"I forgive you this time. Just don't let it happen again, local boy." She winked and took hold of his right hand. "Krista was up half the night after a bad dream. I would have been a basket case. Are you free tomorrow night? I'd love to have you over for dinner and introduce you to her. She wants to meet you."

"Wouldn't miss it for the world. What are you having? I have a very particular palette, you know."

"So I've seen. I'm making what any self-respecting Italian girl would cook for dinner. Pasta, meat sauce, and eggplant, with a big loaf of garlic bread. Can you be there at about five?"

"Perfect. I'll take four hours of comp time and turn my phone off so I don't get jammed up with something. You know how that always happens with planned events."

"I'm starting to find out. Guess we FBI types just aren't as important as you guys."

"I won't go near that one." He smiled and made a gesture covering his mouth so he wouldn't say anything. "I better bug out, Anne. That remaining stack of reports I need to file waits for no one. See you tomorrow at five. Thanks for the invite."

It was three fifteen when the phone rang at his desk. "Intelligence division, Detective Tomczyk, can I help you?"

"Detective Tomczyk, this is Demetrius Simms. I'm a friend of Bobby Heard Jr. I met you at our football game at Pulaski Field."

"How's it going, Demetrius? You're Lightning, right?"

The other side of the line went silent for a couple seconds. "You remember that?"

"C'mon, Demetrius. You're a young man after my heart. Back in the day, I may have been as fast as you, but you got the jukes, brother. I could never make those lightning cuts."

"Thanks, detective."

"Please, call me Declan. What can I do for you?"

"Declan, can I meet you somewhere? I want to run something by you. I spoke to my mom this afternoon, and she said I should speak to someone on the police department about this. When I showed her your business card, she told me to call you right away."

"Great advice, kid. Where you at?"

"How about I meet you at Sub Shop on East Capitol Drive? I'm in that area now."

"Fantastic. Give me about twenty minutes."

"Okay, see ya. And thanks."

Interesting. What would some seventeen-year-old high school football star want to talk to a detective about? Just hope he didn't get himself into some trouble and wants me to bail him out. That's all I need. Tomczyk was in his unmarked squad in less than five minutes and jumped on the expressway. He pulled into the restaurant parking lot and walked into the popular sub-sandwich restaurant. Demetrius was sitting in a booth in the corner.

He got up and shook Declan's hand. "Thanks for meeting me, sir. I hope this won't be a waste of your time."

"Never a waste. What's up?" Tomczyk responded as he took a seat on the bench across from the handsome young black man.

"I took the liberty of getting you a bottle of juice so you can listen while I talk. Is that okay?"

Declan was definitely taken aback by that comment. "Ah, sure. Are you certain you're only seventeen? You have the manners of someone much older. Your parents did quite a remarkable job."

"Thanks. My dad was a police officer. He got killed a couple years ago on the job. It's just Mom and me now."

"Bobby told me all about it. I only met your dad once or twice. A fine person."

"He sure was. I miss the heck out of him now and wish he was still around. Sure could use his wisdom."

"I understand, Demetrius. I was working that day and heard it on the radio. What a terrible tragedy."

"Appreciate your comments. It's been tough, but Mom and I are doing it. Declan, there's no other way for me to explain this other than just starting at the beginning."

"Go."

Demetrius carefully laid out his initial contact with George, with as many details as he could about what George told him. Declan took a drink from the bottle and almost choked on it when Demetrius spoke of the two police stations being bombed on Halloween night in 1935. This mirrored the recovery of the two bombs found in a plastic bag in the alley after the bombing at District Five the night before. *I bet these guys were going to bomb another police station.* Finally, Declan nearly jumped out of his skin when Demetrius named the two detectives who had questioned George about the bombings eighty years earlier. Demetrius finished his story by mentioning about a Richie who had previously worked at the nursing home and who George had also told his story to.

"What really bothered me the most was when George told me how Richie acted when George said something about pissing on those detectives' headstones. I kept wondering, why would someone want to bomb a cemetery? It just didn't make sense. That's when I thought about the connection. Have to tell you, though. A couple dudes at school who make a career out of being stupid and getting into trouble with cops may have considered blowing up a police station, but would never go through with it."

"I get that. Demetrius, I could give you a big man-hug right now! You've just filled in some *big* pieces that were missing in our investigation. Now it's becoming clearer. We kind of had a line on this whole Mad Bomber and Idzi stuff from plugging info into the computer, but we couldn't make sense out of any of it. I mean, how do you connect any crimes that happened that long ago to today? Did George ever mention Richie's name or give you any other information about him?"

"No, he didn't. Richie worked for about a month after I started, which was six months ago. My supervisor, Tim Scott, would know him because he would have been his boss also. He could probably give you all the info you need. I'm guessing you'll have to check with the HR people also."

"You're a regular junior detective. I don't know how to thank you enough. Do you know how long HR is open at the nursing home? I could take a ride up there right now."

"Until five."

"Fantastic." He noticed that it was ten after four. "Do me a big favor. Go ahead and tell your mom about our conversation, but no one else. I'll get back to you and tell you what I can."

"Thanks for listening, Declan."

Declan had to laugh at that one. "You may have just broken this massive investigation wide open, and you're thanking me? I want to meet your mom. I bet she is one fantastic woman, raising a great kid like you."

"She sure is." As much as he liked Declan when he first met him at the football game, he doubled that admiration after talking to him now. Demetrius squirmed in his seat. "Do you mind if I ask you something?"

"Not at all. Go ahead."

"Do you regret not going pro?"

"Whoa, where did that come from? And who told you?"

"A day or two after Bobby introduced us to you, he told us all about your college career and how you passed up a high NFL draft pick to go into the Marines. Told us about your sub-4.5 second 40-meter sprint and how you benched 225 for 41 reps at the combine. Not many people can do that. No disrespect, Declan, but I don't see you clockin' in that fast."

"Now you are really funny." He gestured a fist in Demetrius' direction and smiled. "That was well over a decade—and a couple hundred donuts and bagels—ago." He patted a stomach that had seen more than its share of "ab" workouts. "I'm probably at about nine flat by now." Tomcyzk sat back in his seat for a second before he answered the young man sitting in front of him. "Great question, Demetrius. Coach Alaveres asked that exact question when I told him I was going into the Marine Corps—besides a couple other comments he made. He understood my answer, wished me the best of luck, and gave me one of those 'bear hugs' that a father gives a son. He made me promise that I would go to the NFL combine in case I changed my mind or didn't get into the Corps for some reason.

I wanted to be a Marine more than anything in the world. When my successes on the football field kept coming, I questioned my goal and my decision, but stayed true to my word. After my wife was diagnosed with cancer and I had to get out of active duty to become a cop so I could be closer to her, I did some serious soul searching. By then, it was too late to try out for a team. One night, we'll have that serious talk and discuss your future. I'm sure your mailbox has been full of college scholarship offers. If becoming a Wisconsin Badger is one of your goals, I still have some juice in that area. That is, if coach isn't ticked off at me still. Just kidding. We go out to lunch or dinner occasionally. He's just a great, great man."

"That's what I needed to hear. Personally, I thought you fell off the cart and straight onto your head not goin' pro. Now it all makes sense. I respect your answering me . . . and your service. Can't tell you how many times my dad used to tell me how much he loved being a cop. His eyes always had this unbelievable glow whenever he shared the job with me. You know how many questions a son can ask their father."

Where did this kid come from? I've got to meet his mother. Declan stood up. "I promise; I'll be in touch."

They shook hands and said goodbyes, walking out separate doors to leave.

Chapter 24

IDENTIFICATION OF A MAD BOMBER

eclan got onto the expressway and was at the River Hills Nursing Home in less than twenty minutes. Walking in the main door, he stopped at the front desk and asked the attendant for the human resources department. She directed him to an office down the hall on the right.

"I need to speak to a supervisor regarding one of your former employees." Within two minutes, a middle-aged woman greeted him at the counter.

"Can I help you?" she asked in a matter-of-fact tone. "We're ready to close."

"I'm aware of that, ma'am. I apologize for coming in so late, but this is an urgent matter." He showed her his detective badge and police identification on the back of the badge holder. "I'm looking for information on a former employee. All I have is 'Richie' and that he worked in your maintenance department."

The woman was less than impressed with his credentials. She asked him into her office. Out of the corner of his eye, he noticed one of the front office female employees staring at him the whole time. He liked to think it was because of his good looks and build, but her eyes and body language told a story of something else. He'd worry about it later.

"Again, ma'am, this is a matter of high urgency. We're seeking to get information on this 'Richie.' He worked here until about four or five months ago."

"I don't have to do this without a subpoena, you know."

"I'm aware of that, Mrs. Sanders," reading her name from the fairly large wooden name tag on her desk. "I can request a subpoena, but this is a matter of life and death."

The woman thought for several seconds, then opened the middle file cabinet and fingered through a number of manila employee files.

"Here it is." She removed it from its alphabetical listing in the "former employees" section. "His name is Richard John Zuber, birthday of June 15, 1989. The last address we have is 4879 North Eightieth Street in Milwaukee. Is there anything else you need?"

"Just his current status, ma'am."

"He was terminated five months ago for having too many unexcused absences and coming to work with marijuana on his breath. We have a zero-tolerance policy as far as drugs are concerned."

"Thank you, Mrs. Sanders." He handed her his business card. "If there's something we can help you with, please give me a call."

"Doubt it, but I'll keep your card. Good day, Officer."

"It's Detective Tomczyk, ma'am." Declan couldn't stand her uppity, North Shore attitude. She led him out of her office and back into the hallway.

"I'm guessing you can find your way out from here, Detective."

"Yes ma'am, they tell me I'm a professional investigator. I'll figure it out."

Without responding, she walked back into her office.

What a gem, he thought to himself. He got what he needed; no sense pushing the issue.

———

"What are you talking about, Maggie?"

"Look, Richie, I'm at the nursing home and some detective dude from Milwaukee is asking about you. He just went into mega-bitch Sanders' office. I stepped outside for a smoke break to call you. What's going on? Plus, I haven't seen you in a couple weeks, and I'm missin' your lovin'."

"Nothin' goin' on. Everything's cool. I'm right in the middle of something, but I'll call you in a day or two. I'm missing that hot bod of yours, but I told you we would only be doing part-time sack time since I moved in with Angie."

"I know, but you roll around better than most, and I crave it."

"No worries, Maggie. I'll be in touch. Thanks for the call." He disconnected the phone. "Dammit!"

———

Tomczyk walked back over to the information desk and asked the same woman where he could find the maintenance supervisor and if he was still working.

"Tim left at four today. Said he was going to his son's basketball game. Can I ask who you are?"

He again produced his badge and police identification.

"Why didn't you say so?" the woman asked. "Tim's a friend of mine." She wrote something down on a piece of paper and handed it to him. "Here's his name and cell phone number. He'll help you in any way he can."

"Thank you very much. One last question. I'm also looking for one of your residents named George. I was told he stays in room 126."

"Easy enough. Straight down the hall on the left. There's been some activity there in the last couple hours. I heard he's been coughing a lot recently."

"You've been more than helpful, ma'am."

"Good luck, Detective. Have a great evening."

"You, too." *Man, what a difference—meeting Cruella Deville and Cinderella, all within five minutes of each other.* He walked down the hallway to room 126. Peering into the room, he saw an elderly man lying in bed with an oxygen tube in his nose.

"You gonna stand there all day or come in and talk to me?"

Declan walked in and stepped over to the side of the bed. "Detective Declan Tomczyk, sir, Milwaukee Police." He produced his detective shield and showed it to the man. "Is your name George?"

"Well, don't this beat all. I've stayed out of trouble all these years, and they send me some detective to finally come and arrest me. Who woulda thought?" George put both his arms out. "Handcuff me, flat foot. I'm guilty."

George was as Demetrius described. He had to smile and admire a guy in his upper nineties who obviously still had it going on.

"Sir, you're lucky the jail is full up, so I can't take you with me." He pointed his right index finger at him and shook it gently. "But don't let it happen again." They both laughed as Declan relayed the conversation he just had with Demetrius.

"That young man is one of the nicest kids I've ever met. He better not be in trouble, or you will have to take me to jail. I'll fight for Demetrius all day long and then some."

Tomczyk shook his head. "That's what I thought you would say. I just spoke to him for a half hour, and that's the same impression I got. Guess we'll both be his blockers so no one can tackle or hurt him."

"Now you're talking, Detective. What can I do for you?"

Tomczyk sat down in the chair close to the bed. "Do you mind if I ask you some questions?"

"Go ahead. I have to admit it's been decades since I've spoken to detectives, and the last time wasn't very positive."

"I understand. Would you mind going over that interview with me and who it was with?"

"It was on a Sunday night in November 1935. The two detectives' names were Harold Schlundt, S-C-H-L-U-N-D-T and Stanley Strychalewski, S-T-R-Y-C-H-A-L-E-W-S-K-I. I'll never forget 'em. For many years, I thought they were a couple of sons of bitches, but I came to realize they were just doing their job. You may have heard the story at some point during your career. I'm not very proud to admit it, but we pulled off some bombings and some other things in Milwaukee, and one day my two best friends blew themselves up making a big bomb. All I ever did was drive the cars, but I was there when it all happened, so I'm just as much to blame for not telling anybody. That poor little girl was killed. Many people were injured. A whole lot more could have been killed, including some of your badge-wearing predecessors. I've had to live with that. Never told many people about my involvement over the years, but did tell a kid in this nursing home named Richie. He seemed like a smart kid who was rough around the edges. Reminded me of me.

I thought I'd share parts of my story and hopefully scare him into staying a good kid. He asked many questions, and I gave him most of the answers. He seemed to change a little, though. The last time I saw him, I remember telling him about the two detectives who interviewed me and how I wanted to urinate on their graves after they died. Didn't get a chance to tell him I never went through with it and finally understood why they were so mean to me. This strange look came over Richie's face, and he left. Never saw him again and didn't give it another thought until the bombings at the cemetery and the police station. Please don't tell me Richie's involved in that stuff."

"We don't know yet, George. That's why I'm here. Do you know where the detectives are buried?"

"One's at Holy Cross and the other at St. Adalbert's. I remember seeing an article in the paper years ago about Strychalewski dying and how he was one of the main detectives on the bombing investigation. Ya know, he and Schlundt were the only two Milwaukee detectives assigned to the 'Dillinger Squad' in 1934, so it means they were damn good at what they did. Guess I should take pride in knowing two of Milwaukee's best put me away in prison for those years." He chuckled. "They definitely showed me the light, and I got over my anger after a while."

Declan wrote down the information. "What can you tell me about the police bombings you were involved with?"

"Like I told Richie and Demetrius, I was the driver on every one of the bombings and the robberies we pulled off at the pharmacies and was also involved with the stolen squad car in West Milwaukee. The West Milwaukee deal was a hoot. All the others were a little scary, but definitely an adrenaline rush. You have to understand the times, Detective. I can't justify my stupidity back then, and I won't try. Just glad Idzi didn't invite me to help him make the bomb, or I woulda been blown up along with 'em. You wanna know the damnedest thing? Some old psychic predicted the bombings before they even started and how they were going to end, with a big explosion somewhere south of the Menomonee River. At the time, we laughed about it and thought the guy was a nut job. Guess he wasn't."

"I'm not a judging panel here, George. You paid your debt back to society by going to prison and serving your country. I have great respect for military. Was a grunt myself—seven years Force Recon, Second Marine Division. Urrahhh."

"Well, I'll be. Semper Fi, young man." George gave Declan a solid "thumbs up" and continued his story, relating nearly all the details

Demetrius described to Declan earlier, with a few that a seventeen-year-old didn't need to hear. He paused for a drink from the large, white Styrofoam cup on the table in front of him.

"Can't say I'm proud of it, but can't go back in time to change my life."

"Amen to that, sir."

"I'm not sure where Idzi learned how to wire up and detonate the dynamite. We had an auto mechanic class at Boy's Tech High School, and he did well, but the rest of his grades were bad. Always wondered what went wrong for that last bomb to detonate. Forgot to mention something. For some reason, we liked this one stolen car and even put the siren and light from the stolen cop car in the back of it. We also left a shotgun from the pharmacy robberies and a couple extra bombs in it—in case we decided to blow something else up. We kept a second stolen car in another garage as a backup."

"Unbelievable. Demetrius said you told him about how the cars were found in different garages?

"Yeah, about a month after the bombings, the police found the cars and recovered everything we had in 'em. There were even pictures in the *Journal* newspaper. I was still in the county jail because I couldn't make bail. Those two detectives came to my cell and grilled me on it, but I had my story down pat and stuck with it. They were mad as hell and woulda just as soon beat me like a dog than talk to me. Can't tell you how happy I was to get that interview over with. They nearly broke me. All I kept thinking about was going to prison for the rest of my life."

"That's a good motivation. What can you tell me about Richie? Can you give me a description, any scars, marks, or tattoos you may have seen on him? Did he ever tell you where he lived?"

"Detective, you sound like Agent Gibbs from *NCIS*. I still love that show." He smiled and thought for a couple seconds. "Like I said, he seemed like a good kid. He was one of the maintenance guys here. I'd say he's about six foot, average build, maybe a buck ninety or two hundred. Really short, brown hair. Noticed he had an earring hole in one of his ears. Don't think they let men wear earrings at work in this place. He always wore long sleeve shirts, but this one time he rolled his sleeves up, and I noticed tattoos on both of his arms. I asked him about them, but he shrugged it off. Said he got them when he was younger." George closed his eyes and thought for a moment. "On the left inside wrist was a black 'A' inside a circle. On his right inside forearm, right about here, he had the letters 'TMB' with some sort of design underneath it. I have no idea what either of those mean. I have my own tattoos from my Army days, so I'm not one to judge anyone from tattoos. Mine were a bond to my 'band of brothers.' They have sure popularized that statement recently. Used to talk about it during the war, especially when things got tough."

"Been there, done that, George." Declan raised his right sleeve revealing a bold tattoo on his upper arm. It read, "Force Recon" and had a skull with wings behind it. The skull donned an air hose, signifying air and water capable. In the spaces on the bottom part of the circle around the skull were the words *swift, deadly, silent.* "There was a day when I lived, breathed, and ate Marine Force Recon. Had to leave that life to become a loving spouse, taking care of a wonderful woman with cancer."

"Sorry to hear about your wife, young man. So you were a hard-core charger! Glad guys like you were on our team. I was 101st Airborne. They teamed us up with a unit of Marines on a couple missions in the South Pacific late in the war. Solid warriors. My hat went off to those guys."

"Means a lot coming from you. Read a book or two about your generation's exploits during the war. Had to be bad."

"Yeah, it was, Detective. Made a man out of me, though. Stand tough or die."

Declan patted George's shoulder. "Thanks for your service." He put his head down briefly, then brought it back up. "Did Richie ever mention where he lived?"

"All I know is somewhere around Eightieth and Hampton. Wait. He told me the last day I saw him that he was moving in with a woman he'd been dating. Said she lived somewhere in Rivereast, Riverwest, something like that—by the Milwaukee River."

"Very good; it's the Riverwest area?"

"Said she was a bartender and worked at night. What was the name of that bar? Some short, beer-related name. Float, Suds, something like that."

"How about Hops?"

"Yeah, yeah, Hops, that's it!"

"Fantastic. See, you still have a mind like a steel trap."

"Yeah, but I wish my body was a little more cooperative. Works more like a car with a dead battery."

Declan admired this guy, quick witted and a wealth of information. "George, I have a police officer coming up here with something called a photo array. There are going to be six different pictures on a piece of paper. I'm going to ask if you see Richie on that piece of paper. If you do, great; if you don't, great. That sound okay to you?"

"Sure does. I'll help as much as I can."

"Excellent. It's very important that you're 100 percent positive. Do you understand?"

"Completely."

"Anything else you feel might be important to us about Richie?"

He thought about it for a couple seconds. "Detective, I have to tell you I'm very upset over this. I keep feeling this whole thing is my fault and that all I did was possibly create a monster."

"A wolf in sheep's clothing, my friend. By the tattoos you saw, Richie was already on his way. It was bound to happen one way or another.

Don't take it out on yourself. I can tell you about a young, high school football player who thinks the world of you. You've reinforced his good values by volumes."

"Thanks for that. Demetrius means a great deal to me also."

At that moment, a police officer in a navy blue uniform with River Hills Police Department patches on both shoulders entered the room.

"Good afternoon, gentlemen. I'm Officer Hancock, River Hills PD." He looked directly at the younger of the two men and smiled. "Detective Tomczyk?"

They shook hands, and the officer produced a piece of paper from a brown manila folder that he handed to Declan. "Didn't want it to get bent up or anything."

"Good idea. Appreciate the help." Declan looked closely at the photo array, which consisted of two rows of three photos. The men were all similar in hair color, features, facial hair, and build. All were wearing standard Milwaukee County Justice Facility orange-colored coveralls. He needed to ensure it would be a fair representation of individuals, as the courts considered the process a reasonable and fair one for making positive identification. As he looked at each photo on the page, an eerie feeling washed over him as he realized they had their man. It was the eyes, even at that distance in the cemetery, which gave away the driver of the car that horrible day. *The eyes are the window to the soul!*

"Is it okay, Detective?" asked the young officer.

"Perfect." He showed the array to George, holding it about a foot away from him. "Are any of these guys the man you know as Richie?"

"Well, this is simple enough." He pointed to the male in the center photo on the bottom row. "This is him; I'm 100 percent sure. No question about it."

"Very good. Officer, you're my witness." Declan turned the paper over and wrote down the date, time, and location, then handed his pen to George. "If you could sign your name below the information I wrote."

"Hope you're not wanting good penmanship. Been a while since I've signed anything."

"No worries. Just want to make your identification official. I'll put the rest of the details in my report." With that, he shook George's hand. "Can't tell you how much I enjoyed speaking with you. You've been a tremendous help."

"Detective, it's been a long time since I've spoken to the police. It's been a pleasure conversing with you also. Thanks for your comments."

"I'm giving Demetrius a call later today. Anything you want me to tell him?"

"Yeah, that he's the best friend a guy could ever have."

"Fair enough." Declan left the room with the police officer.

While walking out into the parking lot, the officer asked what it was about.

"A couple homicides and bombings in our city. You'll be reading about this one in the papers real soon. Might explode right onto the front page. Thanks again for the help." Declan got into his squad and drove off to a bar in his old squad area.

Chapter 25

PUZZLE PIECES START FALLING INTO PLACE

ome detective is asking about me where I used to work. Time to
split, man. I'll meet you in thirty minutes in front of the building.
You ready to roll?"

"Not really, man. How 'bout forty-five to an hour?"

"I'll give you forty-five. See you at six. Pack a bag for a week or two
'cause we're going south."

"Got it. Later," Madman responded and hung up the phone. *Shit, bad timing. Not ready to leave yet. Got myself into this mess, so I better suck it up and go.*

"What do you mean you're going for a week or two? Where do you think you're going? And what's this about a detective asking about you? What's going on, Richie? Talk to me!"

Spike turned around and saw Angela standing in the middle of the bedroom doorway. "I may have gotten myself in a little trouble. No problem."

"No problem? I heard you talking on the phone earlier to some Maggie chick about her hot bod. You're shacking with me, and I'm paying most of the rent, utilities, and food. Then you got some hoochie mama on the side? That's bullshit."

"It's not like that, babe." As Spike approached her, she didn't see the knife he pulled from the sheath on the right side of his belt. It was over in a second as he pushed the six-inch blade deep into her left chest.

— — —

Tomczyk parked his unmarked squad in front of the corner tavern, one of over one hundred in this once bustling, blue-collar neighborhood. Walking in, he noticed a couple older men at the bar, drinking glasses of beer with empty shot glasses in front of them. A shot and a beer, still alive in this old rust-belt town. Declan identified himself and asked the bartender for the name of the female night bartender and if she was around.

"Her name's Angie. She starts at seven and works till close. Can I help you with something?"

"Nah, just need to talk to her." He looked at his watch. "Do you have her address or cell phone? It's an emergency."

"Can't do that. Confidential. I'll give her a call, and if she gives me the okay, I'll give it to you."

"Tell you what. Give me her last name, then go ahead and give her a call. It's been a while since I've handled tavern violations, but I'm sure I can find a couple here." Declan didn't like the option, but everyone's a lawyer, and he had to choose his battles. It was too late to get a subpoena.

"Okay, okay. I've had enough trouble with city hall. Her full name is Angela Culbertson. She lives in an upper duplex on Weil just south of Clarke. I don't have her address here. It's at my house." He speed dialed her number but received a recording. "Not answering. Here's her cell number."

Declan wrote down the number in his memo book. "Do you know who she lives there with?"

"Some guy moved in with her a couple months ago. Never saw him. Said his name was Richie. Don't have any other info on him, but she said he was a decent guy. Angie's a reliable employee. She smokes weed and drinks a little, but wears tight clothing and is easy on the eyes. All the customers like her."

Declan obtained the information on the owner and left. He drove straight to District Five to get on a computer. While there, he found out John Birke was working and asked the sergeant to call him into the station.

"You got it, Declan. Said he'll be here in ten."

He logged on to the computer and plugged Angela Culbertson into the Milwaukee Police databases for criminal record history and field interviews. He obtained her birthdate and noticed she had a minor criminal record from a couple years ago. *Bingo!* A recent traffic stop showed an address on North Weil Street. Too late to contact his postal inspector buddy for current address confirmation on where she received mail. He went into the City of Milwaukee property tax website and entered the address. It listed a property owner living on the East Side, near the University of Wisconsin-Milwaukee campus. He called the number listed and a female answered.

"Hello."

"Yes, I'm looking for Thomas or Gabriella Barker."

"This is Gabriella Barker. Who's this?"

"Detective Declan Tomczyk, Milwaukee Police. I'm checking to see if you still own the duplex at 2596 North Weil Street."

"Yes, I do. Is something wrong?"

"No, Mrs. Barker. I'm inquiring as to the people who live there. We're in the middle of an investigation and could really use your help."

There was a short silence. "How do I know you're legit? You could be Joe Blow from Idaho for all I know.

"Understood. You can call my supervisor, or you can look up the District Five telephone number in your phone book and give them a call. I'm there now, and they can verify who I am. I'll spell my name so you'll know who to ask for."

"No need for that, Detective. You sound like you're on the up and up. We have an elderly couple with the last name of Thompson living in the lower. Upstairs is a young woman named Angela Culbertson. She's been there just over a year. She notified us several months ago that she picked up a roommate to help her with the rent. Angie never gave me his name and mentioned it was a boyfriend. We didn't have a problem with it since she's been an excellent tenant, and the upper is a two bedroom anyway. Doubt if they're using two bedrooms, though."

"Did you ever see the guy?"

"I think so. I was there about two months ago to get something and saw a man going in the front door, using a key. Must have been him."

"Can you describe him at all?"

"He was wearing a black leather cap, so I couldn't see his hair, but it was bald on the sides. Clean shaven, with a big earring in one of his ears. About six feet tall. Medium build. He had on a black leather vest with some kind of writing and symbols on it. I think one was a capital A with a circle around it. Isn't that some sort of anarchist thing or something? Couldn't read any of the writing on it."

"Very good, ma'am. Anything else you remember about him?"

"All I remember was blue jeans and black leather boots. He smiled at me and even waved. I saw this tattoo on his right inside forearm. Couldn't describe it, except to say it had initials and a design. That's about it. One more thing. This may be a little weird, but I also remember he had intense eyes. Hard to explain."

"Fantastic, Mrs. Barker. I may call you within the next hour or two for some other info. Please don't call Angela or the people downstairs. That's very important. Do you understand?"

"Yes, I do, young man. I'll be home the rest of the night if you need something."

"Thanks again. Good night." Tomczyk hung up the phone. Several minutes after he finished speaking to Gabriella Barker, John Birke walked into the assembly.

"How you doing, Detective? Whatcha need?"

"Doing well, man. On the night of the bombing, did you get a look at either of the two guys in the car?"

"I think I could maybe pick out the driver if I saw him again, but probably not the passenger as I focused on the driver. Just too fast of a look. He never really looked at me . . . just his eyes, if you get my drift."

"Got it—fish eyes. I've tried to explain that to people for years, and they always give me the thousand-yard stare."

"Exactly."

"John, I want to show you a photo array and see if you can identify anyone. It's worth a shot."

"Let's do it."

Declan pulled out the photo array from a folder he was holding and placed it on the desk. "Take your time."

"Wow, didn't expect this." Birke tilted his head toward the ceiling, closed his eyes, and exhaled. He looked down at the paper and placed several fingers from his right hand underneath each photo. Starting from the top left, he slowly moved his fingers to the next one on the right. It was obvious he was concentrating very hard, trying to remember a fleeting face in the night. He went to the bottom row, starting again on the left. When he got to the middle photo, he closed his eyes again.

"This is the son of a bitch, right here. I'll never forget those eyes or that face. The lights in the parking lot illuminated it fairly well, and he gave me a look that told me he was guilty of something. I'd bet my career this is him!"

"Very good." Declan had made several additional copies of the colored photo array just for this reason. He turned the paper over and had the officer sign and date it, positively identifying the subject in position number five as the person driving the car the night of the explosion. Declan wrote all the information in his memo book.

"Do you know where he is? I'd love to be in on this arrest."

"Not yet, but we're working on it. I'll keep you in mind. How long you working tonight?"

"Usual shift. Squad 5258 until midnight."

"I'll be in touch." Declan shook his hand. "You doing okay? That was a tough night."

"Won't ever forget it. I keep seeing those firefighters in my dreams, and I've been sleeping like garbage."

"You see the shrink? That's what they're there for. After my first shooting, the doctor I went to see helped me out."

"You're right. I have a female shrink, and I've seen her once so far. My problem is at night when I'm alone in bed and have time to think about it. I keep reliving how I could have done things differently."

Declan put his arm around the young officer. "I hate to say it, but that's normal. It's going to take a while. Here's my business card, John. When you have those tough times, give me a shout. I've been there and have more than my share of those dreams."

"Thanks, appreciate it."

"Great job. Later."

Tomczyk called the intelligence division lieutenant's extension. "Lieut, Tomczyk. Things are progressing regarding the bombing case at District Five. You got a sec?"

"Talk to me, Ski."

"He related the story to Lieutenant Vohl. From his initial contact with a teenager who provided information, through to the positive identifications of Richard Zuber from George and John Birke, putting Zuber at the police station explosion. "Lieut, this is also the driver from the cemetery bombing. I recognized him right away."

"Fantastic. What's next?"

"I'll need the duty DA's phone number so I can tell him what we have and hopefully get a telephonic search warrant. I think it's enough, but the assistant district attorney has to think so also. I'll head over to the East Side and show the array to the duplex owner to see if we can get a positive ID of Zuber being the guy she saw go in the front door of the duplex. That will shore it up more tightly."

"Good job. Where'd this kid come up with the idea of this Zuber as a possible suspect?"

"The old man gave him the first clue. Then this kid, Demetrius Simms, picked up the ball and ran with it. His dad was Willie Simms, if you remember him."

"Remember him! Willie was a friend of mine. Met his wife, Dorrie, a couple times. She introduced me to the son at the funeral, but he was a couple years younger. A tough time for us all. How's Demetrius doing now?"

"You wouldn't believe what a class act he is. He's also a high school football star who will probably be going to college on a full ride."

"That's fantastic news. Keep me posted."

"You got it, boss."

Declan re-contacted Gabriella Barker and told her he needed to meet her for something. She agreed. Twenty minutes later, he had another positive identification of Zuber. *Great, puts him living there.* He drove over to the duplex to get a detailed description of the exterior for the search warrant. He already had the upper-floor plan sketch from

Mrs. Barker so he could brief the officers doing the entry. Next, he called Duty ADA Deann Skenarz, one of his favorites.

"Deann, this is Detective Tomczyk. How's my favorite assistant district attorney doing?"

"Things don't change, Ski. Haven't heard from you in weeks, and you're already sweet talking me. What do you need?"

"Nothing's changed. Still in love with only you. I have a great story and need your expertise to get me a search warrant."

"Yeah, yeah, yeah. Go for it."

Declan laid the case out to her, which took ten minutes. She asked intermittent questions to clarify some of the information he provided.

"Sounds good. I'll type it up and send it to Judge Wagner. He's still the best judge on the bench for these after-work-hours warrant requests. Is this a good number?"

"Yes. And Deann, thanks."

"Yeah, yeah."

"One more thing. This guy's an expert at secondary explosives and booby traps. I'm having the bomb squad meet me."

"Sounds like a smart idea. I'll get back to you as soon as I have it."

"Later."

It was seven thirty when he received the call from Deann. "I have the search warrant for the upper and the basement, along with a felony arrest warrant for Zuber. I'll scan it to your email address."

"Excellent." He provided her the information.

Declan had already requested for a couple tactical section squads, etc., to meet him at District Five. With search warrant in hand, he briefed everyone in the assembly about the suspect and the contents of the warrant.

"Keep in mind, the duplex could be booby trapped like other places you've read about. This guy really knows his stuff. We'll knock, but if no one answers, we're not making entry until we verify there are no bombs rigged to blow. We'll let the bomb techs do their magic. Understood?"

Everyone nodded their heads in agreement.

Within ten minutes, officers were pounding on the front door of the upper duplex, after shining their lights in the door window to make sure it was clear. Additional officers were staged at the back door, which was common to both the lower and upper level of the duplex. The rest of the perimeter was also covered. Repeated door banging failed to bring an answer. Officers contacted the elderly couple in the lower flat and apprised them of the situation. They related to Tomczyk that they heard Zuber and Angela yelling briefly sometime around five o'clock, then it got quiet. A couple minutes later, they heard someone walking down the back stairs to the basement. They heard that person walk back upstairs shortly thereafter. About thirty to forty minutes later, they saw Zuber leave in an older, maroon Buick, the one they usually saw him driving. The couple said they've heard no movement or other sounds since then. They were placed in a squad car down the block. The homes on both sides of the duplex were also evacuated.

Detective Billy Hammer, bomb technician, secured a ladder from a neighbor's yard and placed it against the rear porch. He carefully climbed it and stepped over the porch railing. Shining his small high-beam flashlight into the darkened kitchen, he observed what they all had suspected.

"Looks like a bomb on the back door." He checked along the inside of the porch door and saw several colored wires, but his viewpoint didn't allow him to see any device. "The inside of this porch door is rigged as well." He took a closer look at the device attached to the back door to give him some idea of what they were facing. Several minutes later, he stepped back onto the ladder and climbed down.

"What do we have, Billy?" Declan asked, with genuine concern on his face.

"Not looking good at all, Ski. The device on the back door looks to go off once that door is opened. We obviously can't disarm it from outside the apartment. I can't see the device on the porch door." He pointed directly above them. "All I can see are a couple wires that your boy didn't hide as well as he could have. We can enter through one of the windows to check out the place for bombs. I think we have a better chance of removing a window to see in. What do you think?"

"I'm game, man. You're the expert."

"My guess is this guy didn't set a bomb at every entry point from what you said the downstairs people told you. He didn't have the time. I'll try one of the windows on the side of the house and see what we got."

"Okay."

Billy climbed the ladder to the second floor and pulled a cutting tool from a full utility belt he had taken from the bomb truck.

"You never know when this stuff may come in handy," he said to the uniformed officer holding the ladder. He shined the light into what turned out to be one of the upstairs bedrooms and surveyed every corner of the window and surroundings to see what he had. The blade screeched along the window as he made a cut several inches in from the window molding holding the glass in place. Declan felt a tingling in his body as he had flashbacks of fingernails raking down a chalkboard.

"Got it." Hammer used a small suction cup to pull the glass out and carried it down the ladder, handing it to one of the police officers assisting him. He climbed back up and slowly placed his head inside the dark room, his flashlight leading the way. Hammer then came back down the ladder.

"This bedroom's clear. Ken and I will enter through the window and see what we're facing in the rest of the apartment."

"You got it, Billy. Zuber's gone, and the neighbors didn't see or hear the female leave. Her car is still in the garage out back."

"Okay. We'll see what we got. Can I get one police officer to come up with us and stay at our six as a go-between? It'll make things much easier."

"See what I can do." Declan walked over to Sergeant Davis and discussed the situation. Within minutes, an officer presented himself.

"I'm your man, Detective. Two tours in Iraq as an EOD guy. Totally understand it's their show. I'm just their eyes, ears, and helper."

"You're a quick learner. What's your name?"

"Josh Zastrow."

Declan looked over at the bomb tech. "Hammer, this is Josh Zastrow. Former Army EOD who wants to be your Boy Friday."

"Okay, good. Name's Hammer." He began discussing strategy as they prepared to enter the apartment window.

Chapter 26

MILWAUKEE RIVERWEST

A cell phone rang at an apartment in Chicago. "What's up, Spike?" "Bad news, cuz. Somehow the cops found out about me. Can't figure it out. The only way would have been the old guy at the nursing home. He told me about the detectives who messed with him years ago and gave me the idea in the first place. Hate to think he ratted me out."

"So what's the drill?"

"I met Madman at the building and loaded the goods into a van we borrowed last week. Ditched my ride over by the building. They'll have a hard time finding it. We're heading down by you tonight to lay low until the big job I have planned later this week. It's much sooner than we thought. Those dirt bags decided not to pay up, and the little payback plan we had didn't work out. That okay with you?"

"Oh, yeah."

"Good. See ya when I see ya. Shouldn't be more than two or three hours, depending on traffic."

"You got it."

Spike clicked the off button. "All set. This should be an interesting week."

— — —

Search Warrant

Fourteen years on the bomb squad taught William 'Billy' Hammer never to overlook the obvious. He was the first one through the window and stood for several seconds to get the feel of the room. As he shined the million-candle-power flashlight slowly around the room again, the additional angle allowed him to notice the tripwire in the doorway leading into the hallway. He locked it into his brain. Continuing around the room, illuminating a section at a time, he noticed nothing else that gave him concern. He motioned for his partner, Ken Smith, to come up next.

The two experienced bomb techs found the source and defused the bomb. They checked it out to see what kind of bomb maker they were dealing with. It had the usual components, but something about it was different from many others they had dealt with. Less weight, which meant less explosives, or a higher quality explosive. They would be checking that out later, but either way, the first one was defused. "Good job, Kenny. Why don't you scope out this short hallway, and I'll call for Josh to come up?"

"Roger that."

When Police Officer Zastrow climbed into the bedroom, Hammer showed him the IED, explaining how and where they found it. Zastrow looked at it and shook his head.

"Okay, Hammer. I won't make a move until you guys give me the high sign. This is nothing like the stuff we had in the 'sandbox.' Most of those scumbags didn't have the knowledge or materials to make something this good."

"That's encouraging at least. Why don't you hang here in the bedroom until we call you?"

"I'm cool with that."

Smith glanced out into the hallway, skillfully short-stepping the ten feet that opened up into the once-beautiful stucco walls. Should he go left or right out of the bedroom? He chose left. He had placed yellow "Do Not Cross" tape on the hallway floor to be sure the others knew it was "hot." A small table light gave him enough illumination in the living room to see fully. Once Billy gave him a pat on the right shoulder, they steadily made their way across the large room. Hammer observed an explosive device attached to the front room doorway.

"Kenny, bomb on the front door." He pointed at his discovery. The rest of the room was clear. Within several minutes, that bomb was defused as it appeared to have been hastily made and set to go off when someone opened the front door.

"Stand by for a minute." Hammer opened the door and peered down the front staircase with careful examination. He flashed his light through the glass of the door at the base of the stairs and unlocked the door. "Two rooms clear, three more to go," he mentioned to two tactical section officers standing on the concrete walk at the base of the porch, MP5s at the ready. "One of us will be back shortly to give the 'all clear' signal for you to come in. We've diffused two so far. I know you don't want to come in yet."

"You're a genius, Billy. We're fine standing right here."

Hammer gave a wink and closed the door. Smith was examining the explosive device as Billy returned to the living room. Zastrow was standing in a fixed position at the entrance to the bedroom, scoping out the uncleared portion of the duplex. It was obvious to the detectives he'd been in this position before.

"All good, Smitty. Ready for the next part?"

"Happy as a pig in mud. Let's do this."

Hammer walked over the yellow tape and the additional five feet of the hallway, looking into the bedroom on his left. He saw a queen-size bed and a set of legs on the floor in blue jeans. The smaller-sized tennis shoes confirmed it was probably a female.

"Josh, why don't you stay on this bedroom until we clear the other rooms? We'll be back in a jiff."

"Got it."

The bathroom was old styled and had seen better days, but was surprisingly clean like the rest of the unit, considering the "monster" who had been living here. It took Smith a minute of observation and searching to reassure himself that no bombs had been placed in the commode, sink, or the bathtub/shower area.

The bomb setup in the kitchen was unique. Zuber had rigged double switches to go off if either the back door or porch door were opened from the outside. The wires led to a device placed inside a red plastic garbage can in the corner of the room. This was where Hammer got excited. As creative as a bomber thought he could be in making and designing explosive devices, Billy's thought process was exponentially more imaginative in diffusing them. Ken Smith shook his head as he watched his long-time partner examine and take apart a bomb, always with a perpetual smile on his face. SCARY. THE MAN WAS JUST PLAIN SCARY.

They walked back over to Zastrow and patted his shoulder. Smith was first into the bedroom. He came around the bed and saw the full body of the slim female lying still on the carpeted floor. Along with the tight blue jeans, she was clothed in a powder blue sweatshirt. They could see the slit caused by a large-bladed knife or other sharp-edged weapon; the sweatshirt was blood soaked. The sickening smell of death and drying blood permeated the air. Officer Zastrow looked in the left corner of the room from his new vantage point and saw something he didn't like. It was just a slight deviation that could have been overlooked by all but the best. A large Koss-brand subwoofer sat in the corner of the large bedroom. About a quarter inch or less of dark blue wire was visible coming from underneath the speaker. It disappeared under a throw rug that had been innocuously placed from the speaker and partially under the victim's body. The reality proved to be much different than the perception.

"Hammer, Ken, check out that blue wire coming from under the subwoofer. Looks wrong to me. How 'bout you guys?"

They glanced over where Zastrow pointed. "You're right. Great eyeballin.' This is one sick dude. Kills his main squeeze. Then sets a bomb to detonate if someone moves her body."

"Bet the medical examiner would give you a big hug, Josh. They would've gone up in the blast once they lifted the body. Let's see if Mr. Zuber left a gift in the speaker." Detective Hammer closely examined the speaker to see if there were any other wires or obvious variations around it. Not seeing any, he unscrewed the back panel of the speaker and found what they suspected. A two-inch diameter lead pipe with circular-lead end caps lay at the inside base of the subwoofer. Hammer examined the pipe bomb carefully for other potential detonators. He cut the blue wire completing the circuit, ensuring no explosion would occur.

"Lead pipe! If an explosion had occurred, it would've fragged and created serious high-speed projectiles in all directions. Knowing this guy's history, there were probably additional shrapnel items such as nails inside the pipe, inflicting injuries to whomever may have been within range of the explosion. This guy's a real SOB."

Now that the connection from the explosive device to whatever mechanism under the victim was defused, Zastrow checked the carotid artery of the lifeless female using his plastic-gloved left hand.

"Nothing." He could see the post mortem lividity setting in.

"Let's make sure there are no other surprises." Hammer got down on his knees and lifted the body about five inches up on the left side.

Smith was in position with his head low enough to check underneath. He observed a black, metal pressure switch placed squarely on the floor between the victim's shoulders. He saw the blue wire from the switch disappear under the navy blue throw rug.

"Looks like we're here to tell our twisted stories until another day." Both detectives stood up.

"We combed through this duplex unit about as thoroughly as a doctor with ten-inch fingers doing a procto." Hammer stuck his right index finger up in the air for effect. "How about you, Josh? You satisfied there are no other devices in this place? We got a total of four."

"I'd be glad to check it once more, if you want. The more eyes, the better. You guys are getting me excited. It's been five months since I was checking places for IEDs from my last deployment. I'm addicted to this adrenaline rush. Hoo-rah!"

"Look at that, Smitty. Another sick dude, just like us. I'll go down and brief Tomczyk. Give me a holler when you guys are finished, and I'll bring him up the front staircase. It's his scene. He should only need a couple guys up here for the search."

Zastrow and Smith completed their final go-through as Hammer went down the front staircase. "Okay, Ski. C'mon up. We're ready for you."

Tomczyk followed Hammer up the front steps. He led him through the duplex, pointing out the devices and where they had been placed.

"This is one sick sonofabitch, bro. Having a device set to blow your dead girlfriend up into pieces just ain't right."

Sick! "You're right there, Hammer. Hopefully, we can find something to give us a clue on where they made the stuff."

"That'd be great. We also checked the basement. It's all clear."

"Bummer. Mind helping me out with the search? The assistant medical examiner and an investigator are on the way. The boss told me their ETA was around thirty minutes."

"Sure. It would be great to find that gold nugget somewhere in here."

They searched for the next half hour and did not find any other clues.

"It's like this Zuber never lived there," Smith summarized the search results.

Just then, Tomczyk heard the doorbell ring, and Dr. Thomas Jenkins and Investigator Danny Williams were escorted upstairs. They asked a million questions like usual, with Tomczyk coming up with most of the answers.

"Officer Zastrow gets the brass ring for finding this one." Tomczyk explained how the pressure switch under the body and attached speaker bomb worked. The eyes of the medical examiner personnel doubled in size.

"That's a first for me. Zastrow gets a big bottle for this one. Tell him thanks."

"Ski, can you come here a minute? I'm in the bathroom."

Tomczyk walked into the small bathroom. Hammer was on his knees.

"So I see this crumpled up piece of paper on the floor behind the garbage can. Check this out." Hammer produced an opened but crinkled up yellow paper that had RECEIPT printed on the top of it. The receipt had a date from a week ago with an address for a rented space.

"It's only a couple blocks away. One of those old buildings on Gordon Place along the Milwaukee River." Tomczyk again looked at his watch.

"Man, Deann Skenarz is really gonna be pissed at me now. I need to get another search warrant."

Chapter 27

CHICAGO BOUND

pike parked the white van in the lot of the apartment building where Sam told him. It was nearly ten o'clock.

"Man, this Chicago traffic sucks." Madman was not happy. "Over three hours to get here. Damn expressway's like a freakin' parking lot. There were a couple dudes I would've loved to jack who almost cut us off."

Spike chuckled. "Stay in that happy mood. Now we have to unload this cargo. I'm not leaving the bombs in this van. Who knows how many thieves live in this neighborhood? They'd hit the jackpot if they broke in and found them. Let me call my cuz and have him give us a little help."

"I'll say. This was a real bear loading it up. Hope he has a couple homies. What floor did you say he lived on?"

"Fourth floor, man, but there's an elevator in there. He was storing the other ones at a different location." Spike speed dialed the number. "We're downstairs, dude. Where we puttin' this stuff?" Several seconds passed. "We'll wait for you. Can't miss us. Bright white van."

Spike looked over at Madman. "He's using a garage a couple blocks away that he said is as tight as Fort Knox. He'll be down shortly, and we'll get this show on the road."

"Good. That fast-food burger just didn't fill my stomach. I'm gettin' hungry again."

"Blah, blah, bitch," Spike laughed. "Work before chow."

Spike saw his cousin jog out the front door of the large brick building. Another guy was following close behind.

"Sam must've hired one of the Chicago Bears. Look at the size of that dude."

"Just so he's legit and we can trust him."

"Pullin' your leg, man. That's my other cousin, Jamie. Smart as a box of rocks, but loyal as hell and built like a brick house."

"Good to know, Spike. Puts me at ease."

They opened the passenger side door and climbed into the back. "How ya doin', Spike?" his cousins greeted him simultaneously.

"Great. Hey, meet my bud, Madman. We've been working together for a while. This is his first time in Chi-town, so don't forget to show him a good time. Madman, meet Sam and Jamie."

"Hey."

Madman felt intimidated by their size.

"Okay. Take a left out of the lot and go straight for a couple blocks."

He turned into the alley they told him to and stopped next to a brick garage, which appeared to be primarily an industrial area.

"You're sure this place is secure?"

"Hell, yeah. No windows and a solid steel door with big locks on it. You'll see."

Sam pulled out a set of keys and unlocked both large locks on the side garage door.

"Look at the size of these things—Master Locks on steroids." He opened the tan-colored steel door and flipped on the light. One of the garage doors opened when he pushed a button on the wall. "Okay, drive that baby in and let's get the heck out of here. Not many cops patrol this area, but I still don't want one seeing us out here. We'll get stopped for sure." Another vehicle was already parked in the two-plus car garage.

"Take a quick peek inside and see what I have so far." Spike opened the rear door to the van and showed them his creations. At about the same time, an older gray Ford Aerostar minivan pulled up in the alley and stopped.

"Good timing, Joe. Okay, you guys, let's bug out of here." Sam activated the switch for the door, and they were in the van a minute later after securing the side door.

"Damn, Spike. How many bombs you make?"

"There are fifteen finished ones and ingredients plus containers and shrapnel for fifteen more. I can knock those out tomorrow. We'll really rock this city. That black box will be my special surprise to Chicago since I couldn't unveil it fully in Milwaukee."

"Really, what is it?"

"Something I cooked up from stuff I stole out of a hospital. You guys ever hear of cesium chloride?"

Sam looked at him in disbelief. "That's that radioactive shit! What the hell you doin', Spike? I don't need to glow in the dark."

"Chill, Sam. It's safe right now. I added an ingredient or two that makes it a special brew. We'll light up that stadium and everyone in it. And they thought Capone and Dillinger made Chicago famous. Wait till all this shit blows up with the cesium chloride—rainbow cloud over Soldier Field."

"You sure you want to waste that many people?"

"Why not? Screw 'em. Just a bunch of useless Bear and Packer fans, along with a crooked mayor and governor. The place is also going to be full of pigs and uniform-wearing, killing-machine soldiers and vets."

"Can't argue with that. What were you going to do with this in Milwaukee?"

"I was thinking small time there. Maybe a Bucks game down at the Bradley Center in a month or two. They have a military/law enforcement appreciation night. Since we had to get the hell out of Milwaukee before they caught us, we might as well go for a little gusto and break up the party at Soldier Field. My drunken old man used to tell me to 'Go for all the gusto!' Well, let's do it. The world will be our stage, and this'll further our cause."

"You're a crazy mofo, Spike. I'll drink to that any day. Speakin' of gusto, we bought a couple cases of beer the other day. Let's grab a couple pizzas and party. They got a great joint down the block from us. What you guys want on it? I'll make the call, and they can deliver."

"Now you're talkin'. Let's go."

They drove back to the apartment and popped the caps off some beer bottles. The five of them sat down at the kitchen table to discuss their plans.

"We need to have some sort of distractive device go off a couple miles from the stadium. Where would be the best place for that?" Zuber took a long drag off his cigarette and a gulp from the bottle of a local craft beer.

"How about somewhere on Michigan Avenue? There will be a crap-load of people out holiday shopping. All the decorations are lit up, and every spoiled brat will be with his parents, buying from all those corporate greed machines. Rich bastards."

"Perfect. You got a map of the city?"

"Yeah, plus I have a laptop." Joey grabbed his laptop off the kitchen counter, opened it, and was on Google Maps in seconds. A map of Chicago came up. He placed it into satellite mode and pushed the zoom-in arrow several times. "Let's see. Soldier Field is right here." He pointed to the oval structure located along the lakefront.

Sam looked at the screen. "Here's the problem. There's no parking lot next to it. Not like any other stadium in the damn country that has car parking within fifty feet. There's no freakin' parking lot for a couple blocks."

"No worries, we'll figure something out. Joey, go farther up along Michigan Avenue. Let's find a place for our diversion."

Chapter 28

THIRTY-EIGHT HOURS TO DETONATION

I t was a quarter of five in the morning when Tomczyk walked into his house. Another twenty-plus hour workday in one week. This case was draining the life out of him. The events of the night swirled over and over in his head like a runaway merry-go-round.

The interviews and positive identifications of Michael Zuber; the two search warrants, discovery of the dead body, and the explosive devices found there—including the IED underneath the body. That second search warrant seals the deal of Zuber cooking up his explosive devices. Just what we need: a true Mad Scientist. Some nutcase on the loose who knows how to make explosives and has a hatred for law enforcement and people. Why did Zuber steal the license plates off his dead girlfriend's car, and what was he going to do with them? Who the heck is he with? Where is he, and what else is he cooking up in his deranged mind? He's no anarchist, cult worshipper, or Hammerskin. This guy came straight from hell.

On a positive note, all the evidence was packaged and inventories were completed. On a negative note, he had a stack of reports to file when he went back into work in the morning, along with spending a half hour briefing his lieutenant and captain. He laid down on the couch in the living room for a two-hour power nap. Max, his acrobatic jet black cat, jumped on Declan's chest and did the rub against his chin. The last thing Declan heard before falling into solid REM sleep was Max's purring.

"Anne, are you able to come to our office this morning? I want to have you here when I brief my bosses. It's nitty-gritty time. That way you'll get the rest of the scoop on the second search warrant and everything we recovered from the first. Pictures will be included, but you'll have to bring your own popcorn. And, sorry to say, you won't be making dinner tonight for us. Sounds like it's going to be a full day."

"Guess so." Tomczyk could hear the disappointment in her voice. "Another day then. What time's the meeting?"

"Nine."

"Guess that'll have to be our date."

Tomczyk was falling for this beautiful woman. Everything about her was fantastic. Would it interfere with his focus? He had grieved enough for the woman he loved and lost. Marie told him on her deathbed to go on with his life, and it was about time he did. Was it possible to fall in love with another woman as much as he had fallen in love with his first? *Do your reports, Declan, and find these homicidal maniacs. There will be time later to pursue your off-duty passions.*

He dialed the phone number to Chicago PD intelligence division.

"Is this a bad thing when you start memorizing a different area code and phone number? What's up, Ski?" came a voice with that unmistakable South Side Chicago accent.

"Mac, we hit the hornet's nest last night and came away with big pay dirt. Can I ask a favor of you?"

"Sure, what da'ya need? Long time, no hear," MacCarthy said sarcastically. They had been sharing information nearly every day with their updates.

"We made a positive ID on our main guy here. He's got to have some connection down by you. Can you run him and see what you have?"

"Go for it. Got some paper and my writing stick. Ready to copy."

Tomczyk gave him all of Zuber's info and a brief synopsis of the night's events.

"Yeah, he vanished like a fart in the wind—for now. I'll be back on the trail this afternoon after briefing my bosses, the FBI, and, of course, finishing this dang blasted paperwork."

"Wow, you have the same issues we have down here. If it ain't written down, it didn't happen, right?"

"You got it."

"Hang on, man. Let me put you on hold and fire up my computer." A minute later, MacCarthy was back on the phone. "Got him. All we have is one crummy field interview card. He was in a car with another guy a week and a half ago on the corner of Twenty-fifth and Lincoln at oh-dark-thirty. Says the cop got called to a suspicious auto complaint."

"That's right by the Biograph Theatre!"

The phone was silent. "How in the hell would some cheesehead detective from Milwaukee know about the Biograph Theatre being at Twenty-fifth and Lincoln in Chicago?"

"C'mon, Mac. I've seen *Public Enemies* six times. And they have this thing called the Internet you can research stuff on. You ever hear of it?"

"I'm still shocked a muscle-bound jock like you even has a brain. FYI, this was a couple days before the cops from the Nineteenth found the 'bogus bomb in a bag' sitting by the front doors of the theatre with the extortion letter. What were they asking for, twenty million bucks or something? These turds had to be scoping it out first."

"Beautiful. Who was he with?"

"I'm running the guy now. Samuel Rider, white male, DOB July 8, 1985. Has an address on the South Side. They were in a maroon Buick Skylark with Wisconsin plates. Rider's a real gem. Three felony convictions and a slew of misdemeanors, along with a pending battery to police officer and resisting charge. Spent about five total years in the pen. Guess he doesn't like the 'popo' either?"

"The Buick is Zuber's. We found it hidden in the bushes half a block from the building where we executed one of our search warrants. It was obvious he didn't want us to find it, but some of the officers at my old district are like Labrador Retrievers in heat. They have the knack of finding stuff people don't want found. The car had altered plates, and it was also observed leaving Milwaukee City Hall yesterday morning. Some bald, white guy left a backpack containing seven big pipe bombs in the lobby. A really alert cop spotted him and saved the day before he could arm the system. She ended up getting a broken sternum when he kicked her, but she's tough as nails and still gave pursuit."

"Damn. That's solid. So what's next?"

"Let me tell my bosses. I'm briefing them at nine. You're a rock star, Mac. And a rock star with a bottle of that cheap Irish whiskey I now owe you."

"Ah, laddy, I love ya. No such thing as a bottle of cheap Irish whiskey, though. You should know that, Declan!"

"Yeah, yeah. I'll talk at you in a couple hours."

"All right. The Chicago PD is here to serve—and to be served."

"Later, Mac." Tomczyk hung up while still laughing at MacCarthy's comments. *This is what it takes to solve crimes. Talking cop to cop.*

It was 8:52 a.m. The buzzer to the main door rang, and the visitor was allowed in. She walked over to Tomczyk's desk.

"You're looking your usual radiant self this morning, Agent Dvorak."

"Always trying to schmooze the feds. Any developments?"

"Just got off the phone with Bill MacCarthy from CPD. You remember him from the meeting, right?"

"How could I forget? It was like you two were long lost brothers who met for the first time in twenty years."

"C'mon, Anne. Was it that obvious we are kindred spirits?" They smiled. "Anyway, he ran Zuber in their databases. Seems he was FI'd by a uniformed squad who was sent to check out a suspicious vehicle across the street from the Biograph Theatre three days before that fake bomb and extortion note were found at the front door. Unfortunately, the two incidents were never hooked up. Turns out the cop handed in the FI card in the next day, then left for a vacation in Hawaii. He was out of pocket when it occurred. Otherwise, I'm sure he would've added two plus two. It didn't get entered into the data base until after the Biograph incident. So the lines were never connected there either."

"Bummer."

"Well, let's go in for the brief. Sorry, you'll have to hear the rerun version of some of this. Great stuff, but I'd wager our bad guy has left Milwaukee. Not sure how he found out we were on his trail, but something sure spooked him." His mind went back to the female at the nursing home. *Should've grabbed her name.*

Upon walking into the conference room, Lieutenant Ned Englebort was already conversing with three other intel detectives. Captain Spinnola came in a short time later with his usual "off the storefront window" look of impeccable dress.

"Morning everyone." In Spinnola's hands were two boxes of Krispy Kreme donuts. "No real meeting starts in any police department until the donuts and coffee arrive. Dig in. Coffee is in the corner."

After the scramble of securing donuts and a cup of joe, Spinnola looked at Tomczyk. "Okay, Declan, you're up. What do we have?"

Tomczyk meticulously walked them through the previous evening's events, starting with the undetonated bomb at city hall and his initial interview of Demetrius Simms. He showed a number of photos that were taken of both scenes, including the explosive devices at each entry point, in the speaker, along with several of the victim, her wound, and the pressure switch under her body. He concluded with a booking photo of Richard Zuber and all the information the Milwaukee Police Department had on him. He also related what he had obtained from Detective MacCarthy.

"Where do we go from here?" asked Lieutenant Engelbort. "How do we know what he did with everything?"

"My guess is Chicago, but I can't be positive. I think they have something big planned. They were kind of mirroring things in Milwaukee and Chicago. If Zuber pulled up stakes here, I'd put my money on him going to Chicago to pull the big Kahuna. Unfortunately, we don't know what that is yet. George from the nursing home said his former dead friend, Idzi Rutkowski, was planning a big hit in Milwaukee. That ended when he and his teenage sidekick blew themselves up making a bomb with over a hundred sticks of dynamite. For some reason, and you can get an FBI behavioral analysis unit agent to either prove me wrong or confirm my theory, I think Zuber wants to become Idzi the Second, thus the whole Mad Bomber portrayal."

Captain Spinnola sat and thought about it for a moment.

"While you're pondering, Captain, a police officer spoke to several neighbors across the street from the warehouse at our second search warrant. They saw a white van parked in front of it at about six last night. Two white males were loading boxes into it. The witnesses weren't overly concerned because people are moving stuff in and out of those buildings all the time. The one subject matched the description of Zuber, but we haven't identified the second guy yet. From the description Officer Bicker provided of the suspect at the city hall incident, that's the second guy. A late-model, windowless, white Chevrolet van was reported stolen four nights ago on the East Side.

Driver left the engine running at the gas station when he went in to buy a soda. Here's the info on the vehicle, along with the license plate number. My guess is those boxes were full of explosive devices or ingredients. I also think they're going to use cesium chloride somehow. The hospital reporting the theft of the radioactive material two weeks ago said six ounces were taken. We've only recovered a fraction of it so far, and that was in the envelope these guys attached to the headstone at the cemetery. That still leaves a lot of bad stuff out there."

"Not good." Spinnola looked over at Agent Dvorak. "What's the FBI's stand on this one, Anne?"

"I'm going to brief my ASAC when I step out of this room. He only had the info up until the close of business yesterday. I think Declan's right. Let me get back to you ASAP. My suggestion is to get Declan deputized by the US Marshal, giving him federal authority. I also think we should drive down to Chicago and dig further into this guy who was in the car with Zuber. No question in my mind he's the Chicago connection for the bombing at the cemetery where the cop was killed, along with the other explosive incidents that occurred there, including the two from last night. I'll get some FBI agents over here to hook up with your detectives and help track down every lead we can about who Michael Zuber is, relatives, and any other associates they can find. Our timeline is unknown, so we better hit the bricks running."

"I concur. I'll call Marshal Evans and get the ball rolling for the deputization sometime today. Sooner the better." Captain Spinnola looked directly into Tomczyk's eyes with a laser glare. "Ski, a hell of a job, but nothing less than the excellence you give us every day. Find these miscreants and shut them down before anybody else gets hurt or killed. Do us proud, son! Anne, make sure Declan doesn't go full Marine on us and kill all the bad guys before we sort everything out."

"You can count on it, Captain. I'll be his sensitive side."

"This meeting's over. You all know what you need to do. Declan, I need all the reports from last night finished before you leave so I can brief the chief."

"Anything for you, boss." Tomczyk closed his eyes briefly, thinking about another marathon day of work, all on two-and-a-half hours of sleep.

Chapter 29

CHICAGO: THIRTY-THREE HOURS TO DETONATION

How's it going, Spike?"

He looked up from his position at the workbench in the garage. "Great, dude. These are coming together nicely. I have ten more to make. Have any problems buying the rest of the stuff I asked for?"

Sam shook his head approvingly. "Got it all. No questions asked from anybody at the store."

"Good . . . if they only knew."

Sam produced two shopping bags full of materials. "Where do you want them?"

"Right there on the floor will be great. I'm keeping the workbench reserved for the devices so I can start wiring them in series of three when I finish each one. I'll do the final wirings before we leave. That way I'll just have to push the timer when we park the van."

"No chance of that stuff going off now, right?"

"Naw. Just like most other explosives. Purrs like a kitten until a detonation device is added. Then the kitten turns into a lion." He chuckled to himself at the analogy.

"So why are you making this a timed detonation instead of the usual way we've been doing it?"

"Because we'll need to get the hell out of there. Can't risk being around when it blows. I'm thinking total pandemonium, and we don't need any drama or obstacles that could screw us up or trap us there."

"Makes sense."

"I was going to give us about fifteen minutes—like we discussed last night. That will be enough to vacate the area and still have a good viewing point for the explosion. Won't be as personal, but I guarantee this baby will be viewed and felt from a long way off. We'll still be close enough to be involved. And we definitely want to be upwind from the cloud it creates. I'm hoping the cesium chloride is going to do some serious damage."

"No shit, Sherlock." They had to laugh at that. "Just so you know, I got what we need for the paint job. Perfect plan, man. None of those badge-carrying fools will suspect a thing."

Twenty-six Hours to Detonation

It was just before five o'clock when Anne and Declan parked the unmarked squad across the street from Chicago PD Headquarters. They walked inside the now-familiar building, produced their credentials, and were waived through the magnetometers.

"You know where you're going?" asked a middle-aged, uniformed officer who looked like he was allergic to a treadmill.

"Yes, Officer, we've been here before."

They were let into the intelligence division seconds after buzzing the door. MacCarthy rose from a desk in the corner and came over to welcome them. There were about ten other personnel in the room, working at their desks.

"How was the trip?"

Tomczyk spoke up. "Oh, you know. The Chicago Factor is always in the air, but it was easier getting downtown on the expressway than the poor people who had to leave and go north. The Kennedy was great, but that Dan Ryan was not my friend. You guys are all saints for having to do this on a daily basis."

"I'd like to say you get used to the traffic, but that'd be lying. I'll show you what we got on your boy, Rider." He opened a newly created folder containing papers. "Here's his arrest record, convictions, sentences, associates, you name it. Where do you want to start? I can tell you the address he gave to the cop the night of the FI with Zuber is no good. According to the postal service and utilities, he checked out of there the end of October. No forwarding address either. He had the same address with DOT and Accurint databases. My guess is he's hanging his hat with a friend or a chick. In a city of nearly three million people, finding them becomes a daunting task."

"We can't help you much. All we bring to the table is a stolen white van, stolen license plates, and a turd bird from our city with an unknown amount of explosives and WMD material. Not a fair trade. The important thing is I brought two bottles of Irish whiskey. The Jameson's for you and the Bushmills Black Bush is for the victory party, whenever that happens."

"Ah, laddy-boy, you're a true Irishman." MacCarthy stood up, holding a bottle in each hand, and addressed his fellow detectives. "See, you guys? Here's a Milwaukee detective who respects and admires the Chicago PD detectives." Laughs and comments came from Mac's newly found audience. He sat back down, looked over at Anne, and raised his right hand. "Special Agent Dvorak, I want you to know the cap off of either of these specimens of beauty will not be removed until the perpetrators of these offenses are on their way to jail and the bombs are safely secured."

"Fair enough for me, Detective Mac. I can be a Bushmills person when the time is right."

"Now you're talking. Well, let's get to work. Do we have cell phone info on Zuber?"

Tomczyk looked at his notepad. "Not yet. No records, bills, or receipts for phone companies were found for him at either search location. The dead girlfriend had one of the big carriers, but Zuber must have taken the phone and either dumped it or turned it off. Haven't gotten any pings off cell towers. We have a subpoena for records, but those won't come until tomorrow morning. I have a detective assigned to tracking down phone numbers, outgoing and ingoing, when we get the info."

"Good. Rider just got off parole three months ago and, of course, his PO had the old address also. She had him working at a small machine shop in the Fillmore District over on the West Side. I spoke to the owner this afternoon. He said Rider quit two months ago, only mentioning that he had found a better job with higher pay. Said Rider was a pretty good employee and never asked for a reference for the new position. He gave me a cell phone number that has since been wiped clean. One of those fly-by-night phone companies. We're working with other internal contacts to find out about the new job, but they're having glitches and can't get me current employment info. They still have him at the machine shop."

"How about prison mates? Maybe Rider's rooming with one of his prison homies."

"Didn't go there yet. Good idea, though. Admin staffs are all gone. We'll have to make it an emergency request. Prison staffs move like frozen molasses sometimes, so it may take a while. I'll get on the horn when we're done. What else can you think of at this time?" MacCarthy touched his forehead as his mind searched for other opportunities of investigation.

"Think we're good for now. What do you guys do for chow around here? We haven't eaten since noon, and I need to feed the beast before I go into a lack-of-food coma."

"Simple enough. Let me place a call to Joliet Prison and get the ball rolling. By the way, all I can tell you is that we better have this wrapped up tomorrow by five. I have season tickets for da Bears-Packers game at seven. It's going to be a big game with a bunch of military and law enforcement officers there for the celebration of Soldier Field and—" He stopped mid-sentence and glared at Declan and Anne. "Don't tell me!"

Tomcyzk nearly fell out of the chair he had just sat down on. "I knew they were playing against each other on Thursday night, but never even considered something like this being a possible target. Why is this game such a big event?"

"Soldier Field is the oldest stadium in the NFL, and will be celebrating over eighty years of operation. It was built as a tribute and memorial to all American soldiers who died in wars. Tomorrow night's a special celebration because of the ninety-five-year rivalry between the Bears and the Packers. There's also a military/law enforcement tribute taking place during halftime. A number of VIPs will be there, including the governor and the Chicago mayor. Holy balls, that would be a media frenzy if something like this happened!"

"Guess this is going at the top of the list for possible targets. Going to be tough covering that place and not causing a massive stir."

"I'll say." MacCarthy was perplexed. "Let me call the lieutenant in here. Looks like your case may have just leaped up into high priority."

"Well, this is not very reassuring," Anne surmised. "Some guys may blow up a major professional football venue in the third-largest city in the United States in twenty-four hours or less, armed with a boatload of bombs, and we don't have a hill of beans to go on but two guys' names, without the slightest idea of where they are. Is that about it?"

"Well, that's not quite everything," Tomczyk said, adding to the difficulty of the situation. "We know they have a stolen, white van with Wisconsin plates on it."

"Sorry, forgot," she said, somewhat hopelessly.

"I'm really hungry now."

Chapter 30

CHICAGO: TWENTY-TWO HOURS
TO DETONATION

We're good on the paint job, Spike. Great idea. I'll finish the striping tomorrow so it'll fit right in." Sam took a gulp from his beer. "Joey and Madman are briefed on the diversion plan and the location. You'll have to tell them how to detonate that bomb and where you want it placed. How 'bout we have a final go 'round tomorrow morning? They'll be back in an hour, and we can finish watching those movies I got at the store. A couple thrillers, just like we're going to do." When he started laughing, he nearly choked on the smoke he had just inhaled from his cigarette.

"Good plan. And don't kill yourself. I fell asleep in class when they were talking about that lifesaving shit, so I can't help out."

"Fair enough. We still have some pizza left from last night. You want a couple pieces?"

"Yeah, that was great stuff."

"Told ya."

— — —

"My butt's dragging, Anne. I'm going to call it a night. I have got to get some solid sleep tonight. If Soldier Field is the target, we'll all need to be at the top of our game. If not, we'll never figure out where Zuber is going to hit and stop him."

Anne moved closer and embraced Declan in the hallway of the hotel. She stroked his wavy brown hair and gave him a long kiss. When they finished, she looked him squarely in the eyes.

"Declan Tomczyk, you're one of the best people I've ever met."

"Feeling's mutual, pretty lady." He returned the kiss. "If you need something, give me a shout. If not, I'll be in dreamland all night. Meet you in the lobby at six forty-five. Is that good for you?"

"Perfect. Time enough to grab some breakfast and head out. I contacted our Chicago office. Five people from their domestic terrorism squad will meet us at CPD Headquarters at eight thirty."

"Good, we'll definitely need the help. I'm hoping my MPD boys will be calling with some info from their leads. The call I got from them today was not very promising. They struck out on every place they hit. Good night, Anne. Sweet dreams."

"Hoping you'll be in one of them."

"Now you're making me blush."

Chapter 31

CHICAGO: TWELVE HOURS TO DETONATION

Declan showed up in the hotel lobby at exactly six forty-five. Anne was seated in one of the large, brown leather chairs checking her emails.

"Here we are in this beautiful, historic hotel on Michigan Avenue and can't really take it all in," she said, admiring the charm of the lobby.

"I hear you. Too much on my mind to enjoy this place right now. Another time."

"Are you asking me out again, Detective?"

Declan's face blushed red. "A figure of speech. Let me remove my size thirteen from my mouth. And for the record, I'd love to ask you out for a date again."

"Great. Right now, a breakfast will work perfectly. I checked the menu, and it's very reasonable."

"Can't tell you how fantastic I feel. Woke up at five and got a great workout in. Quite the monster gym for a hotel. My engine's back running on all cylinders."

They were on the road by seven thirty for the five-mile drive down Michigan Avenue to CPD Headquarters. The eight thirty brief with the other agencies went well, with the exception of "no new news." Tomczyk was getting antsy and questioning himself on whether he made the right choice about Chicago. He kept looking at his watch, wondering if making the drive here instead of staying in Milwaukee and guarding the city he was sworn to protect was the right decision.

"C'mon, Declan. Don't look so glum. You did the right thing. I feel it in my heart of hearts. This was right, you coming to Chicago." Anne rubbed his elbow reassuringly. "Besides, you know a woman's intuition is seldom wrong. You heard what I told you last night, how I feel about you. Totally women's intuition!" She smiled and gently pinched his forearm.

He smiled back. As he was about to respond, his cell phone rang. It was ten-thirty-five. He perked up when he saw who the caller was.

"Ski, this is Blaze. I'm so sorry, man. It took forever to get here, and these people grudgingly gave up the info about their son. We stirred up a cesspool of old and hurtful memories. Remember when they used to talk about Dahmer dissecting rabbits and squirrels at seven or eight-years-old? Well, this dude was blowing them up at that age. Child prodigy with an IQ like Ted Kaczynski who couldn't corral his emotions or temper. They spent a fortune on private and specialty schools, counseling, and psych wards to straighten him out. Dad even got him a job at one of the nursing homes he owns in River Hills as a maintenance man, but the kid got fired for missing too much work, along with a positive urine test for cocaine and marijuana. Neither parent has spoken to Zuber in months. They are definitely distraught over the broken relationship."

"Good work, Blaze. Anything at all for associates in Chi-town?"

"Yeah. That Sam Rider guy. He's Zuber's cousin. Rider also has a younger brother, Jamie Rider. He's 6'6" and over 300 pounds. Heck, that's even bigger than you. They said Sam lives somewhere on the South Side of Chicago, and Jamie may be living with him. They provided us with the parents' addresses and phone numbers if you want them to call for current info."

"No, hold that. Let's see if we can get that from this end. Don't want to spook the parents and have them tip their kids off. They may have issues, but they're still their kids."

"My exact thoughts. "We'll finish up here and head back to the office to man the hoses. There's a couple other small things we want to check out that may help you."

"Fantastic, thanks for the call. You perked me up. Thought I went down the wrong rabbit hole coming here."

"I think you're in the right hole. Now, we need to find that rabbit."

"Keep me posted, brotha, and thanks." Tomczyk hung up the phone. "Okay, back on the trail. Sam Rider is Zuber's cousin. Sam has a younger brother named Jamie. Mac, get them magical fingers of yours running and track these guys down. They've got to be our connection to Zuber."

His cell phone rang again. "Detective Tomczyk."

"Ski, Susie from intel. Phone company finally came through with the phone records from Angela Culbertson's cell. There's a recurring record to and from a cell phone number of 414-220-5555. It's gotta be your guy. And here's a bonus. The cell phone they found on that homicide victim in Gordon Park had at least ten phone calls to and from that number. The last call was made from Culbertson at 2:11 p.m. on the day she was murdered. We checked the number, and it doesn't come back listed to any of the major carriers, so I can't get any provider or customer info for you. Sorry. One last thing: An agent from the Secret Service just called. Said something about finally getting into a thumb drive you gave him several weeks ago. He apologized a couple times. Said the pass protection was amazing and something he's never seen before. Needs to speak to you ASAP. Mentioned it was a matter of national security, but it had to be on a secure phone since the info was all classified."

"Fantastic news." He thought for a second. The hidden thumb drive found in Squirt's boot was classified. *That's not good.* "Did you tell him I'm on a mission here in Chicago?"

"Sure did. He just said at your earliest convenience."

"Thanks, Suze. Lovin' ya."

"I know. Later, and good luck."

Tomczyk disconnected the phone, and the adrenaline started pumping back into him.

"Now we're cooking. Man, I needed those calls." *A matter of national security. That'll have to wait. We have major drama going on right now.*

"Jamie Roger Rider, DOB, January 2, 1989. Last known address as of three months ago is in an apartment over on Sixty-sixth and Halstead. Nothing major as an adult: drug possession, a couple thefts, and property damage. Armed robbery and burglary arrests as a juvie. He was obviously just trying to find his way."

"Of course. Young man trying to grow his wings."

"Ever cynical." Anne shook her head.

"You're right. But after the thousandth guy you run across with the same story, your mind gets tainted. Happens to the best of us." Mac shrugged his shoulders. "Not saying it's right, just keepin' it real."

"Mac, can you do anything with a cell phone? The phone records of Zuber's dead girlfriend came back and our intel analyst is almost positive it's his. Said it's not a major carrier customer number, though."

"I have a contact at Cell Tower Central. Give me the number, and I'll run it."

In five minutes, MacCarthy was back with an answer. "Good stuff. That number pinged off a cell tower in the Englewood area on Tuesday night at about ten. Nothing since. I told them to put a flag on it in case anything goes back in or out of it."

"Smart move. Narrowing it down. The scumbag kills his girlfriend, then rigs the apartment with bombs set to blow off when the 'popo' come knocking. He loads up a stolen van with explosives, drives down to Chicago, and hooks up with his cousins to plan something big. We need to confirm that Jamie Rider, and hopefully Mr. Samuel Rider, are living in that building and plead with a district attorney for a search warrant." Tomczyk was growing happier by the minute.

"I can go one step further. They got partial fingerprints off some evidence from the bomb hoax bag left at the Biograph. Couldn't match it with anybody at the time, but if the ID people have known ten prints, they can get enough PC for a warrant based on that."

"Now you're talkin', Mac. Let's do it."

Chapter 32

CHICAGO: FOUR HOURS TO DETONATION

I t was nearly three o'clock when the Chicago PD SWAT Team stacked outside the apartment building. Plainclothes officers had been "eyeballing" it for the last two hours, with no movement of anyone matching the photographs or vehicle info they each had of the suspects. The ten heavily armed and tactical-gear-wearing police officers were let into the building by two CPD plainclothes bomb technicians. One of them was holding onto a leash attached to a jet-black lab.

"Smokie didn't smell any explosives in there. Have fun breaching the door."

The sound of the apartment door being smashed in a minute later and, "Police, search warrant," was easily heard by residents in the building.

A short time later came the words over the portable radios, "All secure, send in the detectives."

"Okay, looks like it's show time. Let's go!" MacCarthy walked over to the SWAT supervisor. "What do we got, Sarge?"

"Looks good to me. Didn't see any weapons, explosives, or anything to worry about. Unfortunately, no bodies. Just a typical dirty apartment with guys living in it."

"Good, thanks. We'll handle it from here. If you don't mind leaving one squad behind to cover us while we do the search, we'd be much appreciative."

"You got it, Mac." The sergeant looked over at two of his men. "Jives and Walters, hang out with the detectives until they're done with this place. Put yourselves back in when you're done."

"Copy that, Sarge."

The apartment was bigger than expected: three bedrooms, a kitchen, living room, and dining room area. Ornate construction from a long, lost time. McCarthy took the lead.

"Let's split her up and knock this place out. I'll grab photos of the door and doorjamb damage, then all the rooms before we start. Two people to a room. Fair enough?"

"Excellent. This is your stage, Mac; we're only support." Tomczyk was now in his element. He loved the mystery of doing searches. Dope, guns, records, and paperwork, all revealing secrets about individuals and their activities.

"Right. Whose stage is this again, smart aleck?"

"Okay, maybe we have a little more than a bit part."

The complete search was over in an hour. Two backpacks containing clothes, personal property, and hygiene products were in a back bedroom with two day beds in it. No identification markings were in either pack. Personal-use stashes of marijuana were in the living room and burnt marijuana butts in several ashtrays. Utility bills of Jamie Rider were located, along with property and identification paperwork of Samuel Rider to confirm his living there. An old table in the dining room contained the most revealing evidence. A map of Chicago was spread out across the table and a Dell laptop computer sat next to it. There were several pieces of paper with writing and doodling on them: "650 Michigan Ave"; "Two should be enough." Also printed on the paper was "Soldier Field, game starts at seven." Tomczyk read the letters and numbers on the other piece of paper. "APJ173." Below it was written "ABU478."

"You gotta be kidding me!"

"What do you have, Declan?" Anne asked as she, MacCarthy, and CPD Detective John 'Duke' Dukeyser walked over to him.

He pointed to the top line. "This is the plate number to Zuber's dead girlfriend's car. We put it into NCIC as stolen and taken in connection with the homicide. See the next line." He slid his finger down where he wanted them to see. "They made some adjustments and now have a whole new plate. Hopefully, we'll be seeing these again real soon."

The large, tan garage door opened up in an alley off of Sixty-third Parkway and Green Street in the CHIRAC neighborhood of Chicago, and a blue van with white horizontal striping drove out and stopped. A second vehicle pulled out after it. The driver of the car stepped out and walked back into the garage. Shortly afterward, the electric door closed again. The same white male, wearing a black leather jacket and blue jeans, reappeared from the side of the garage and got back into the car. Both vehicles drove away through the alley. Thousands of activities occur daily in major cities across the country and are never seen by anyone. This time, the white lace curtains in the kitchen window of the sole single-family house on the block slowly moved back to their original closed position. The elderly woman removed her hand from the curtain and wondered why a Chicago Public Works van would drive out of a private garage, followed by a separate vehicle. It was suspicious enough for her to remove the wall phone receiver and dial the general number for the Chicago Police Department.

— — —

"Honestly, are these the best tasting Chicago Hot Dogs you've ever eaten in your life?" On their way back to headquarters before heading over to Soldier Field, they made a quick stop at one of Chicago's famous hot dog stands, knowing it could be a long night. It's nearly impossible to do great police work on an empty stomach, and they were famished.

"Dang straight, Mac. Hot dogs are the last true American meat. Pretty much everything in 'em except the kitchen sink, but they sure do taste fantastic with all the Chicago-style toppings."

MacCarthy happened to have his portable radio tuned to the frequency of the police district they were in. "Squad 6287, meet the caller at 6315 Parkway Drive regarding a suspicious vehicle. Plate number on a blue with white-stripes Chicago Public Works van was ABU478. Be advised, no record for that plate number."

The four of them looked at each other in amazement, knowing they had the exact same thought at the exact same moment.

"Duke, you and Anne head to that call and get the details. Ski and I will shoot over to Soldier Field and give the supervisors the latest and greatest. They're all aware it's a possible target, but now we have additional info to get them up to speed."

"You got it, Mac. We'll keep you posted on what comes up with the call."

"Excellent. Ski, you ready to go?"

Tomczyk slammed down the last bite of his third hot dog and gave a "thumbs up." "Let's rock and roll." He grabbed the cup containing his ice-filled drink.

Chapter 33

CHICAGO: ONE HOUR PLUS
TO DETONATION

I t was just after five thirty when an older green Ford Aerostar minivan
stopped along the curb in front of a large home decor and furniture
specialty store in the six hundred block of North Michigan Avenue.

"I'm going to take a slow ride around the block. You know where
to place the bag. I'll be parked facing northbound on Rush Street, the
next street over." Joey pointed west to make sure Madman understood.

"Got it, dude. See ya in a couple." Madman got out of the van and
began walking. He rounded the corner and headed westbound on West
Erie Street. When he reached the end of the white building, he ducked
into the alley and placed the blue Nike backpack on the concrete next
to it. He then continued on Erie and saw the minivan parked along the
curb at the first parking meter. He climbed in the front seat.

"All good."

Madman pulled the cell phone out of his left coat pocket and
unlocked it.

"You know how to work that thing, right?"

"Damn straight I do. Move it!"

Joey made a right turn to go east on Erie and slowly drove down the street. Just as they were passing the spot where Madman placed the backpack, he pushed some buttons, activating a detonation switch and completing the circuit. A loud explosion rang out. Laughter erupted from inside the van. "All right, that bitch worked! Let's get the hell out of here."

Joey looked in his rear view mirror and watched the chaos beginning to form on the south side of Erie Street. Cars were stopping, and a crowd of pedestrians were gathering. He couldn't tell if anyone was down from the explosion or not. *Collateral damage if there was,* he thought to himself. *This was urban warfare against all these nasty, consumer-glutton whores!*

— — —

"All squads, be advised. We have a report of an explosion that just occurred in the south alley on West Erie between Michigan and Rush Street. Chicago Fire and Rescue are en route. Unknown casualties or damage. Advise if responding. Updates forthcoming."

A number of squads "miked" into the radio, notifying the dispatcher they were responding.

MacCarthy and Tomczyk were nearing Soldier Field when the call came over all channels. Tomczyk punched his right knee. "Dang it! Not good."

"You want me to start heading over there?"

"I'm not feeling it. Zuber's going big and an explosion in the business district along the Magnificent Mile isn't a big enough fish for him. I'm convinced that phony Chicago Public Works van is the key. We find the van, we'll find Zuber and the explosives. I'll keep my money on them showing up at the game. By the way, if you HAD been going to the game tonight, where were your seats going to be?"

"Oh, sure. You buy me a bottle of whiskey and now you think you own me. My stomach is still sick at the thought of my brother-in-law sitting in the seat next to my wife because I'm in a squad car working with some useless detective from Wis-CON-sin when I should be getting ready to watch da Bears mishandle the Packers."

"Where's the love? By the way, did you notify all the squads at the stadium about the van?"

"Oh, yeah. My guess is every cop in Cook County is searching high and low for that baby."

"That's what I like to hear."

"You see the black smoke up there? That's the residuals of the explosion."

"Yeah. Let's hope casualties and damage are kept to a minimum."

MacCarthy took the Soldier Field exit off South Lake Shore Drive and made the right turn onto East Eighteenth Drive. The street changed into Museum Campus Drive. Straight ahead, Declan could see the hundreds of boats moored at Burnham Harbor on Chicago's famous lakefront. Beyond that were the alluring sky blue waters of Lake Michigan. Since it was the second half of November, he reminded himself the water was great to gaze at or ride a boat on, but way too cold to sunbathe at or swim in. He thought about the dozens of times his dad had taken him out on the lake for fishing and to reflect on life. They were disrupted by the reality of iconic Soldier Field stadium to the left and Detective MacCarthy's voice.

"Ski, we'll stop off at the command post and check in. Roll call was at four, but I'm guessing they'll understand our tardiness because of the circumstances."

"Okay by me."

MacCarthy parked the black Crown Victoria next to a number of other marked and unmarked vehicles in the lot on the northeast side of the stadium. They stepped into the mobile command post vehicle and were met by the uniformed lieutenant assigned as the event commander.

"How ya doin', Mac?"

"Good. Lieut, this is Detective Declan Tomczyk, Milwaukee Police. He's the lead investigator on their case."

"Thanks for the help, Declan. So this Zuber guy's a pretty bad hombre?"

"Yes, sir. We're almost 100 percent sure he's responsible for at least three of our homicides and possibly the killing of the police officer at the cemetery here in Chicagoland. He's also good for the attempted homicide of a Milwaukee detective and several other recent bombings we've had in our city. Oh, yeah. He's a class-A piece of crap."

"Got it. We have about two hundred officers here, inside and out, along with three bomb tech units and a WMD team. They all have the pictures and other info on Zuber and the Rider brothers. All the outside units have the vehicle info on the van. Duke and the female FBI agent, Anne, checked in just before you and gave us the description of the other vehicle that came out of the garage with the van. They said the witness only got a partial plate number, and we broadcasted the info to all units."

"Then you're up to speed. I'm guessing you already know about the explosion on Erie Street."

"Unfortunately, yes. That was my beat a thousand years ago. Knew every square inch of that area and can picture where they placed that bomb. Some of the best years of my career were on the Mag Mile."

"Back in the good ole days of police work, I'm sure," Declan responded.

"No question. But that discussion is for another day."

"Amen, brother!"

"We'll cruise around and remain on the outside," MacCarthy reassured the Event Commander. "Let's go, Ski."

"Ski?"

"It's a long and boring story. Good to meet you, sir." Tomczyk shook the Lieutenant's hand.

"Likewise."

As they walked back to the squad, Tomczyk noticed it was 6:29. MacCarthy drove north on Museum Campus Drive and pointed to the squad blocking traffic on their left side. "We shut down the tunnel on both ends from here to McFetridge Drive. No sense even giving those guys a chance to detonate anything under the stadium."

"Good work."

MacCarthy drove up to the circle drive in front of the Shedd Aquarium and stopped.

"Can't tell you how much time I spent down here as a kid." He pointed out the Adler Planetarium and the Field Museum, all within walking distance of each other. His memories took him to a faraway time. "Enough for my walk down memory lane. FYI, there are squads patrolling every one of these lots and other areas, looking for the van and the other car in case they decide to hide out then attack around game time. I will take it real personally if they try to damage any of my best friends here," looking at each of the internationally renowned buildings.

"You rock, Mac. That's what I love to hear. Let's go find these maggots and put them where they belong."

They gave each other a fist bump, and MacCarthy cruised along McFetridge Street between the Field Museum and Soldier Field. Two marked CPD squads were blocking the other entrance to the tunnel under the stadium. He drove back eastbound, then south on Museum Campus Drive. Turning right onto Waldron Drive, which ran along the south side of the stadium, MacCarthy stopped the squad along the curb. They sat for a couple minutes looking in all directions for a vehicle they were positive would appear in the next couple hours.

Duke was the first one on the radio. "All squads. A blue van with white stripes and Chicago Public Works written on the side just stopped along the curb in the northbound lanes of Lake Shore Drive, less than two hundred yards north of Waldron. It's probably the closest they can get to the west side of the stadium. One white male wearing navy blue coveralls got out and placed orange pylons behind the van. A second white male wearing the same outfit exited the back. Both now walking to the front. Hold on. A black, four-door Charger stopped in front of the van, and they're getting into the car. We're southbound on Lake Shore Drive and can't turn around. Get on that Charger!"

"Okay Mac, let's go!"

Chapter 34

CHICAGO: DETONATION TIME

efore Duke finished his broadcast, Mac was already in gear, heading out toward Lake Shore Drive with tires squealing. "Okay, there's the van. Where's the Charger?"

As they passed the blue van, Tomczyk saw the ABU478 license plate on the back, which now had a blue background and black lettering instead of the familiar white background and black lettering of Wisconsin plates. The darkness made it difficult to locate the auto. Thankfully, Lake Shore Drive was not filled with heavy traffic and was well lit. Tomczyk searched his memory banks for the configuration of the taillights of a newer-model Dodge Charger.

"There it is!" he shouted, pointing the auto out to MacCarthy. It was in the left lane, four cars in front of them, traveling with traffic at about forty-five miles per hour. "We have to take that car out!" Tomczyk heard the scene commander on the squad radio in the background, ordering bomb tech units over to the van. "Mac, we have some really quick decisions to make. If they have a detonating device in that car, we're screwed if we try stopping them with the *Kojak* light," pointing to the red police light on the floor. "If the bombs are on a timer, your techs will have half a chance to diffuse it before the clock runs out. Let's PIT 'em. Hopefully they'll get confused and won't be able to detonate."

"I have to get an okay before I attempt a PIT! We don't even know if Zuber's in the car."

"I'll take that chance! The book says you have to be an emergency vehicle before you can do one. If you become an emergency vehicle, those killers will detonate the device for sure. Mac, put it ALL on me. I'll take the blame and the jail time. Now let's do this."

"You're a crazy SOB, Ski! This is gonna cost you."

Both vehicles drove through the green lights at East Balbo when Mac made his move. He drove up on the right side of the unsuspecting driver and passengers until the front of his bumper was about equal to the rear tire of the Charger. Just before MacCarthy started moving across the lane to nudge the back right quarter of the Charger, the back seat passenger turned and looked at the two detectives, realizing instantly who they were. Tomczyk looked straight into the soul of a monster.

"That's Zuber. Do it, Mac! Do it now!" The unmarked squad pushed into the Charger perfectly and the force of the contact caused the driver to lose temporary control of the auto as the Charger spun around in a 360-degree clockwise turn and came to a stop. MacCarthy tapped the brakes to get out of the way and stopped directly behind and slightly to the right of the car. The passenger in the front seat stepped out in the middle of Lake Shore Drive and pointed a dark handgun at their squad. Tomczyk's department-issued .40 caliber pistol was already out of the holster. In quick succession, he fired five shots at the target through the squad windshield. He had trained countless times to automatically fire three quick rounds to the upper torso and two to the head. This was completed in less than two seconds. Richard Zuber rushed out and attempted to do the same thing with his Glock Model 22, but was quickly dispatched to the same deadly fate by both MacCarthy and

Tomczyk. Neither detective noticed the driver get out of the car during the shootout and flee west toward Grant Park.

"Ski, that big dude's getting away!"

Tomczyk was out of the squad in a second and in hot pursuit. Jamie Rider made it across the southbound lanes of Lake Shore Drive and reached the large concrete walkways of the park. *No way, big boy. You're mine.* Tomczyk holstered his weapon for an easier and faster pursuit of the suspect but was ever watchful with his cat-like reflexes if he needed to redraw and engage.

As Jamie Rider reached the walkways that ran around historic Buckingham Fountain, he turned and placed both hands at chest level and tightened them into fists. "Okay, pig. I hope you're ready for me—unless you'd rather be a chicken shit and call for some backup."

"Squads are already on the way. If you're in the mood for fighting, go for it."

Jamie flicked open a switchblade knife he had hidden in his right hand and charged at Tomczyk. He was able to hit pay dirt on Tomczyk's left forearm, causing blood to surface on his maroon sweatshirt sleeve. The highly trained detective used Rider's large frame against him and performed a quick double kick to the body and one perfect punch to the jaw. To Tomczyk's surprise, Rider was able to do a leg sweep, causing the detective to fall to the concrete. Rider attempted to get up and attack again, but Tomczyk finished the fight with an amazing, forceful right-leg kick to the chest. Rider flew onto his back and slammed against the hard surface. The knife fell harmlessly away. He rolled the suspect over and used two sets of handcuffs to secure him.

"When you get released from prison in sixty years, I suggest you think before you attack someone who knows what he's doing. And by the way, you're under arrest for a whole lot of things. Too bad your family members probably didn't make it. Pointing a gun at a police officer is a bad idea."

Several marked vehicles arrived and took custody of Jamie, placing him in one of the caged squads. Tomczyk walked back to MacCarthy's unmarked squad with an obvious limp, favoring his right leg. Michigan Avenue was lit up like a Christmas tree with red and blue police lights. Spotlights illuminated the Charger. Anne ran up to Tomczyk and embraced him with all her might.

"Thank God you're okay, Declan. Mac told me about the PIT maneuver and how you had to shoot those guys. Why are you limping?" She also noticed the fairly large, wet blood spot on his sleeve.

"Just a scratch. PIT, the precision immobilization technique," he accentuated with an overly studious look, "when used properly, is a cop's best friend in ending a pursuit. Mac's execution of it was pure textbook. Are either of those guys still alive?" He looked over at the paramedic ambulances near the Charger. "I did my best to neutralize them. Think I twisted my knee when I turned and ran for that big dude. Old war wound. Guess I'm no longer in my prime."

"You look awfully good to me, but let's get that arm looked at. I'm not sure about those guys, though. Mac probably has more answers."

They walked over to Detective MacCarthy, who was conferring with a uniformed lieutenant. Upon seeing Tomczyk, he put out his arms and bear hugged his fellow law enforcement officer. "I will be your partner, anywhere, anytime!"

"Same goes for me, Mac."

"The bomb techs were able to defuse a helluva bomb in the back of the van that was on a timer. You called it. We just received word that a Joseph Shipley from Chicago and a Thomas Friend from Milwaukee, AKA Madman, were picked up as they parked a minivan at the building on Halstead and tried going into the apartment we did the search warrant at. I'm positive they're good for the bombing in the alley downtown."

"Madman! Excellent. How about Zuber and Sam Rider? They can't be doing too well."

"Zuber definitely bought the farm—he'll be DOA. I don't give Sam Rider much of a chance of survival either. Interesting shooting through the windshield, by the way."

"Didn't have time to get out of the car before Rider was starting to take aim. He sure was out in a flash. Besides, the engine block is safer than that TV 'behind the car door' stuff as far as cover's concerned. Seen bullets go through doors too many times."

"I hear you on that one. Did you see the expression on Zuber's face? He recognized you instantly."

"Sure did. He was the driver the day my former partner was hurt in the cemetery—even gave me the finger. We only locked eyes for a split second. His are just plain scary."

"I could see that evil-eyed SOB, and I was concentrating on hitting the car in the right location. Let's go down to HQ. We have much work to do."

"Okay. Anne, we'll see you and Duke at the PD." He gently touched her right hand with an 'I'm okay' look. She returned a relieved smile.

"Good enough."

Within ten minutes, MacCarthy drove the squad into the police parking lot across the street from Chicago Police Headquarters. Detective Dukeshyer pulled in next to him, and they all got out. MacCarthy went to the trunk and pulled out the bottle of Bushmills, along with four small, plastic white cups.

"Didn't think it would look very professional having a shot of Irish whiskey on Michigan Avenue and making the ten o'clock news. We just saved a whole lot of people and have you two to thank for it. The City of Chicago owes us this one." Mac poured the four of them a drink and toasted their health and friendship. "Great stuff," he said as they swallowed it down. "Promise I'll share the rest of the bottle with my intel buddies; however, the Jameson's coming home with me."

They all laughed. Tomczyk grabbed Anne gently by the arm and gave her a long, tender kiss as he held her close. "Thank you, Anne. You're the best federal agent I know, and I want to get to know you a whole lot better."

"I love the sound of that! Well, Detective Declan, looks like we have some paperwork to do. No one else I'd rather do it with."

"C'mon, you two. There's no kissing in police work!" Detective Bill MacCarthy put an arm around each of his newfound friends' shoulder, and the four of them walked into the building together.

"What a night! And what a great ending, working with some of the best. Doesn't get better than that."

This was why Tomczyk chose a life of service. "Mac, do you have a secure phone in your office? We may have another major 'fire' to put out. I also promised to make a phone call to a great kid named Lightning."

TIMELINE FOR THE 1935 REIGN OF TERROR

This timeline is based on information taken from numerous newspaper accounts in the *Milwaukee Journal* and *Milwaukee Sentinel* archives during the time period.

October 1: One hundred fifty sticks of dynamite, four hundred fifty fuse caps, and two hundred feet of fuse stolen from the locked storage sheds at the Civilian Conservation Corps camp in Estabrook Park.

October 12: Loud explosion heard in the city of Wauwatosa by the railroad tracks in the vicinity of Seventieth and State. Later theorized that it was related to the bombers practicing with the stolen dynamite.

October 16: Whitefish Bay Armory broken into, eleven guns stolen from locker. Offense possibly involved with the timeline of The Mad Bomber.

October 18: Seventy-year-old "psychic detective" Arthur "Doc" Price Roberts told Milwaukee Police Detective English, before the explosions, that there were "going to be lots of bombings—dynamitings! I see two banks blown up and perhaps the city hall. Going to blow up police stations. Then there's going to be a big blowup south of the Menomonee River, and it'll be all over." Roberts was known for his strange talents, so extra precautions were taken by local law enforcement.

October 20: Attempted armed robbery of Kemp's Rexall Pharmacy in Shorewood, where a shotgun round was fired at a clerk but struck the wall clock behind him.

October 22: West Milwaukee Police Department squad car stolen from police garage.

October 26: Shorewood Village Hall explosion.

October 27: Citizen Bank explosion at Thirty-sixth and Villard on Milwaukee's North Side.

- Armed and masked robbery of Kemp's Rexall Pharmacy in Shorewood.
- Armed and masked robbery of Druschke Rexall Pharmacy on Milwaukee's East Side.
- First Wisconsin Bank explosion on Milwaukee's East Side.

October 28: Note found at Palmer Street Elementary School, along with a dynamite fuse, demanding $125,000. The note was written on a typewriter found in a room in Idzi's house.

October 31: Bombing of Milwaukee Police Station at Third and Hadley at 6:45 p.m. Bombing of Milwaukee Police Station at Twelfth and Vine at 7:00 p.m.

November 1: Letter received at Milwaukee Police Station at Sixth and Mineral stating, "You're next, no kidding." A note was also sent to Detective Captain Prohaska, demanding $100,000 or his house would be blown up.

November 3: Rutkowski and Chovanec, "The Mad Bombers," die in a garage explosion behind the house at 2121 West Mitchell Street.

- Nine-year-old Patricia Mylnarek was killed in the explosion and a number of others were wounded.
- George Sujewicz and juvenile Elmer Gritz were arrested. They admitted to being in a stolen car during a hit and run accident on October 24. Milwaukee Police investigators were unable to connect either with other crimes.

December 6: Two stolen cars were found in a garage at 2960 South Thirteenth Street that had been rented by Paul "Shrimp" Chovanec in October. One of the cars contained a light and siren from the WMPD squad, along with four bombs, two shotguns, a rifle, and pistol—along with five sets of license plates. One of the bombs was made up of six sticks of dynamite.

SIDE NOTE

May 1, 1939: Twenty-year-old Edward Malinowski was in possession of 150 sticks of dynamite stolen from a quarry in March 1939. Also found were 458 blasting caps in his attic, taken from a different quarry. Newspaper articles of "Idzi" Rutkowski were found in Malinowski's attic, along with the contraband.

AUTHOR'S NOTE
FACTS

We as a society continue to be enraptured by a period in our history that occurred over eighty years ago. The Great Depression struck on "Black Monday" in October 1929 and thrust the United States into its darkest financial period. Our parents, grandparents, and even great grandparents, now mostly gone, may have shared with us what it was like during those times. Countless books, magazines, and movies have chronicled the pain and misery that swept the nation.

The names of Eliot Ness, Melvin Purvis, J. Edgar Hoover, and others have etched an indelible mark in the annals of our history in that bygone era. The well-written and well-chronicled book *Public Enemies* by Bryan Burrough became one of my inspirations to start this project.

This book is based on factual events that occurred; however, it is a fictionalized account. Except for the names of Hugh "Idzi" Rutkowski, Paul "Shrimp" Chovanec, and a couple of others, the characters are the products of my imagination.

During a short period from late October to early November 1935, Milwaukee came under siege during the "Reign of Terror" by someone termed "The Mad Bomber." This fictional book is based on that small snapshot of time.

I include the cast of characters during the *Public Enemies* era because it sets the stage for this book by showing some of the notorious criminals of that time. Or as Bryan Burrough put it, "America's Greatest Crime Wave and the birth of the FBI, 1933-1934."

Courtesy of the Theodore C. Sliwinski family

"HAPPIER TIMES"
Top Row: Sigmund "Sig" Powalisz (1914), Gus Sliwinski (1908), Unknown, Hugh "Idzi" Rutkowski (1915)
Middle Row: Alois "Bingo" Powalisz (1910), Charles "Charlie" Sliwinski (1910)
Bottom Row: Theodore C. "Bevo" Sliwinski (1912)

Photo of neighborhood friends and baseball team members, taken between 1933 and 1935.

CAST OF CHARACTERS DURING THE PUBLIC ENEMIES ERA

- **Al "Scarface" Capone** (born 1899): Probably the most notorious of all the criminals during this era. He was imprisoned at Alcatraz in 1931 and died of cardiac arrest on January 24, 1947.
- **Bonnie Parker** (born 1910) and **Clyde Barrow** (born 1909): Outlaws, robbers, murderers; died of multiple gunshot wounds on May 23, 1934, in an ambush on a rural road in Bienville Parish, LA, by four Texas police officers.
- **John Herbert Dillinger** (born 1903): A gangster and bank robber; Public Enemy Number One. He and his gang did a number of bank robberies in 1933 and 1934, along with pulling the big prison escape from Indiana. He left the Biograph Theatre in Chicago on the night of July 22, 1934, after watching a movie with Polly Hamilton, his girlfriend, and Anna Sage, the infamous "Woman in Red." The trio were confronted by FBI agents and local police, including Melvin Purvis, Special Agent in Charge of the Chicago FBI office.

Dillinger drew a weapon and attempted to flee; he was shot three times and died at the scene.

- **Charles Arthur "Pretty Boy" Floyd** (born 1904): Bank robber; he became the primary suspect in the June 17, 1933, gunfight known as the "Kansas City Massacre" that resulted in the death of two FBI agents and two Kansas City police officers. Committed a number of bank robberies. Died of gunshot wounds in a cornfield on October 22, 1934, in northern Ohio while being pursued by local police and FBI agents.
- **Lester Joseph "Baby Face Nelson" Gillis** (born 1908): Known under the pseudonym George Nelson; bank robber and murderer. He killed more FBI agents in the line of duty than any other single person. Gillis died on November 27, 1934, in a running gun battle with FBI agents in what became known as the "Battle of Barrington," in Barrington, Illinois. Two FBI agents, Herman "Ed" Hollis and Samuel P. Cowley, were also killed.
- **The Barker Family**, AKA the "Bloody Barkers":
  ◊ **Kate "Ma" Barker** (born 1873): Born in Ash Grove, Missouri. She was the mother of four sons: Herman, Lloyd, Arthur (Doc), and Fred, who were all born in Aurora, Missouri. Believed to be the leader of the twenty-five-member Karpis-Barker gang responsible for three kidnappings, ten murders, and thefts of more than one million dollars during a three-year period that began in 1932. Ma Barker and son Fred were killed by FBI agents on January 16, 1935, while hiding out on Lake Weir in Ocklawaha, Florida.
  ◊ **Herman Barker** (born 1893): AKA Fred Hamilton; committed suicide on August 29, 1927, in Wichita, Kansas.

He shot himself during/after a shootout with police to avoid arrest for murder.

◊ **Lloyd William "Red" Barker** (born 1896): He spent twenty-five years in Leavenworth Prison (1922-1947) for robbery. Barker was killed by his wife in 1949 in Denver, Colorado, less than two years after his prison release.

◊ **Fred Barker** (Born 1903): Bank robber, kidnapper; he and his mother were killed by FBI agents in 1935.

◊ **Arthur R. "Doc" Barker** (Born 1899): Bank robber, kidnapper; he was arrested in Chicago by FBI agents, including Melvin Purvis, on January 8, 1935. Sentenced to Alcatraz in 1936 and killed by prison guards while trying to escape, January 13, 1939.

• **Alvin "Creepy" Karpis** (born 1907): Bank and train robber, kidnapper; after Ma Barker and Fred Barker were killed, Karpis became Public Enemy Number One. While holding that distinction, he committed a bank robbery in July and a train robbery in October 1935. He was arrested by FBI and local police in New Orleans, Louisiana, on May 1, 1936. Karpis was confined at Alcatraz Prison with other Karpis gang members. He was then transferred to another prison where he once taught guitar to a young Charles Manson. Paroled in 1969 and deported to Canada. Died in Spain in 1979.

• **George "Machine Gun Kelly" Barnes** (born 1900): Gangster, bootlegger, and businessman; arrested in Tulsa, Oklahoma, for smuggling alcohol onto an Indian reservation and sent to Leavenworth Prison for three years. He married Kathryn Thorne, who bought Kelly his first machine gun. Kelly and others kidnapped a wealthy Oklahoma City resident and a friend in September 1933. He was arrested shortly thereafter and sentenced to life in prison. He spent seventeen years at

Alcatraz where he was known as "Pop Gun Kelly" because he was a model prisoner and not the hardcore criminal his reputation depicted. Kelly died at Leavenworth Prison on July 18, 1954.

I would also like to give tremendous gratitude to *Wikipedia* and the *Milwaukee Journal/Milwaukee Sentinel* archives, along with several other open sources, for being very valuable and helpful in the writing of this book.

Larry Powalisz

ACKNOWLEDGEMENTS

Terrorism is not a new phenomenon in our country. Up until September 11, 2001, Milwaukee had the dubious honor of having the most police officers killed in one day in United States history. This occurred on November 24, 1917, when a bomb exploded at police headquarters and five police officers, three detectives, one police alarm operator, and a citizen were killed. Anarchists were suspected to be behind the bombing. The case remains unsolved.

Law enforcement has been much of my life for over four decades. This book is dedicated to all the police officers, detectives, supervisors, and support staff with whom I worked at the Milwaukee Police Department from 1973-2001. It is also written in memory of those who died in the line of duty and whose names are forever inscribed on the marble walls of the National Law Enforcement Memorial in Washington, DC, to all those who have since died, and to the millions who have ever stood watch and who still stand watch on "the thin blue line." You have my utmost gratitude and respect. God bless you all!

Thanks to my friend, Cary Collins, for tightening up the manuscript and providing his strategic use of action words. To Morgan James

Publishing and their wonderful staff. Thank you for giving me a chance and taking on CIRCLE OF TERROR. I would also like to thank Angie Kiesling and her talented team at Editorial Attic for doing such a great job on the final professional editing.

Finally, this book is lovingly dedicated to the memory of my father, Sigmund. Along with a number of other friends and acquaintances, he was taken into custody by Milwaukee Police Department personnel in November 1935, and questioned concerning his activities and friendship with a neighbor and fellow Boy's Tech High School attendee, Hugh "Idzi" Rutkowski, AKA, "The Mad Bomber." Without the stories my father shared with my siblings and I years later, this story would never have been written.

Larry Powalisz
CIRCLE OF TERROR

A free eBook edition is available with the purchase of this book.

To claim your free eBook edition:
1. Download the Shelfie app.
2. Write your name in uppser case in the box.
3. Use the Shelfie app to submit a photo.
4. Download your eBook to any device.

Shelfie

A free eBook edition is available
with the purchase of this print book.

CLEARLY PRINT YOUR NAME ABOVE IN UPPER CASE

Instructions to claim your free eBook edition:
1. Download the Shelfie app for Android or iOS
2. Write your name in **UPPER CASE** above
3. Use the Shelfie app to submit a photo
4. Download your eBook to any device

Print & Digital Together Forever.

Snap a photo

Free eBook

Read anywhere

Morgan James makes all of our titles available
through the Library for All Charity Organization.

www.LibraryForAll.org